LIES

WE

NEVER

SEE

A novel by
MICHAEL LINDLEY
Sage River Press

LIES WE NEVER SEE

Book #1 in the "Hanna Walsh and Alex Frank Low Country Mystery and Suspense" Series

THE AMAZON #1 BESTSELLER FOR MYSTERY AND SUSPENSE.

The Low Country of South Carolina is the setting for this twisting tale of betrayal, upheaval and new hope in this *"unputdownable"* first book in the Amazon bestselling "Hanna and Alex" mystery and suspense series.

Free legal clinic attorney Hanna Walsh finds her life in emotional and financial ruin when her philandering husband is found murdered and his ties to a ruthless crime family reveal a twisting web of betrayal and deceit in this emotional and captivating story of shattered dreams and hard-fought deliverance.

A novel by

MICHAEL LINDLEY

Sage River Press

The *"Troubled Waters"* Suspense Thrillers by

MICHAEL LINDLEY

The *"Charlevoix Summer"* Series

THE EMMALEE AFFAIRS
THE SUMMER TOWN

The *"Coulter Family Saga"* Series

BEND TO THE TEMPEST

The *"Hanna Walsh and Alex Frank Low Country Mystery and Suspense"* Series

LIES WE NEVER SEE
A FOLLOWING SEA
DEATH ON THE NEW MOON
THE SISTER TAKEN

Michael Lindley Amazon Author Page

DEDICATION

A quick note of thanks to the many readers, publishing partners, book retailers and fellow authors who have been so supportive in the pursuit of these stories.

The Reckoning...

The lawyer was late as usual for his next *meeting*. Looking away from his watch, he pulled the leather strap of his bag up higher on his shoulder and looked both ways before crossing the street.

It was another hot afternoon in Charleston and traffic was building again downtown for the rush to get home. He held his summer suit coat under his arm. His white dress shirt was already damp from the stifling humidity. He had an appointment, *of course it was a date,* he thought to himself, with a woman from another law firm he had begun seeing recently. It was listed in his calendar as a *meeting* for the sake of his office assistant... and his wife.

He was thinking of the young woman he was about to see for a cocktail and then perhaps a trip back to her downtown condo for more intimate fun as he turned down an alley in the middle of the block to get to the bar where she was waiting. He knew he was becoming obsessed with this woman, but it wasn't the first time and certainly wouldn't be the last, he thought with resigned amusement.

The shade in the alley between the two tall buildings offered some relief from the heat. He pulled his tie loose and glanced at his watch again. A restaurant worker wearing kitchen clothes came out from a door ahead and threw a bag of garbage in a dumpster before going back inside.

The lawyer wiped at the sweat on his forehead. The sound of footsteps approaching from behind caught him by surprise. He turned to see another man coming toward him. He recognized the face immediately and sighed in frustration. He looked back down the alley and kept on toward the street ahead.

"Hey!" he heard from behind. He turned again as the man approached. They were alone together now in the narrow alleyway. The man came up and stopped a few feet away, seeming to catch his breath and sweating heavily. He took a cap off his head and wiped at the sweat on his forehead.

"I'm late," the lawyer said impatiently and turned to move on.

"I need to talk to you!" the intruder insisted.

"What the hell..." the lawyer said, turning and seeing the gun now in the man's right hand. His senses went on full alert, but before he could react, the barrel of the silencer on the semi-automatic was pressed against his forehead. He felt a rush of panic and his bag fell from his shoulder and his jacket dropped to the ground.

"What are you doing?" the lawyer said. "Just be cool."

"I thought we could work this out," the man said calmly, not taking his eyes off the lawyer's face who now had his hands in the air, the gun still pressed to his head. Then the man turned and looked back behind him for a moment. There was still no one else in the alley. The lawyer watched as the man looked back and a grim smile came across his face.

"There was enough for both of us, but you just wouldn't listen."

The chill from another wave of panic swept through the lawyer. He struggled to answer. "We can work this out. If it's about the money..."

The two men stood staring at each other for a moment as the man seemed to consider the lawyer's protest. The thin smile on his face disappeared. "We're past that now."

The lawyer watched the gun lower from his face and for a moment, a brief sense of relief swept through his brain. He started to step away when the gun came back up. When it reached chest level, he heard the soft whispered pop of the silencer as the gun fired the first round into his heart. The blow was staggering and the pain excruciating as he stumbled back. The second round a moment later caught him again, higher in the chest. He fell back and his head smashed hard on the concrete. The pain quickly faded to a numbness and a cold rush all through his body. His vision blurred as he saw his assailant come up and stand over him, the gun pointing to the ground now. He tried to hold a hand up in defense but couldn't seem to move.

"Like I said, we're past that now."

The lawyer heard these final words, but his mind was fading, and he could no longer bring reason or response to the situation. His last conscious thought was not about the woman he was rushing to see, but a wife who he had betrayed on too many occasions and who would now be left with an unimaginable burden.

The gun whispered one more time, and the lawyer had the vague sense the side of his forehead had just been blown away before all went dark.

Chapter One

Hanna

Charleston, South Carolina *Present Day*

So, this is how it all ends, now, she thought.

Hanna Walsh stood on the red stone walk that wandered through the secluded garden behind her house on South Battery, a home she and her husband had acquired ten years earlier. She turned to see the many colors of the season in the shrubs and plants that were bursting forth as the warm nights of spring came to the homes along the confluence of the Cooper and Ashley Rivers forming Charleston Bay. Behind her, the old house rose three stories through the live oak, crape-myrtle and palmetto palms, a crisp whitewashed façade against the greens and bright colors of the gardens and trees.

In the past, she found great peace and comfort in this quiet space. She remembered gatherings of friends and family at the long dining table beneath the vine-covered pergola behind the house. She walked by the neat herb garden her son had helped plant some years ago. The black iron gate to the crushed gravel drive along the side of the house was an elegant reminder of the grace and beauty of the house that had originally been built by a local sea captain in the late 1700's.

The home had somehow survived the relentless battering of storms and weathering decay. This would be her last day at the house she at one time felt would be her home for the rest of her days.

At forty-four years of age, she found herself mostly alone now in a world that once included a traditional family, a cherished son, a large group of friends and a career that was both satisfying and incredibly challenging.

A black crow startled her as it flew into a tree above her, squawking back at something that disturbed it. The distraction brought her back to the moment and a familiar realization that so much had changed so quickly in her life and so much was gone.

Never overly concerned about her looks or fashion, she let her light brown hair hang straight past her shoulders, parted to the side and frequently pulled back behind her ears. Her routine in the morning to prepare for the day had little time for makeup. Her face was balanced and pleasing, her complexion pale and shadowed with a hint of freckles beneath her brown eyes. Casual and comfortable were her normal wardrobe choices, even at her law office.

She heard a car pulling into the drive, the low rumble of the sports car her husband had purchased for her son, Jonathan, on his sixteenth birthday. She watched as he came through the old iron gate, still amazed at how he had grown in the last two years, now well over six feet just a few weeks after his eighteenth birthday. At his high school graduation the previous week, she had been unable to hold back an overwhelming sorrow, knowing her son would be leaving soon for Chapel Hill and college classes that would begin in the fall. Her friend, Grace Holloway, had been there with her that night in the school auditorium and had to steady her as they stood to watch the graduating class throw up their mortar board caps and join in the celebratory march out of the hall.

Jonathan closed the gate and pocketed his keys as he came toward his mother. He reached out and took her in his arms. She felt the warm comfort of all that was left of her family.

"Mom, I'm sorry," she heard him whisper.

She felt the tears coming again and held him closer.

"Mom, please."

She pulled back and wiped at her face with the sleeve of her shirt. "Grace is coming out to the island with me tomorrow. Can you come for a few days?" she asked as she looked up into her son's face, his own tears leaking out on his tanned cheeks and dripping down onto his University of North Carolina blue t-shirt. He had his father's blond hair and strong features. His deep brown eyes matched his mother's. "I really need your help in packing up," she pleaded.

"Mom, I've told you... I have to start work up at school. I need the money before classes start."

Hanna cringed as she thought of more than just the spending money her son needed to start school in the fall. *Where in hell am I going to cover these tuition checks for four years at one of the best schools in the country?*

"It will only be a few days," she said.

"Do we really have to sell the Pawleys Island house, too?" he asked. "How many years has it been in your family?"

"Forever," she answered, trying to block out the guilt she was feeling in having to sell the place her family had embraced for generations.

"There has to be some other way?" her son said, but she barely heard him as she found herself drifting back to times shared with her own parents on the shores of the Atlantic in front of the historic old beach house when she was a little girl.

Hanna and Grace drove across the south bridge to Pawleys Island the next morning, the heat of the day already building and burning off the low haze, now just a fading whisper above the row of houses along the beach ahead. They were in Grace's black Mercedes sedan, the windows up to keep in the AC. Hanna always enjoyed rolling down the windows on this drive and taking in the familiar smells of the low country marshes, but she found no will for it at the moment.

She glanced down at her watch. It was five minutes past ten. "We'll be late to meet the man from the consignment shop," she said. "I may have them take most of the furniture. I have no idea what we'll do with all the other things." She started searching in her purse for her cell phone.

Grace reached over and took Hanna's hand in hers. "Honey, we'll figure this all out."

Hanna had met Grace years ago when her husband joined the law firm that also employed Grace's husband, Phillip. Their friendship had quickly grown very close and they had become confidants through life's many challenges and surprises. Grace was two years older than Hanna. She was a Charleston native and spoke with the heavy South Carolina accent that was so prevalent in the city. She was tall and lean, always dressed immaculately and kept her blond-accented hair cut short in the latest style. Her wrists were typically weighted down with too many bracelets and the wedding ring on her left hand often turned heads.

"I thought most buyers would want the place furnished, but Thomas has some interested clients and the wife wants to bring in her own decorator," Hanna said. Thomas Dillon was her real estate agent and old family friend on the island. "Some of that furniture dates back to when my family first built the place. Thomas says they would totally gut the place."

Her friend answered, "Seems a crime to take all that history and charm out of there."

Hanna found her phone and looked for the number of the man from the furniture store. She got him on the line and apologized for being a few minutes late, then hung up and looked out across the marshes. She pushed the button for her window and felt the hot breeze blow into the car. The familiar and comforting scents of salt and the sea life of the Low Country quickly followed as she watched the low-tide water pulling back to expose the black mud along the marsh grasses. Two men in a small fishing boat drifted along a deep channel, casting to the edges for redfish. She remembered days fishing with her husband and Jonathan. The boat had been sold just last week, as well as the Jeep they kept out at the beach.

Hanna was startled back to the present when Grace turned right at the end of the causeway, then again, a few minutes later when she pulled the big car into the drive at her family's beach house. Two historic log outbuildings, a crumbling cabin that once housed slaves and a storage shed sat to the side, a stark reminder of her ancestor's heritage. The old gray cedar shingles on the sides of the beach house had been replaced a few years earlier, but already looked like they'd been there for years with the relentless toll the beach weather took on these old homes. The man from the consignment store was already there, standing by his car at the end of the drive.

Hanna took a deep breath and tried to block out the gloom that seemed to invade her every waking hour. *So, now this ends, too,* she thought.

Chapter Two

Amanda

Pawleys Island, South Carolina November 1866

The young woman stood on the broad gallery of the weathered house in the bracing chill of the morning, the narrow sand path down to the ocean lined with beach grass and bleached shells and tall sea oats moving with the push of a light wind from across the dunes. A cup of coffee was warm and steaming in her hands. She watched as a flock of gulls just offshore staged above a pod of bait fish and plunged over and over into the calm water, screeching and diving for an early meal.

The scent of rosemary and gardenia drifted up to her from the sparse garden below the porch and the sun made its way full above the far horizon, orange and shimmering through the haze like the yolk of an egg on a vast gray canvas. A dark wall of clouds from an earlier shower pushed to the south leaving the air charged and sodden.

She pulled the knit shawl close around her shoulders, catching the loose curls of red hair blowing across her pale face and sat on one of the worn wicker chairs along the rail, resigned in knowing the day ahead held little promise or expectation.

Down to her left a lone figure walked slowly along the shore break of the water, a faded long black coat pulled up tight around his neck and a wide-brimmed dark hat low over his eyes. Amanda watched him move along, aimless and unhurried. She couldn't see his face but noticed long brown hair falling from under the hat. The man reached down and picked up a piece of driftwood. He brushed some loose sand from the length of it. The gulls seemed to catch his attention and he stopped to look out across the water. He watched for a few seconds and then threw the driftwood far out into the low ocean swells.

When the man turned to continue along the beach, he looked up toward her on the porch of the old house. As their glances met for no more than a moment in what seemed at first a casual, unintended connection, she made out just the slightest hint of recognition in his shadowed eyes before he turned away and kept on down the beach.

She watched until the man was far down the shore, nearly to the end of the island before he turned and disappeared up into the low dunes. Only then did she pull her shaking hand from the purse in her lap and the grip on the cool metal of the pistol she always kept close.

Amanda reached for a book and a pen that rested in an inkwell on the table beside her. The worn leather cover had no title. She opened the book and leafed through several pages until she found the place she was looking for near the middle of the book. The diary had been a present from her mother on her sixteenth birthday. In those early years she had found little time for entries, but since her husband's departure for the war, she found the diary to be a sanctuary, not only to capture her thoughts and deepest emotions, but also to chronicle the devastating impact of the war on her family and a way of life that was so quickly fading away across the South.

Her name was Amanda Paltierre Atwell. She was a twenty-three-year-old widow and daughter of Louis and Miranda Paltierre. Her family had been in the Low Country of South Carolina for nearly 100 years and her ailing father now oversaw what was left of the rice plantation the Paltierres had nurtured through storms and pestilence for generations. It seemed now the end of the war with the northern states would be the final dissolution for the Paltierre plantation long known as *Tanglewood* and the privileged way of life they had come to embrace as their birthright.

Each day she heard her father's concern grow more urgent in the face of defeat of the Confederacy and the imposed sanctions and declining markets that were sure to take the last of their livelihood. The past few years had brought on times of previously unimaginable deprivation and hardship. Her mother had passed just a year earlier as the strain of dispossession finally took its toll. Her father had faded noticeably as well, now a slight measure of his previous vital self. He spent his days walking slowly across the barren acres of their once abundant land, often pausing to look back at the great house that now sat in disrepair and faded neglect.

Amanda's earliest memories were of servants loading the wagons each summer with supplies and necessities to move the family from the harsh heat and constant threat of fever and disease in the sweltering days of the Low Country plantations, to move out to the island for the few months of cooler breezes and chilling ocean water along the shores of the Atlantic. Amanda treasured the memories of learning to swim and catching crabs and fish with her older brothers along the marshes; of the walk to church with her family on Sunday mornings and pleasant afternoons with abundant feasts of food and drink spread across tables on the wide porch of the beach house with family and friends. She remembered the steady procession of young men coming to call upon her father to ask permission to take her to a dance in Georgetown or attend one of the many parties at the other homes along the narrow strip of land known as Pawleys Island.

Her three brothers and most of her suitors had not returned from the war. Over the long months, the families from Georgetown County continued to get word of another of their own lost in the battles between the states.

It had been over a year since a young Confederate lieutenant had stopped his horse in front of the big plantation house and asked to speak with the wife of Captain Jeremy Atwell. Amanda knew what the officer was going to tell her before he even began to speak. There had been no word from Jeremy for months even after news of the treaty signed at Appomattox reached the remote regions of South Carolina. Her mother held her as the lieutenant read softly from a dispatch from the War Office in Richmond, Virginia. Her husband had been killed in battle in a remote coastal area of southern Texas, inconceivably, weeks after the treaty was signed and all forces were to have put down their arms.

Even as her mother tried to hold her, Amanda fell to her knees as the officer rode away. She placed her head down in the folds of her skirt and let the racking sobs come, one wave after another.

Amanda Paltierre was a woman of proud bearing and elegant features. She was known for her gentle manner and caring ways. Her red hair was striking and almost alive with its own energy, like glowing hot coals in a summer beach fire against the soft pale skin of her face and neck. But, her grief at the news of the loss of her husband had been staggering and profound and took all joy and light from her soul. For months, she was unable to speak or even leave the house. She would wake each morning and feel the burden of loss and anguish lay on her spirit like an immovable weight that took all breath from her lungs. She became obsessed in knowing how her husband had died. Several letters to military command in Washington had gone unanswered. *How could Jeremy have been killed so many weeks after the War had ended?*

Chapter Three

Hanna

Pawleys Island, South Carolina *Present Day*

Hanna sat with Grace in two of the worn Adirondack chairs facing the ocean on the long deck of the beach house. Both had a glass of white wine resting on the arm of their chairs. The Atlantic was a deep blue and nearly mirror calm with only a breath of wind blowing from the west across the marshes. Several families had set up chairs and umbrellas along the shore for the day in the sun. Two fishing boats drifted by slowly about a mile out. The sounds of gulls and children playing in the surf went unnoticed by Hanna as she was consumed by her own thoughts and emotions.

The furniture man had left an hour ago after a tortuous tour of her home and assessment of all the family treasures she would either sell to new owners of her house or ship off to this consignment man to dispose of for a fraction of what it was worth if the new buyers didn't want it. She felt overwhelmed in all that would have to be done to deal with dishes and books and clothes that, until just a few months ago, had been a normal part of the routine of her life. Soon, it would all be gone, along with the house and any semblance of the life she had come to take for granted.

She took a sip from the wine and felt the damp condensation formed on the outside of the glass in her hand. The wine was already warm in the mid-afternoon sun. "Where in hell am I supposed to go?" Hanna finally said aloud, more to herself than to her friend sitting beside her.

Grace reached over and placed her hand on Hanna's arm, but didn't respond to the question.

"By the time we deal with the mess Ben left behind, there will be nothing left," Hanna said. "Your husband talked to me the other day about filing for bankruptcy, for God's sake!" Grace's husband, Phillip Holloway, was Ben Walsh's former law partner and was helping Hanna sort through the financial calamity her deceased husband had left her.

Grace said, "You'll keep the clinic open, won't you? You can certainly stay with us until you find another place in Charleston."

Hanna had run a free legal clinic in the city for many years. She had two young attorneys volunteering time to help with the caseload but the work had been piling up with all the distractions she'd been dealing with over the past months. She was seriously considering closing the office but was struggling with leaving so many of Charleston's under-served families without a resource for their legal issues. Her husband, Ben, had never been supportive of the endeavor, constantly reminding her she could put her legal talent and prestigious Duke law degree to better and more lucrative purpose. It had been one of the serious issues in their marriage. She was realistic in accepting the fact now that if she continued to practice law, there would have to be income to pay the bills.

Hanna's cell phone rang inside the house where she had left it on the kitchen counter. She rushed in to answer it, thinking it might be her son reconsidering his decision to come out to the island to help her sort through everything in the old house. She didn't recognize the number on the screen and hit the receive button as she was coming back out on the deck.

"Hello, this is Hanna," she said, standing at the wood railing, looking out at the water.

"Miss Walsh?" the caller asked.

"Yes, this is she."

"Miss Walsh, this is Alex Frank from the Charleston Police Department. I'm the detective assigned to your husband's case."

"Yes, I remember."

"I'm sorry to bother you again about this," the detective said.

"What is it?" Hanna asked and looked back at Grace with a confused stare.

"We've come across some additional information in your husband's death I need to discuss with you."

"New information?"

"Yes, I really need to speak with you," the detective said.

"I'm out of town for several days," Hanna said. "What is it?

There was a pause before the detective said, "I need to speak with you in person."

Hanna turned to Grace and covered the phone. "It's the police. They want to talk about Ben, again."

"What on earth?" her friend said.

To the detective, she said, "I'm up at our place on Pawleys Island for the week. Can it wait?"

"I'm afraid not. Would you mind if I drove up to see you later this afternoon?"

"Is it really that urgent," she asked.

"Yes." He paused again. "I can be up there by 5 o'clock. What is the address, ma'am?"

After agreeing to meet with the police detective at 5, Hanna heard a knock at the back door. She knew her real estate agent wanted to come by. She had known Thomas Dillon since she was a little girl growing up here on the island in the summers. His parents had been friends of her own. There had been a brief romantic spark one summer during high school, but by the following year they had both moved on to other attractions, but the friendship had endured.

Hanna walked through the house to the door. Through the window, she could see her old friend standing on the back porch, a cell phone to his ear. He ended the call as she opened the door. "Hanna," he said as he stepped inside and gave her a big hug and peck on the cheek.

"You're such a dear to help with all of this," Hanna said and then took his hand and led him out to the front deck.

Grace and Thomas exchanged greetings. Grace said, "Would you like some wine?"

"Yes, that would be great, thanks."

Grace went inside. Hanna and Thomas stood at the railing, looking out over the ocean. "So, you're sure you want to do this?" Thomas asked.

"It's not a question of *want*. There's no other way," Hanna said and looked down at her hands gripping the wood rail. "Even with what you've told me we'll clear on the sale, I'll still be nowhere close to what I need to settle Ben's affairs."

"Even with the Charleston house?"

"Yes," she answered in barely a whisper.

Thomas put his arm around her shoulders and pulled her closer. "I'm so sorry, Hanna. I wish there were some other way."

Grace came out with the bottle of Chardonnay and another glass which she filled for Thomas. She returned to their chairs and filled the two other glasses, coming back to hand one to Hanna.

"I'm not going to take any commission on the sale," Thomas said. "I've already cleared it with my broker. We'll have to pay the buyer's agent, but..."

"You don't have to do that," Hanna protested.

"It's done," Thomas said. He was Hanna's age but looked older with black hair gone mostly gray and deep creases on his tanned forehead and around the corners of his eyes from too many years sailing in the sun. "I hope you have a good attorney."

"Grace's husband is representing me," Hanna said. "Ben's old partner."

Thomas nodded, turning to look at Grace. "You're a good friend."

Grace took a big gulp of her wine and said, "This is all so devastating...I mean, it's just killing us to see what Hanna's been left with."

Thomas said, "Well, I hate to say this, but we need to talk about these buyers who are desperate to see the house one more time before they make an offer."

"I know," Hanna said. "That's why we're here."

"Would tomorrow afternoon be okay? They're coming in from Atlanta."

That's fine. Grace and I are going to start sorting through all the clutter. I met with the consignment house this morning in case we have to clear the place out."

"It's looking that way," the real estate agent said. "I'm sorry, Hanna."

"If these people move forward, how long will I have to get out of here?"

"Plan on about a month for appraisals and inspections and closing."

"Dear God," Hanna said.

Chapter Four

Amanda

Pawleys Island, South Carolina 1866

As Amanda sat overlooking the deserted beach along the Atlantic coast of South Carolina, she thought back to the days she had first met her future husband. Jeremy Atwell had been introduced to Amanda at church when she was seventeen years old as they attended a wedding for the daughter of a family friend to both the Paltierres and Atwells.

Her first glimpse of the young Mr. Atwell came as the final guests made their way into the church pews for the ceremony to begin. Jeremy came in with his parents and younger brother and sat two rows in front and to the side of Amanda and her family. He glanced back before he sat down and happened to catch Amanda's eye for just a moment. She saw him smile at her and then look again before he sat down. She watched the back of his head through the entire wedding ceremony, hoping he would turn again, hardly hearing the preacher leading the wedding vows. Only when the new bride and groom came down the aisle and the congregation stood to welcome the couple, did she see Jeremy turn again in her direction as he began to slide out of the pew with his family.

He looked at her with an embarrassed grin as he passed, following the wedding party out of the church.

When Amanda emerged from the church sanctuary with her own family around her a few minutes later, she looked across the crowd assembling on the lawn for the young man who had captured her attention. She walked down the steps and then was startled as she was touched on the arm from behind. She turned to see her good friend, Jessica Samuels.

The young woman said, "Amanda, you look like you're lost."

"Lost?" Amanda replied, still looking across the lawn.

"He's over there," Jessica said, pointing to a line-up of carriages on the side of the church. "I saw you watching him through the entire ceremony. For goodness sake, have some pride!"

Amanda saw him helping his mother into one of the carriages.

"Would you like me to introduce you?" Jessica asked. Amanda didn't answer. "His name is Jeremy Atwell. He's from Georgetown. His father is a lawyer and they're friends with our family." Georgetown was a small hub of a community inland a few miles to the south.

Jessica took Amanda by the arm and started walking across the lawn toward the Atwells. Amanda resisted at first and then decided to follow. As they approached, Jeremy turned and saw them coming. He smiled again and walked toward the two women.

Amanda noticed his well-tailored suit and brightly polished black boots. He was a bit taller and walked confidently with an easy stride. His dark hair was combed back, and his face gave an overall impression of kindness and even spirit, a self-assurance that was not born of pride or arrogance, but more a sense of ease about his place and purpose.

"Good morning, Jessica," he said as they all came together.

Jessica said, "Jeremy, you wouldn't leave without saying hello?" He was staring now at Amanda. "This is my best friend, Amanda Paltierre. She lives over at *Tanglewood*. You know, the plantation just west of the island."

"Good morning," he said, finally taking his eyes off Amanda and acknowledging his friend, Jessica. "It's very nice to meet you, Miss Paltierre. I'm sorry we were in such a rush to leave. My mother's not feeling well, I'm afraid."

Amanda smiled and held out her gloved hand which Jeremy reached for. He bowed slightly and said, "My pleasure."

"Good afternoon, Mr. Atwell," Amanda finally replied and then found herself totally at a loss at what to say. She was frustrated with her embarrassment. It wasn't like her to be so silly with boys, she thought. She held Jeremy's hand just a bit too long.

From a distance, they heard Jeremy's father call out, "Hurry now, son. We have to get your mother home."

"So, you won't be going to the reception?" Amanda said and then silently chastised herself for sounding so desperate.

"No, I'm sorry," he said, looking intently at Amanda.

"Ride with us," Jessica said. "I'll have my brother get you home later."

Jeremy looked relieved and quickly said, "Just a minute." He let go of Amanda's hand and ran back to his family. After a quick discussion, which the girls couldn't hear, he came back over. "I guess I'll be joining you," he said.

"Excellent, Jessica said. "Why don't you ride with us. Amanda, we'll see you at the party?"

"Of course," Amanda said and then watched as her friend walked away with young Mr. Jeremy Atwell.

The reception was held at the home of the bride on one of the large rice plantations just two miles south of *Tanglewood* and the Paltierre's home. As Amanda rode in the family carriage with her mother and father, she saw the large white house emerge through the canopy of live oak trees ahead along the curving drive. The tree limbs were draped in brown Spanish Moss that swung lazily in a light breeze. The azalea bushes were in bloom and bright colors of white and red blossoms spread through the trees along the drive and up around the grand house. In the distance, she could see the broad sweep of rice fields flooded and just coming into season. Her three brothers followed on horseback, joking with each other about which girls they'd be dancing with. Amanda shut out the chatter and tried to calm herself. She hadn't recovered from her uneasiness in meeting this new young man. It wasn't as if she was unaccustomed to being around suitors. There had been many in the past couple of years since her formal coming out. *And why haven't I met this Mr. Atwell previously,* she thought.

Later, she stood with Jessica next to a long table spread with more food than this assembly could ever possibly eat. A young black servant was at the end of the table carving from a large ham as people passed along the buffet. The spacious drawing room in the plantation house was filled with groups of people holding drinks and conversing loudly. Many more had their food at tables arranged across the back lawn, the sun now beginning to set across the long expanse of marshlands to the west. A small band was set up near the back gallery playing dance music. A few children were dancing with their parents or aunts and uncles, but the many young people attending had yet to begin dancing.

Amanda had seen Jeremy when she first arrived, talking with a group of young men near the bar and leering at the procession of unattached women streaming into the reception. He caught her eye for just a moment before one of the other men pulled him back into their conversation.

"So, tell me about Mr. Atwell," Amanda said as she reached for a piece of cheese on the table.

Jessica was looking at another young man across the room but turned back. "He'll be attending school in Charleston in the fall," Jessica said. "I'm told he plans to join his father's law practice."

"Why have I never seen him before?" Amanda asked.

"He's been away at school since he was young. His father has sent him to Charleston to work at another law firm in the summers."

Amanda watched as an older gentleman with who appeared to be his daughter in tow, approached the group of young men Jeremy was conversing with. Introductions were made, particularly between Jeremy and the young woman. Jeremy bowed and took the girl's hand and led her out the back door toward the small group dancing on the lawn.

"Well!" she heard her friend say as Amanda felt her face flush with disappointment, and then she chastised herself for her reaction. One of the others in the group of men Jeremy had been speaking with came toward them and asked Jessica for the next dance. As her friend excused herself and walked away, Amanda could see out through the door as Jeremy Atwell danced quite elegantly with his new partner. He seemed to be enjoying himself more than she would have preferred. She looked around the gathering room and met the gaze of her father. He walked over to her and gave her a warm hug.

"You're the most beautiful belle at the ball," Louis Paltierre said. "My God, don't see how you could be standing here alone with all these eligible young men around. May I have this dance, daughter?"

She went out and danced across the lawn in her father's arms. She knew she was fortunate to have a father so loving. He had always treated her as the princess of their family, often to her mother's dismay. The music stopped for a moment and her father said,

"There's your mother. I'll have this next dance with her." He kissed Amanda on the cheek. "You be careful with all these boys around, you hear!" He smiled and walked off.

Amanda walked back into the house then out the grand front doors and down the steps through the many horse-drawn carriages assembled along the front drive. She kept on past several white-washed farm buildings and storage sheds. She saw a cluster of rough cottages to her left in a deep growth of trees where the servants lived. She reached a grass-covered bank at the edge of the rice fields and paused to take in the vast scene before her.

The sun was hanging low to the west, just above the tree line, casting a bright reflection back across the wetlands. A pattern of low clouds was tinged in purple in the fading light. The faint sound of music from the wedding celebration was behind her. She didn't hear anyone approach and was startled by the touch on her sleeve. She turned to see the face of Jeremy Atwell.

"I've been looking for you," he said. "My friends told me you had headed out this way."

"Isn't it beautiful?" she said, looking again across the fields.

"Certainly," she heard him say and when she turned back, he was staring at her. "May I have this next dance?" he asked as he reached for her hand. Before she could answer he took her in his arms and they began a slow waltz to the distant music, right there on the grassy levy.

She watched his gentle smile as they turned gracefully across the field and when their eyes met, she was caught in the deep brown colors that reflected back at her. They didn't speak for some time and then the music stopped, but they kept on close together, turning to the rhythm of the silent waltz in their heads.

A call from behind interrupted them. "Amanda!"

She turned and saw her mother coming toward them. As she approached, Amanda saw her concerned face and couldn't help but smile at Jeremy.

"Amanda, you really must come back inside," her mother scolded. "Everyone's been asking about you."

"Mother, this is Jeremy, Mr. Atwell from Georgetown."

"Good afternoon, Mrs. Paltierre," Jeremy said with a calm confidence as he reached for the woman's hand. "Forgive me for stealing your daughter away."

"Yes, right," Miranda Paltierre said. "We must get back, Amanda."

"May I escort you, ladies?" Jeremy asked, holding up both his arms to lead them back. Amanda saw the exasperated look on her mother's face but ignored her glare and turned to take Jeremy's arm. She knew there would be terse words later about her *scandalous* behavior, but it wouldn't be the first time.

Their formal courtship began that May when he returned from school. During that first summer, Jeremy convinced his father he could stay in Georgetown and work in the family practice before heading off to college in the fall. Jeremy spent every spare moment with Amanda, often out at the Paltierre family house at the ocean, although under the watchful supervision of three brothers and her ever-suspicious mother.

Amanda knew she was in love with Jeremy when he left for a week to travel to Charleston with his family. All she could think about was his return to Pawleys Island. Every night he was away she lay awake thinking about their time together, the touch of his hand on hers as they walked along the beach, the lingering sensation of their first and only kiss when they found themselves alone on the front steps one night before she had to go in.

At Christmas, Jeremy had met with Mr. Paltierre to ask for his daughter's hand in marriage. The Paltierres had approved of young Mr. Atwell from the beginning. He was from a respected family with excellent South Carolina lineage. They were married the next spring and traveled to Savannah for their honeymoon. They spent three marvelous nights at the Marshall House hotel on old East Broughton Street.

It was only a few weeks after they returned that news of the war with the North swept through every home and business and tavern. Jeremy and his brother and father, as well as the men from her own family, were offered commissions in the new army due to the high position and education of both their families. Suddenly, all the men in her life were gone to fight the Union Army. Only their fathers stayed behind due to their age and physical health, although both held the honorary rank of Colonel throughout the war.

On the day Jeremy left with his commission as a young lieutenant in the gathering Confederate Army, they spent the early morning together walking along the beach. It was a morning Amanda would often think back to. They had made love earlier for the last time as the sun brought light into their room overlooking the ocean. The sound of gulls and the low tide breaking along the beach comforted them as they lay together, each unsure how long it might be until they were together again.

As they walked along holding hands and feeling the cool water wash across their feet, Amanda tried without success to prevent tears from escaping down her cheeks. Jeremy turned and held her close as they looked out across the water. She felt her tears soak into his shirt and she took in the smell of him and the warm comfort of his embrace.

No words were spoken until later that morning when they stood in the front of the house and kissed for the last time. As Jeremy mounted his horse, he placed his gray hat over his head and then reached for Amanda's hand as he said, "I'll be home soon." He hesitated for a moment, then said nothing more.

Jeremy kicked the horse and it started off slowly. Amanda wouldn't let go of his hand and she walked along beside her husband as his horse moved off down the long gravel drive to the main road. She held her skirt up with her free hand to keep from tripping, not taking her eyes off Jeremy's. He squeezed her hand tight and she saw he was crying and trying to wipe away the tears. When they reached the road, Jeremy pulled his horse to a stop and leaned down low to kiss her again.

"I love you, Amanda."

"I love you, too," she said, finally letting go of his hand. "Please tell me you'll be back safe."

He jumped down from his horse and pulled her close, his tears now flowing freely. "Nothing will keep me from getting back here and soon. I promise." He held her face in his hands and wiped her tears from her cheeks. "I don't want you worrying about me."

"You know I'll worry every minute," she said, pulling him close again. Then, she remembered the chain in her pocket with the cross she'd found in Georgetown. She pulled it out from a pocket in her dress and put it over Jeremy's head. "But, I know you're coming back to us."

He let her go and mounted his horse again. "I'll be back... soon. Those damn Yankees'll be licked in no time and back where they belong." He turned the horse and started away again. They watched each other until he was around the far bend in the road and out of sight.

As Amanda saw him ride away that morning down the road inland, she felt a sadness that was overwhelming. She fell to the ground and lay her face in the sand, letting her arms close around her and the tears flow. Her mother came out some time later looking for her and helped her up and into the house, offering words of comfort, but providing little in the end.

Chapter Five

Jeremy

Palmetto Ranch, Texas May 12, 1865

Captain Jeremy Atwell sat astride his horse in the morning heat, hands resting on the saddle horn as he looked east across the barren sand and scrub chaparral bushes toward the approaching enemy. The horizon was obscured with a low haze and small sand hills as the sun just began its ascent from across the Gulf of Mexico. Seabirds from the coast drifted high up in the currents and the acrid smell of animal waste from the paddocks around the old ranch buildings were rank in the air.

Scouts had alerted them to a significant force of Union soldiers now approaching from the east along the Brownsville Road from Boca Chica and Brazos Island on the Gulf coast. The past evening the Federals had overrun a small abandoned Confederate guard post and encampment at White's Ranch further east and downriver towards Brazos Island. The scouts had hastily come back to join the small cavalry company that had been stationed at the distant outpost at Palmetto Ranch, fifteen miles to the east of Brownsville along the Rio Grande River, just for this purpose.

Atwell and his men had been patiently waiting out the final days of the war, somewhat comforted in knowing of the agreement reached between commanding officers of both armies in Texas to cease hostilities and prevent any needless losses when the final surrender of all Confederate forces was clearly at hand.

The war had taken its toll on the young man's face, now hardened and creased with deep lines filled with the dust of the Texas plains. He had let his black hair grow long and stopped shaving several years ago, his beard raggedly trimmed just above his collar.

Back at Fort Brown in Brownsville, under the joint command of Colonel John S. "Rip" Ford and General James E. Slaughter, the remaining Confederate troops were presiding over the final disposition of men and supplies, all in hopes of returning home soon to family and loved ones. The word of Lee's surrender at Appomattox had reached them weeks earlier and was met with mixed reactions; both despair at the devastating loss following years of death and hardship across the Confederacy, but with no small measure of relief in knowing they had survived the great conflict and would soon be returning home

While they all knew the battle for the independence of the Southern states had been lost, Atwell's unit had not been ordered to lay down their arms, despite the unwritten agreement to cease armed conflict. There was still the uncertainty of the formalities of the end of the war and the ownership and protection of weapons and horses in Brownsville. There were also valuable stores of cotton shipped south for eventual transport to distant markets. Captain Atwell and his small force of just sixty-five men held reconnaissance to the east to make sure there were no surprises or unwelcome intrusions of Union forces prior to clarification of treaties, pardons and the disposition of arms and other goods.

Earlier that morning, Jeremy sat at a makeshift table in the old barn at Palmetto Ranch and penned his latest letter home to his wife, Amanda, in South Carolina. He took the letter now from the satchel at his side and read it one more time before placing it back in the envelope and then the side pocket of his bag. He would send it out in the post on his return to Brownsville, hopefully very soon with hostilities winding down and thoughts of home and the warm bed of his beautiful wife never far from his mind. He had been gone for nearly four years from his home in Georgetown near his wife's family plantation west of Pawleys Island.

The scout's hurried return and reports of the Union assault at White's Ranch had startled him into a worried sense of alert and caution. *How could this be happening after all the talk of surrender and cessation of conflict?* He took one more look out across the prairie, no visible signs yet of the Union advance. He pulled his horse up sharply and turned back to the ranch.

With his officers assembled in the small ramshackle outbuilding that had been used for the post command, Jeremy briefed his men on the situation and how he proposed to deal with it.

"It seems there are about three hundred Blue Coats on their way through here, I assume on their way to Brownsville," he said. He placed his dusty gray hat down on the table beside him as the men murmured among themselves. "From the way they came charging into White's Ranch last night, I don't think this will be much of a social call."

Jeremy paused and looked around the room at the faces of his men, most showing the confusion he was still troubled by. "I know General Slaughter reached an agreement with the damn Federals that we'd quit fighting and wait for Lee's surrender to make its way out here to Texas. For some reason, this outfit on Brazos Island either doesn't know or doesn't care."

Sergeant Miller, a large husky man standing on the perimeter pushed his way to the front and spat before he said in a loud forceful voice, "Cap'n, no way we gonna let them bastards just march through here, is there?"

Several others in the room voiced their agreement with the sergeant. Jeremy looked around at the faces gathered in the low and dusty light. He saw the frustration, fear and anger in their current situation.

Finally, he said, "Boys, I think we take it to 'em this morning."

The small assembly of soldiers erupted in their assent. Jeremy began issuing orders. Knowing they were badly outnumbered, he knew they would have to use the element of surprise and many of the "hit and run" guerrilla tactics they'd learned from their commander, Old Rip Ford.

Chapter Six

Amanda

Georgetown, South Carolina 1866

Later the day Amanda saw the stranger on the beach, she was driven to Georgetown by Atticus, their long-time servant, now a free man following the end of the war, who had chosen to stay with the Paltierres. Amanda's father had owned ten slaves through the war who all lived and worked on the *Tanglewood* plantation. Five had stayed, including Atticus and Tulia. In the back seat with her was Tulia, a black woman who had been with the family since before Amanda was born. She had helped raise all the Paltierre children and continued to be Amanda's closest confidant.

Two old horses they had managed to keep from the Yankees pulled the family's carriage into Georgetown. The town had grown along the banks of the Winyah Bay at the confluence of the Great Pee Dee, Waccamaw and Sampit Rivers, a long twelve miles to the south and west from Pawleys Island across the marshes to the mainland. Amanda had an appointment with her father-in-law regarding her financial affairs. As they made their way down the narrow streets of the town, Amanda looked out across the gathering of small shops and eating establishments and assorted storefronts. They passed the Episcopal Church on Broad Street where she and Jeremy had been married and then the imposing white courthouse on Screven, before the tall clock tower of the Old Market building came into view as they turned on to Front Street. She recognized a few people along the way and waved a quiet greeting. Familiar sights brought back memories of her time here with her late husband, happy and even giddy times when their greatest concern was simply finding ways to spend more time together.

Atticus pulled the carriage over to the side of the dusty, hard-packed street and reined the horses back in front of the Atwell Law Office, a classic red brick two-story structure with a stark white front door and brass kick plate. The old black man slowly got down and came around to help Amanda off the carriage.

Amanda nodded at Tulia and said, "I won't be long. Will you pick up those things we need down at the store? They'll put it on our account." She turned to take Atticus's hand to step down from the carriage. She thanked him and walked around the horses and up onto the wood-plank walkway that stretched the length of the main street in Georgetown. As the carriage pulled away, she turned to go through the wrought-iron gate up to her father-in-law's office. She smoothed her long white dress and checked the pin that held the small sun hat on her head.

She looked up when she heard a horse come up behind the carriage and stop along the walkway. Sitting on the sweat-soaked brown mare was the man from the beach, the stranger who had passed her that morning. He apparently didn't see or care to notice her this time. She watched as he threw his leg over the horse's rump and got down, leading the animal to a post to tie up. The long coat was gone now in the heat of the day and he wore a brown leather vest over a white shirt rolled up to his elbows, the big hat still low over his eyes. His faded denim pants were tucked-in to high worn boots coated with a layer of dust from the road.

Amanda kept on up the walk to the office but looked back again to see him pass by the gate behind her. This time their eyes met at close range and she saw a face weathered and lined at the corners of his dark eyes. His skin had an ashen pale beneath several days' growth of beard that flashed hints of gray at the ends. He walked with a slow shuffle, his heavy boots barely lifting above the wood planks. The strap of an old leather satchel hung around his neck and he held it close to his side. Again, she felt some hint of recognition or familiarity in his gaze and she stopped on the walk. His free arm lifted, and he reached for the brim of his hat, tipping it down and bowing his head slightly, and then he moved on down the walk like there had been no interaction or connection between them. She watched him move away, passing other people as if they weren't there, almost like he could walk right through them and not interrupt their path. He pushed open the door to the old tavern on the next block and disappeared inside.

Her business with Jeremy's father, Orlando Atwell, was brief. The financial future of the Paltierre and Atwell families was threatened by the declining economy in the South. Without the abundance of slave labor to manage the rice crops, the local production was falling off and markets had generally declined through the war. Speculators were everywhere trying to buy up cheap land, mostly for the vast forests to be timbered. Amanda had chased two men away from *Tanglewood* the previous day when she found them bargaining with her addled father on the purchase of his holdings.

Orlando Atwell was a squat man, somehow managing to keep an ample waistline through the deprivation of the war.

His head was shaved down to a full beard reaching to the top of his shirt collar, now mostly gray. His clothes were well-tailored and crisply pressed. Two medals for service during the war hung from his suit coat pocket, though he had seen no action against the Union armies.

He continued his financial review with his daughter-in-law, sitting behind a large, ornately carved mahogany desk. "Now, Amanda, remember there is considerable value in your father's real estate holdings," he said. "The problem, as I've told you before, is there is virtually no income to cover the carrying costs of these properties, let alone money to live on each month. I've talked to your father to help him get the plantation back into crop production, but even then, markets are slow to recover, and he's lost most of his labor for the harvests."

Amanda said, "So, what are you suggesting, sir?"

Atwell hesitated in answering, shifting some papers on his desk. He finally looked up at Amanda and said, "Dear, there is little hope of getting *Tanglewood* back into production that would provide anywhere near economic viability." He paused again before saying, "Particularly with your father's current state of health."

Amanda listened to the man's dire prognosis. In her heart, she knew he was right, but she continued to hold out some desperate hope for a solution to her family's financial challenge. "Is there a market to sell off some of the land?" she asked.

Atwell considered the question for a moment and then responded, "Yes, there's a possibility your neighbors would have interest in adjoining properties. I can begin making some inquiries if you would like."

"Yes, please."

"I should caution you, however," he said, "your surrounding neighbors are dealing with many of the same issues as your father."

"Yes, of course," she said.

Atwell finished the exchange with a summary of bank balances remaining. The accounts she held now with her deceased husband were nearly gone or held in worthless Confederate currency. Atwell had also been brought in by her father to help manage their family accounts which had suffered considerably as the war pressed on. There was virtually no time left before all their remaining money would be gone.

Amanda was not surprised by the polite exchange with Jeremy's father. She didn't push for further explanation as he outlined the dire financial situation she faced and the prospect of having to sell her family's assets to settle bank debts her father had incurred in recent years to keep the operation functioning.

Her father-in-law invited her to stay in town for the night to have dinner with him and Jeremy's surviving brother, Jackson. Jeremy's mother had passed away a year into the war from a fever that took her quickly. When Amanda hesitated about the offer of dinner, her father-in-law persisted until she reluctantly agreed.

Out on the street, Atticus and Tulia were waiting with the horses. "We'll be staying the night now down at Mr. Atwell's," she said. "I need to pick up a few more things first. Would you please wait here for me?" Atticus nodded his head in acknowledgment and turned to climb up into the carriage.

Tulia said, "You hurry, now. It's too hot to be out in this sun!" The old woman was always fussing at Amanda but loved her like a daughter.

Amanda moved away down the narrow walk, her leather boots slapping on the old planking, the smell of horses and wood fires thick in the air. Layers of dark purple and gray clouds pushed in above the main street buildings leaving only a splash of the sun's rays breaking through far to the west. As she walked by the tavern, she couldn't help but look inside the open door for the stranger. She saw him with his back to her at the long bar, alone except for the bartender who replaced the empty glass of beer in front of him. The old satchel sat on the bar beside him. The man turned when he heard her footsteps as she came through the door. He took off his hat and placed it over the satchel. He looked at her again with those haunted eyes. Amanda crossed the short distance between the two of them. He stood and pushed the barstool aside. She held out her hand. "My name is Amanda Atwell."

The man stared at her for a moment, holding her hand. "Yes, I know," he said.

"How do you know me?" she asked, pulling back, nervous and unsure of the man's intentions.

"Would you sit down with me for a moment?" he asked, pointing to a table near the wall.

Amanda continued to look into his face, searching for some recognition or knowledge of the man. He pulled the satchel from the bar and followed her as she moved over to sit at the table. He sat across from her, placing his hat on the back of the chair and the satchel between them.

"What is your name, sir?" Amanda asked.

The man took a deep breath and then let it out slowly, not able to meet her gaze. When he looked up, she noticed wetness forming in the corners of his eyes. His face was strained and tense with deep creases formed in the pale skin of his forehead.

Finally, he spoke in a whispered voice and she had to lean across the table to hear him. "My name is Heyward, ma'am," he said.

"And why are you here, Mr. Heyward?"

"Just Heyward," he said. Again, he took in a deep breath, this time looking directly into her eyes. "I have news of your husband, Miss Atwell," his voice now gaining some purpose and assuredness.

"My husband?" she asked, pushing back, her hands pressing down hard on the table between them. "Where did you know Jeremy?"

Heyward didn't answer but pulled back the flap on the satchel and reached inside. His hand came out holding a wrinkled and folded piece of paper which he held between them and then reached across the table to hand it to her. She saw it was a piece of white stationery, though stained and torn at the edges. She looked back at him for an explanation, but he just nodded at the letter.

When Amanda opened the two folds of the paper, she was stunned to see the familiar handwriting of her husband. She felt the air drawn from her lungs. With hands shaking, she started reading, the voice of her lost husband speaking to her in the comfortable and accustomed tone she had nearly forgotten.

My dearest Amanda,

By now I'm sure you've heard of the treaty signed by General Lee. We were all shocked to hear of the defeat of the Southern Armies as we had yet to even raise our weapons against the Yankees since we arrived in Texas. We were making plans to abandon the outpost here at Brownsville to return home. It's been so long and I was lifted, even in defeat, knowing I would soon be home and in your arms again.

This morning our scouts spotted a large force of Union soldiers approaching from Brazos Island to the east. I'm not sure yet in their purpose, but it seems clear they're looking for a fight. We're leaving now to stage along the river near the old Palmetto Ranch. Some of our officers think they're coming for our weapons and horses.

One thing I've learned in this war, things don't always turn out to be what they seem.

I'm sure to be home soon. All my love,
Jeremy

Amanda's hands fell to the table, still trembling as she held the letter. She looked up at the man who called himself, Heyward. "Where did you get this?" she asked. When he hesitated, she said again, "Tell me where you got this!"

"Your husband died at Palmetto Ranch in south Texas, Miss Atwell," he finally said, his voice low and restrained, his hands gripping the edge of the table to find some feeble grounding.

When he paused, she lashed out, "But why, the war was over for weeks?"

The man found the resolve to continue as he brushed the hair back from his face. "My outfit was ordered to muster at Fort Brown and support your husband and his small unit of cavalry who were holding off the Federals down along the river to the east of Brownsville. Your husband was a brave man, Miss Atwell." He hesitated, clearly unsure in how to continue.

"But why?" she pleaded. "What was the purpose? He said they wanted horses and guns?"

Heyward looked down at the letter in her hands but couldn't answer. Finally, he said, "I found this letter in this satchel on your husband... on his body, after the fight. I thought you should have it."

"My God," she gasped. "You were there with him?"

He nodded but didn't answer, trying to hold her insistent stare. The sound of the old clock on the wall ticking was all that broke the silence between them.

"You need to tell me!" she said, leaning across the table.

"Your husband led a series of attacks against the Federals," he finally said. "He and his men had kept them hemmed in since the previous day. When we arrived with Colonel Ford and reinforcements on the second day, Captain Atwell continued to harass the two units of Union fighters to the south while Colonel Ford set up a counterattack to the north.

"Tell me what happened," she said, squeezing the letter tighter in her hands.

"Your husband was shot and killed as he led another attack on one of the Union skirmish lines," he said and then paused to gather himself. "He fell as their horses made another rush at the Union position. When the fight ended, I checked to see if he was alive. I found the letter in an envelope with your address here in South Carolina. It was in this satchel he carried that day," he said as he touched the bag on the table between them.

She pushed her chair back. "And you've come here to tell me you saw my husband die?" He didn't answer. "Why did you wait? It's been over a year."

He nodded as if that would be answer enough, but then he spoke. "It took some time for..." and then he hesitated. "There were things I needed to attend to after we were sent home."

"But why did you come?" she asked, pleading for some sense of understanding.

"I had Captain Atwell's letter." he said, "I knew I had to someday get it to his family, to face you and tell you what really happened."

Amanda continued to look into Heyward's eyes. She glanced down at the letter and the satchel on the table and saw the words of her husband on his last day, penned across the page. A tear ran down her cheek and fell on the letter, the spot widening as it soaked into the soiled paper. She folded it and held it gently.

When she got up, Heyward stood as well, pushing back his chair. They looked at each other across the table, the clock ticking above them, the bartender cleaning glasses behind the bar. She stood staring at the man, holding the back of the chair to steady herself. Thoughts and images of that last battle rushed through her mind, Jeremy falling from his horse mortally wounded as the man before her watched his life ebb away.

Heyward stood with his hands at his side, the satchel still resting on the table. His face held a look of both expectation and doubt. When she finally spoke, there was an air of uncertainty in her words. "Mr. Heyward," she began and then held her hand out to him. "I must thank you for coming all this way."

"Miss Atwell... " he began, but she stopped him.

"No, you need say nothing more," she said.

"But ma'am..."

"No, it was good of you to come. It was right for you to come."

"Your husband was a fine officer, ma'am," the man named Heyward said.

Amanda paused, considering his comment. "I'm having dinner with Jeremy's father tonight," she said at last.

He nodded.

"I think you should join us," she said. "I want you to meet Jeremy's father and brother."

He looked down for a moment, hesitating. "It would be my honor," he said at last, standing straight and bowing slightly as if he was still in uniform. He reached for the satchel on the table and handed it to her with nervous reverence. She took it and held it to her breast.

Amanda told him the address and time and then turned to leave. She stopped and looked back at Heyward. She went over and stood before him. She saw his face tremble slightly at her nearness. She leaned in closer and could smell the scent of horse and leather and beer on the man. She reached out her hand and Heyward looked down and then held it softly.

"Thank you for making this journey, sir."

Without waiting for a response, she turned and walked out the door. She put her husband's letter back into the satchel and pulled the leather strap over her shoulder as she walked back out into the heat of the coming day.

Chapter Seven

Hanna

Pawleys Island, South Carolina *Present Day*

The detective was fifteen minutes late and apologized as she let him in the door. Grace and Thomas had left a half hour earlier to get some dinner. Hanna had no appetite, but they promised to bring back some take-out.

Detective Alex Frank looked to Hanna to be on the older side of his thirties. He was taller than her and seemed quite fit. His white dress shirt was turned up at the sleeves and slightly damp under the arms from the heat of the day. He wore no tie and his shirt was unbuttoned at the neck. His slacks were a pressed khaki, although wrinkled from the drive up from Charleston. He had comfortable looking tan loafers on his feet. Hanna looked at a face she remembered from three months ago during the dark times of Ben's death. It was a kind face and his demeanor had been the same during those difficult days.

"Thank you for seeing me so quickly," he said as she led him into the kitchen.

"Of course," Hanna said. "What on earth is this all about?" She motioned for him to take one of the stools set at the long kitchen island. "Can I get you something to drink?"

"A glass of water, thank you."

She went around to the sink, took down a glass from one of the cabinets and poured the glass full. She set it down and stood across the island from him. "So, what couldn't wait 'til next week?"

"We kept your husband's case open these past months, ma'am," he started. "As you know, there was no killer apprehended. The one suspect we had proved out to be the wrong guy... the street dealer, you remember."

"Yes, I remember," Hanna said. "I told you from the beginning, Ben didn't do drugs."

"Yes, we know. No need to go over all that again, but there seemed to be enough evidence at the time to place him as a suspect," the detective said.

"So, what now?" Hanna asked, watching as the man laid a shoulder bag on the counter and pulled out a file he opened between them. He sorted through some of the papers without comment. She winced when she saw crime scene photos of her husband lying on the sidewalk near downtown Charleston, a pool of blood from the gunshot wounds on the side of his head and chest.

The detective noticed she was looking at the photos and covered them with some other papers in the file. "I'm sorry," he said, now pulling out several other documents and a spreadsheet. "We continue to learn more about your husband's financial affairs, Miss Walsh."

"Please, Hanna."

He looked up at her from the papers. "Yes, Hanna. Now about this new information..."

"What, that I'm dead broke and have to sell everything I own, and I'll still be in hock for the rest of my life."

Frank considered her comment for a moment and then said, "Yes, that and more."

"There's more! God, no!"

The detective continued. "Are you aware your husband was working with some very questionable characters in the business dealings he had leading up to his murder?"

"What are you talking about?" Hanna said, now with her full attention focused on the man. "I certainly know someone stole every cent Ben had invested in the deal, which happened to be every cent we had."

"The real estate developers he was working with on the golf course and homes project just on the mainland near Savannah," he said.

"Yes, I'm well aware of the Osprey Dunes project, Detective. "Now that it's all gone south, it's going to cost me everything I own, including this house that's been in our family for God knows how many years."

"I'm sorry," Frank said.

"Nothing to be done about it now," she said, her voice quivering.

"Miss Walsh... Hanna, it seems the company your husband was investing with and representing for the legal work on the project was apparently just a front for a group based out of Miami."

"Miami?"

"The FBI has been working this..."

"The FBI!" Hanna said, her eyes growing wide.

"Yes, a few weeks ago we began to see some of the connections in this case and we needed to call in the Feds... excuse me, the FBI."

"What connections?" Hanna asked.

"We started following the money, ma'am."

"What money?" she said with exasperation. "There is no damn money!"

"Oh, there was plenty of money."

"What!"

Frank continued. "Problem was, it all seems to have ended up down in Miami with some very unscrupulous people."

Hanna came around the island and sat next to the man. "Are you telling me my husband was dealing with the mob?"

"It appears so, Hanna."

Chapter Eight

Amanda

Georgetown, South Carolina 1866

Amanda sat on a rusting wrought iron bench in the small garden behind her in-law's house, the letter from her husband open on her lap. The once vibrant green space that had graced the Atwell home before the war with the colors of azaleas, primrose and trumpet vine now lay unattended and overgrown with weeds and kudzu. The back of the house which sat at the far western border of the small town of Georgetown had two boarded-up windows.

The Union Army swept through the area a year earlier and ransacked most of the homes in their path. The Atwells had only regained occupancy of their house a few months ago and were staggered to find most of their possessions stolen or burned as the Federals passed through. The small stable at the back of the property was burned to the ground and the charred ruins remained as a reminder of the invading army's relentless assault. Orlando Atwell had slowly attempted to make the place livable again, finding furniture and other household necessities down in Charleston that had been shipped back.

Jeremy's father had done his best to protect their financial assets, but much of their wealth had been lost in now worthless Confederate currency. The Atwell law practice had survived the war, apparently because the family had some remaining resources to fall back upon when local clients grew scarce.

Amanda looked again at the letter in her lap and thought about the strange man, Heyward, who made the trip to South Carolina to deliver her husband's note personally. He was obviously still dealing with difficult emotions from the war and it seemed particularly so about the battle that had taken Jeremy's life. *Palmetto Ranch*, she thought. *What a godforsaken place it must be.*

While she had never been to Texas, she imagined it from stories and news items she had read as a barren and bleak landscape, devoid of all but the most inhospitable outlaws, Indians and snakes. She thought again about the Union attack on her husband's position. *Who was responsible for this senseless effort? Who should be held accountable?*

She hadn't asked Heyward where he was from, perhaps Texas, although Jeremy's letters over the past years described his unit as mostly men from the Carolinas. When she told Jeremy's father earlier she had invited the man to their house for dinner that evening, he seemed genuinely pleased to meet a member of his son's Company and was certainly interested in learning more about how his son had perished at Palmetto Ranch. Jeremy's brother, Jackson Atwell, had been less enthusiastic. He wanted to know more about the man named Heyward and had asked numerous and skeptical questions.

The Atwell's long-time slave and now paid servant, Sadie, poked her head out the back door of the house and said, "Miss Atwell, your guest at the front door."

"Thank you," she said to the thin black woman. "Tell him I'll be right there."

"Yes, ma'am," she responded before disappearing back inside.

Amanda placed the letter back in her purse. She stood and walked around the side of the house feeling a hot breeze blow up and rustle the leaves and hanging moss in the live oaks and low through the sawgrass. When she came around to the front, she saw the man named Heyward standing on the front porch speaking with her father-in-law. Both men noticed her and moved aside as she made her way up the few steps to join them. She tried to block out thoughts of the past and took a deep breath before she reached out her hand. "Mr. Heyward, I'm glad you were able to join us tonight. You've obviously met Mr. Atwell, Jeremy's father."

"Good evening, ma'am," said Heyward. "We were just getting acquainted." Heyward had changed clothes from earlier at the saloon. He had clearly bathed and put on a clean shirt and thin tie, as well as a dark gray coat and pants pulled down over his still worn boots. His long brown hair was combed back wet from his face.

"Shall we go inside?" Atwell suggested.

He opened the door and the two men followed Amanda into the house and then to the left into the main drawing room. Sadie was there with a tray of white wine poured in tall glasses. They all reached for drinks and the elder Atwell raised his in a toast.

"Managed to keep a few bottles from the Yankees," Atwell said. "To my son, Captain Jeremy Atwell, and to his fellow soldier-in-arms, Mr. Heyward." He paused a moment. "And to the Confederacy!" The three of them touched their glasses and took a sip of the wine. He continued, "As I was saying, Heyward, thank you again for coming all the way out to Carolina to deliver Jeremy's letter. I'm sure it must have been a burden for you."

"No, not at all," said Heyward, a bit reluctantly. "I wanted to make sure it arrived safely."

Amanda said, "I didn't ask how far you traveled, sir. Where do you make your home?'

Heyward took another sip from his wine and then said, "I've settled in Texas for now."

"Then you'll be going back soon?" Atwell asked.

Heyward just nodded.

"It must be a considerable journey," Amanda said and again, Heyward bobbed his head in affirmation. "We'll be anxious to hear more of your time with Jeremy, sir. Perhaps over dinner?"

"Certainly, ma'am," he said.

"My other son will be coming in soon from town to join us for dinner," Atwell said. "Jackson served with one of Lee's regiments from Virginia. We were fortunate to see him return in one piece. He saw quite a lot of action."

"I'll look forward to meeting him, sir," Heyward said.

"Shall we sit a moment?" Atwell asked, motioning to a circle of chairs and a long couch. The two men took chairs facing Amanda after she sat on the end of the couch. "So, you served in my son's company?" Atwell continued.

"No, another company of Colonel Ford's regiment," Heyward said.

"But you knew my son, you say?" asked Atwell.

"Yes. Yes, I knew him. He was a fine officer, sir."

"Thank you, Mr. Heyward." Atwell took a long drink from his wine. "And you were there the day he died?"

"Just *Heyward*, sir and yes, I was there."

The three of them turned as the front door opened and Jackson Atwell came in, taking off his Confederate officer's hat and hanging it on a stand. He turned and came into the drawing room to join the others. The men stood to greet him. Amanda bowed her head a touch as he approached. She always thought him a slighter version of his brother in both size and demeanor. While there was a resemblance to her husband, the younger brother Jackson had always struck her as duller in features, less pronounced in spirit and manner. They had always had a cordial relationship since her marriage to Jeremy, but she could not say they had grown close. She had seen him on only a few occasions since his return from Virginia, just a month before they learned of Jeremy's death, although he had called on her twice out at Pawleys Island, asking of her health and well-being following the news of Jeremy's passing. Amanda continued to be surprised when Jackson would wear articles of his military apparel, as if that would better define his position and accomplishments. The smell of bourbon and cigar smoke came into the room with him.

Orlando Atwell spoke first. "Son, please meet one of Jeremy's fellow officers."

"Heyward," the visitor said, interrupting his host. "It's my pleasure to meet you, sir."

"Welcome to our home," Jackson Atwell said, his speech noticeably slurred from drink. "We appreciate you bringing us news of my brother, sir." As the two men shook hands, the younger Atwell stared intently into their guest's eyes and held his hand longer than necessary in an overly firm grip.

"Certainly," said Heyward.

"Shall we go in for dinner?" Orlando suggested.

Sadie was hovering near the door to the dining room and nodded as the group followed Amanda in for the meal. The old woman scurried off ahead of them into the kitchen, barking low orders to others who were preparing the food. Mr. Atwell held a chair for Amanda next to his place at the head of the table. Jackson sat to her other side and Heyward in the seat across from her. When they were all seated, Sadie came through the door with another bottle of wine and filled their glasses.

This time the younger Atwell proposed the toast. "To our fallen brothers of the Confederacy," he said as they all raised their glasses and drank. "And to the loveliest woman in the Carolinas," he continued with a bright smile that seemed out of place and improper to Amanda. Again, they all took a sip from their drink, more hesitantly on this occasion. Jackson drained his glass and looked for the bottle to refill it.

"So, Mr. Heyward," Jackson continued, "you served with old Rip Ford in the Texas Cavalry?"

Heyward nodded as they all looked to see Sadie and Amanda's servant, Tulia, with two other servers coming in with trays of food. There was a young black girl and an even younger little boy. While they were being served, Atwell said, "We've heard this Rip Ford was a heck of a fighter."

"Yes, sir," Heyward replied. "Between scrapes with Indians and Mexicans and the Union Army, he's seen his share. I can testify he's a darn fine battlefield commander."

With Sadie's and Tulia's help, they all passed food and began to eat. Amanda looked across the table at the man named Heyward. "Tell us a bit more about yourself," she said.

Heyward looked at the faces around the table for a moment and finished chewing his last mouthful of food. "Ma'am, there's not much to tell," he said. "I'm just released from the Army. I'll be headed back to Texas and hope to find a piece of land to get a ranch going."

"Do you have family back in Texas?" Amanda asked.

Heyward took a sip from his wine before he answered. "No, ma'am. There's no family"

"I don't recall Jeremy ever mentioning you in his letters," she said. "Were the two of you close?"

"No, I wouldn't say close. Fort Brown was a big garrison with a lot of officers."

Jackson put down his knife and fork and looked across the table at their guest for a moment. "Seems strange you'd come all this way, seeing you weren't even friends."

Heyward noticed they were all looking at him. He glanced down at the table for a moment. "I felt it was something I needed to do," he finally said. "Bring the letter I mean. I saw Captain Atwell fall to the enemy's guns. I stopped and tried to help with his wound, but it was too late. I took his bag so it wouldn't fall into the wrong hands."

"He died quickly then?" Amanda asked.

"Yes, I think he may have been gone before he even hit the ground. I'm sorry, ma'am."

Amanda sighed and pushed the food around on her plate. "Well, thank God for that," she said, a note of resignation and despair clear in her voice. "We've never heard where he was buried, sir."

Heyward hesitated for a moment. "There's a small cemetery at Fort Brown in Brownsville."

"I'll have to make the trip someday soon," she said.

"It's no place for a woman, Miss Atwell. The Mexicans and the French are stirring up trouble again."

"Well, someday."

Orlando Atwell put his fork down and wiped his mouth with a napkin. "Can you help us understand why this damn fight even happened, Captain Heyward?"

Before he could begin to answer, Jackson raised his hand to interrupt, knocking over his full glass of wine. "The goddamned Blue Bellies ignored the damn treaty!" he spat.

"Jackson, that's enough!" said the man's father. "And you've had more than your share of drink today. I suggest you excuse yourself."

The man stood unsteadily, his hands on the table for support. He glared at his father for a moment with glassy eyes, then at Amanda. "Please forgive me, Amanda dear," he mumbled and then pushed back his chair. "Mr. Heyward," he continued, "it's been my pleasure, sir." He turned and walked on wobbly legs through the door into the kitchen. They all heard the back-door slam as he left the house.

"I'm sorry for my son's behavior," Orlando said. "He's struggled since he's been back. I'm sure you understand, Heyward."

"Of course, sir."

Orlando said, "Again, I ask, what could possibly have caused this fight? Lee's Army had laid down their arms weeks earlier and I understand the commanding generals of both armies in Texas had agreed to a truce to wind down the war there even before that."

"You are right, Mr. Atwell," Heyward answered, looking at Amanda as he spoke. "There was no good reason for the Union attack."

"Then why, sir? What did my son die for?"

Sadie had apparently heard the voices rising and she came into the dining room. "Can I take the dishes, Mr. Atwell?" she asked.

"Later, Sadie," Atwell snapped. "Give us a few more minutes," he continued, this time in a softer tone as he watched her back through the door into the kitchen. He looked back at his dinner guest. "No good reason, you say."

"No, I'm afraid not, sir," Heyward replied, clearly uncomfortable. He placed his napkin on the table. "The Union commander at Brazos Santiago was a colonel named Barnett."

"Barnett," said Amanda.

"Yes, ma'am. I'm not sure, but it seems this man, Barnett, felt the need to show his mettle before the war wound down completely."

"And what did he hope to accomplish?" Orlando asked.

"No one seems real clear on that."

"And how many men did he get killed besides my Jeremy?" Amanda asked.

"Too many, ma'am," he said quietly. "Too many."

"This man, Barnett," she continued, "did he survive the attack?"

"Yes, he did," the man said slowly.

Amanda paused, staring at their dinner guest, then said, "And were there any consequences?"

"Consequences?" Heyward asked.

"Was this man dealt with for ordering such a senseless attack?"

Heyward looked back at her and then over to her father-in-law. Finally, he said, "I've heard this man, Barnett, received no disciplinary action. Others in his command were brought before a Courts Martial for their role in the defeat of the Union forces during those two days at Palmetto Ranch."

"In their defeat?" Orlando asked.

"Yes, sir. When Colonel Ford arrived with considerable support for the Confederate defense, more cavalry and even artillery, the Union positions were overrun. Many surrendered... or were killed, but most were able to escape and return to their garrison on Brazos Island."

Amanda wiped at tears forming in her eyes as she listening to the man's account. She said, "So it was all for nothing?"

"Yes, ma'am."

"And this man, Barnett, he escaped?" she asked.

Heyward looked down at his plate and then said softly, "Yes, he led the retreat."

There was only silence in the room and then Amanda stood abruptly, knocking her chair back. She threw her napkin down on the table and rushed away into the kitchen. The two men could hear the back door open and then slam as she ran out into the night.

Chapter Nine

Hanna

Pawleys Island, South Carolina *Present Day*

They were on the deck now. Alex Frank had agreed to join her with a glass of wine, seeing that it was after five o'clock and he was technically off duty. Grace and Thomas hadn't returned yet from dinner.

Hanna was still staggered from the detective's revelation her husband had been doing business with the mob in Miami. Her hand trembled as she took another sip from the wine.

"I'm sorry to upset you, Hanna," he said. "I can't imagine how hard this has been for you."

Hanna looked out over the water trying to compose herself. The beach was nearly abandoned now. The low sun turned the water a shiny gray and small swells pushed up onto the beach.

She heard Frank say, "So, again, you never heard your husband talk about any organized crime elements in Florida?"

Hanna swallowed hard and shook her head. "No, I told you, I didn't know Ben had ever even been to Miami, let alone doing business with people like that."

"The FBI will want to talk to you about this," he said.

She looked at him with alarm in her eyes. "What could I possibly tell the FBI?"

The detective turned and leaned back against the deck rail, holding the wine glass in both hands. "They've put together a considerable paper trail on this whole episode. They want to confirm a few details that you may have some recollection of."

"I've told you, Ben never talked about anything related to Miami or..."

Frank interrupted, "I know you think that now, but they may be able to help you remember even some small details that could help."

"Help with what! My husband is dead. Everything we owned and cherished is gone. I have no idea how I'm going to get my kid through school."

"I would think you'd want to know why your husband died."

"We know why he died!" she said, slamming her hand down on the deck rail. "He was robbed, and the animal shot him."

"Yes, that's what it appears to be, but the Federal investigators aren't so sure."

"What, they think some mobster killed him over this damn real estate deal?"

"They'll share the information they've obtained," he said with a calm and reassuring voice. "They'll want to know if you can confirm or elaborate on any of their information."

Hanna looked at the man for a moment, trying as best she could to control the anger and fear that was building, but then all attempts to keep her composure melted away and she threw her wine glass as hard as she could against the front wall of the house. The glass shattered against the cedar shakes and the wine spilled down onto the deck with a thousand pieces of broken glass.

"None of this is going to bring Ben back!" she screamed. "None of this will save my life from slipping down this hellhole!"

"I'm sorry, Hanna." He bent over and started to pick up the broken glass. "I wanted to warn you about this. I didn't want the FBI to show up unexpected on your doorstep. They're just trying to find who's responsible for all this."

Hanna slumped to the floor of the deck, her back against the old wood spindles of the rail. She put her arms around her knees and buried her face. She took a deep breath to gather her composure then remembered back to the afternoon just three months ago when the detective and another plainclothes policeman came to her front door in Charleston to tell her of her husband's death. The same numbing sense of disbelief and fear she felt that day swept over her again.

She didn't hear Grace and Thomas come out on the deck until Grace cried out, "What in hell is going on here!"

Chapter Ten

Jeremy

Palmetto Ranch, Texas March 12, 1865

Atwell stood beside his horse with a dozen of his small cavalry patrol along a line of chaparral and mesquite bushes that hid them from the skirmish line of Union soldiers two hundred yards to their east. The sweat smell from the horses and black flies buzzing around his head barely caught his attention, his senses acute to the nearness of the enemy. He could see most of the Federal soldiers who looked to be about fifty strong. They were stationed along a thin perimeter lying prone to the ground with rifles aimed at a possible Confederate attack, taking cover where they could behind small sand hills or scrub. Three officers on horseback rode along the line behind them. The smoke fires from the main Union force could be seen back towards White's Ranch, perhaps a mile away, rising in gray plumes against the early morning sky.

If the Union commander planned to keep on toward Brownsville, Atwell had detected no visible signs yet. The enemy skirmish line he now faced seemed clearly to be in defense of the main force back at White's Ranch. Earlier, he had given his men orders to begin a series of attacks that would be more harassment than a real threat to the enemy. In his mind, their best chance to delay or even head off a direct assault on Brownsville would be to continue to pester the Federals with quick assaults to make their own defensive force seem much more formidable than it really was until reinforcements arrived from Fort Brown.

Atwell motioned to the first man down the line from him and signaled to spread the word. He drew the pistol from the holster at his side and took aim through the cover of the bushes at the Union soldier closest to him across the open field. He saw all his men do the same. He took a deep breath and fired off the first shot. The deafening crack of the pistol and ensuing weapon's fire echoed through the early morning stillness and caused his horse to startle and lurch backward. Birds resting in the low bushes suddenly took flight with irritated squawks and screeches. He saw his shot strike the sand hill in front of the enemy position as a small cloud of dust was pushed up. The sound was followed by a continued chorus of gunfire and screams from Jeremy's small force.

The horse of one of the Union commanders reared up and whinnied loud as the men along the skirmish line pulled their rifles close to take aim at an enemy they had yet to see, other than smoke from gunfire drifting up above the far bushes. All three enemy officers began screaming orders as they raced up and down behind the small line of soldiers.

Jeremy's men kept firing and yelling, moving to new cover every few moments. The enemy's return fire began to come in, breaking branches in the chaparral, sometimes whistling too close to one of their heads. After just a minute of this first quick assault, Jeremy ordered his men back as previously instructed to another line of cover, just out of range. Their retreat was visible to the Federals who continued to fire.

Twice more, Jeremy ordered his men up for a quick assault under cover of the Texas scrub, more noise and bluster than any serious peril to the enemy. Within a half hour, he could see the main force coming forward from White's Ranch, marching quick in orderly rows under the full colors of Union and regimental flags. A senior officer was out front barking orders to the men around him.

Jeremy sent word to his small patrol to continue their planned retreat back toward Palmetto Ranch. Throughout the morning, they would repeat their quick attacks on the approaching enemy, only to draw back again behind cover. Two more patrols from Jeremy's command joined them and spread out along the route of the advancing Union force to keep the surprise and pressure on the enemy. Jeremy was quite certain they had created the appearance of a far larger force to the enemy command, but if anything, they were only slowing the inevitable march of the Federals toward Brownsville.

By noon, they had fought and then retreated as planned all the way back to Palmetto Ranch. They had suffered no casualties and only a few insignificant wounds. Jeremy was uncertain of the damage inflicted on the enemy, but he thought it slight, at best. He called his officers together quickly outside the main outbuilding and gave the order to move back again toward Fort Brown, leaving the desolate outpost of Palmetto Ranch to the approaching enemy. He had yet to receive word on any specific support coming from Colonel Rip Ford in Brownsville but knew it would be best to continue to wait on a major assault on the enemy until reinforcements arrived.

He watched as his men rode off quickly to the west, the dust of the Texas prairie drifting up behind them. He took one more look as the enemy force came around a series of low hills, still in formation along the main road. His command would be leaving behind a few head of cattle and food supplies but nothing of real strategic value. He kicked his horse and turned to follow his men back into cover about a mile west of Palmetto Ranch.

At midday, Captain Atwell stood with two of his officers looking east toward the distant cluster of buildings at Palmetto Ranch from the rise of a long hill stretching to the north. The small company had reassembled after their quick retreat an hour earlier. As he listened to one of his men speculating on what course of action the Federals might take next, Jeremy saw a plume of dark gray smoke rise from the direction of the small ranch they had just abandoned. The smoke trail grew larger and then was joined by two others in obvious close proximity.

"They're burning the damn place down!" Jeremy said in disgust.

One of his scouts pulled up quick in front of them with his horse. Without dismounting he said, "Looks like the full lot of 'em got into Palmetto Ranch. They took everything they could find and then started to torch the place, even the house."

Jeremy shook his head, looking out to the east as he considered the situation. He knew the Orive family who had owned the land for generations. "Did you get a good count on their numbers?" he asked the scout.

"Pretty close to three hundred, as we saw yesterday," the young scout said. "They was moving down along the river, taking the high ground to the south of the ranch."

"Those sons of bitches!" Jeremy hissed. "First, they come roaring in looking for a fight, never mind the damned treaty. Now they torch that family's ranch." He turned to the officers beside him. Their numbers had grown to near 200 through the day as word had spread west to other small

63

Confederate outposts on the road to Brownsville. "Have the men assemble, six companies again." He signaled to have his own horse brought up. "They're gonna think the whole goddamned Confederate Army's coming down on their asses this afternoon!"

For the next three hours, Jeremy's small attack parties continued to harass the Union forces dug in south of Palmetto Ranch along the Rio Grande. Despite defensive positions on high ground, the sporadic and fierce assaults of mounted Confederate cavalry coming from ever-changing directions seemed to confuse and intimidate the enemy. Finally, at about 3 p.m., Atwell began to see signs of a Union retreat. He ordered his teams to continue the offensive, keeping the pressure on the enemy even as they pulled back from Palmetto Ranch. Eventually, the Union forces pulled all the way back to White's Ranch again where their command ordered defensive skirmish lines as night fell.

Chapter Eleven

Hanna

Pawleys Island, South Carolina *Present Day*

Detective Frank had left over an hour ago. Hanna was unable to eat any of the food Grace and Thomas brought back from dinner. Thomas had also just left as the day was ending and the sun held just above the rooflines to the west of the long barrier island.

Grace had convinced her to take a walk on the beach. They walked south now along the hard-packed sand near the water line, the ocean still calm and serene to their left, the sun a large orange ball to the west, still leaving the air stifling hot. The cool chill of the water was the only comfort from the heat.

"The FBI is coming out here?" she heard Grace ask.

Hanna didn't answer at first. She had filled her friend in on most of the conversation with the Charleston detective. Her mind was still overwhelmed with the new information the man had shared.

Grace said, "Phillip will be furious they haven't contacted him," referring to her husband who was also Hanna's attorney.

"What...who?" Hanna finally said. "What are you talking about?"

"The FBI should inform your attorney they need information from you. The Charleston police know he's representing you."

"Why on earth for?" Hanna said. "I don't have anything to hide."

"That's not the point," Grace said. "They're obviously fishing for something and you need to be represented and protected."

"I can't believe this," Hanna said. She turned and walked deeper out into the water and then stopped when she reached her knees. The calm water slapped gently at her bare legs. A formation of five pelicans came low over the water from her left and continued south for their evening's roost. The air felt metallic in her mouth and smelled of dried seaweed and early bonfires.

Hanna said, "Can they possibly think I was involved in all this?"

"We don't know what they think," Grace said. "I'll call Phillip when we get home. Let's see if he can come up tomorrow to speak with you before the FBI gets here."

"I don't want to look like a suspect with my attorney sitting in the room."

"That's not the point," Grace replied.

"What is the damn point to any of this?" Hanna said, turning to her friend and walking back toward the shore.

She decided to start in the attic. The sun was down now, and she flipped on the light at the base of the stairs. Grace followed Hanna up as a stale smell drifted in the air from above. They both screamed as a bat came at them and then turned to fly back up into the attic.

I am not going up there!" Grace said, backing down the narrow flight of stairs. "Don't you have some closets or something I can sort through?"

"Why don't you start in the kitchen pantry. There are some trash bags in there for all the food. Just throw it all away. I'll help you sort through the pots and pans later."

"You sure you want to go up there?" Grace asked.

"Those bats have been there for a hundred years. We used to go up as kids to try to roust them. They're harmless."

"Just scream if you need me," Grace said as she turned to go back down to the kitchen.

Hanna reached the top of the stairs and found another light switch on the wall that illuminated the old attic with two bare bulbs. The space was stifling hot and the musty smell was consuming. She looked across the room filled with old furniture, taped-up boxes and more junk than she thought she'd ever have time to sort through. She almost turned to leave it was so overwhelming but then decided she would have to deal with it sooner than later.

After an hour, she had made some progress in sorting out the few items she thought she should keep and place in storage somewhere, although she had no idea where. The rest was trash that would have to be hauled away. She realized she would have to get a dumpster brought in to hold all of it.

She started in on another pile of boxes and saw an old trunk sitting behind them. She pushed the boxes aside and slid the dust-covered trunk out closer to the overhead light. It was made from old leather with tarnished metal fittings and edges. She struggled with the clasp on the front before it finally broke loose. She opened the heavy lid slowly, a little afraid of what she might find... *hopefully not another damned bat*, she thought.

She saw layers of old clothes and an even heavier smell of mildew and decay made her turn her head to take a clear breath. She thought for a moment about just sliding the whole mess into the trash pile but then sorted down through the top layer of old dresses and jackets. She tried to place the age of the clothes and figured they had to be at least late 1800's. Further down she found several small boxes filled with what was probably costume jewelry and a few coins that looked like old silver dollars. She placed the boxes on the floor next to the trunk and kept digging down.

There were several books and she pulled the first out to examine the cover. It was a very old copy of a James Fennimore Cooper novel, *The Pioneers*, the cover badly worn and nearly falling off. She looked through several others thinking they may be worth a few dollars to a collector but wasn't sure she even wanted to deal with trying to sell them.

The last book didn't have a title on the cover. It had a black and very worn leather cover like an old Bible. She opened it and saw faded writing on the yellowed pages, an elegant script handwriting barely legible now after years of decay in the old trunk. Near the middle of the diary was a folded piece of notepaper. She pulled it out carefully, worried that it might fall apart in her hands. As she gently unfolded the paper, she turned to get more light and began to read. She was halfway through the note when she whispered, "Oh, my God!"

Chapter Twelve

Jackson

Georgetown, South Carolina 1866

The younger of the Atwell brothers tripped on the door stoop as he staggered into the dimly lit barroom. Catching himself before he fell, he glanced around and saw the two men he had come to meet. He motioned to the man behind the bar to bring a bottle and made his way across the near-empty saloon to join the men.

Both were dressed in fine suits which seemed out of place for this dingy bar. The first was a broad-faced man with a well-trimmed gray beard and thinning gray hair. The other was far slighter and his clothes hung loose on a thin frame. His hair was dark and greased back away from his face, dark circles rimming the bottom of his bloodshot eyes.

Atwell staggered as he pulled out a chair and sat to join the men. The bigger man, Westerman, spoke first. "Where the hell you been, Atwell? We've been waiting over an hour."

Jackson looked over his shoulder as the bartender placed a bottle of whiskey and a shot glass in front of him. He poured a drink and offered the bottle to the others. He watched as they poured the whiskey into their glasses, then he held up his glass to the men and said, "To our bright future in the fair state of South Carolina."

The two men acknowledged the toast and all three threw back their drinks. With glasses back on the table, Westerman said, "We spoke to the old man out at the Paltierre place yesterday, as you said."

"The old fool has lost his mind," Jackson replied.

"Has a daughter who ran us off the place," the thin man named Sullivan said.

Jackson poured another round of drinks. "She's a fine one. I told you she's my brother's widow."

Westerman and Sullivan both nodded. The bigger man said, "You need to talk some sense into that woman."

Jackson said, "I can take care of her."

Chapter Thirteen

Hanna

Pawleys Island, South Carolina *Present Day*

Hanna wasn't sure how much time had passed. She sat against the old trunk, the diary open in her lap. She looked up when she heard Grace yell from the bottom of the steps up to the attic.

"Honey, you okay up there?"

"Fine, I'm fine," Hanna said, still engrossed in what she had been reading.

"Can I get you anything?"

"No, really. I'm fine, thanks."

"We're gonna need a dumpster for all this junk," Grace yelled up.

"I know. We'll call in the morning."

"Do you need any help?" Grace asked. "Did the bats get you yet?"

"No, I'm almost done. I'll be down in a bit." She heard her friend walking away and muttering to herself, "I need more wine."

Hanna looked again at the first page of the diary. It had a name and date written in the same faded and elegant handwriting... *Amanda Paltierre 1857.*

She was familiar with the name. A few years ago, she had spent time on *Ancestry.com* tracing back some of her family's past. The Paltierre family had been early descendants on her mother's side of the family. Further research revealed they had owned this house on Pawleys Island and a large rice plantation to the west on the mainland that was named *Tanglewood.* The old plantation house was a private home now, restored by another family.

Hanna spent several weeks in her spare time searching online historic registries and books about the area and time. She learned more about the Paltierres and the home her family still shared on the island, as well as the old plantation that sat between Pawleys Island and Georgetown to the south. She had contacted the new owners of *Tanglewood,* and they invited her to tour the property.

It was three years ago that she and Grace spent a half day walking through the old house and the grounds where her family used to grow rice and where they lived out the Civil War. They drove up from Charleston on a cool morning in November, Hanna sitting in the passenger seat reading to her friend the history of *Tanglewood* and the Paltierre family from the file she had assembled.

At the time of the Civil War, the Paltierres had four children, three sons and a daughter, Amanda. None of the sons returned from the war and the mother died of an unreported illness while they were away. The daughter, Amanda, had married into another local family, the Atwells. Her husband, Jeremy, had been a Captain in the Confederate Army. It was unclear just how long the plantation had stayed in the Paltierre family after the war and Hanna was anxious to meet the new owners and hopefully learn more about the history of the place and her family.

Hanna had the address in her phone GPS and was navigating for Grace as they drove through the dense South Carolina countryside that morning. Deep forests were broken on occasion with recently harvested farm fields and green pastures with cows and horses grazing, the open land pushing up across the hillsides. A lingering fog still drifted through the trees and lay across the low wetlands as they drove on. The sun filtered through tall pines and sentry-like live oak with huge branches draped in Spanish Moss spreading across the old road.

At the turn into the drive at the *Tanglewood* plantation, there was a black iron gate anchored by tall brick columns. A bronze sign embedded in the brick had *Tanglewood* written in an elegant script. The gate was open, and the drive angled up through a heavy canopy of trees. The tires of Grace's car crunched over the old shells that covered the drive. They made several slow turns and still there was no sign of the house. Hanna remembered there had originally been over 500 acres when the Paltierres owned the property. She wondered how much of the old estate was still intact.

As the drive made another turn, Hanna felt her heart beating faster as the house came into view. She had seen pictures while doing her research, but she was unprepared for the grandeur of the setting and elegant lines of the house, not the iconic two-story columned plantation home that was prevalent across the South, but a low, sprawling ranch house with a long-covered veranda across the front. The white-washed façade of the house was framed by a gray and faded cedar shake roof. Two tall red brick chimneys rose up on each end of the house.

Off to the left, partially hidden by the massive trees on the property, Hanna could see a large white barn and several more smaller outbuildings. There was a long expanse of green meadows beyond, framed by a brown three-rail wood fence. The drive ended in a circle in front of the house. Hanna took a deep breath as Grace pulled the car to a stop. They both had their windows down and a cool breeze blew through the car. She could hear a collection of birdsong from the trees. She noticed feeling a bit unsteady as she reached for the door handle.

A young woman came through the front door. Hanna guessed her to be in her mid-thirties. She was dressed casually in jeans and a loose gray wool sweater against the early morning chill. Her blond hair was tied back in a small blue ribbon. She waved as she came down the steps to greet them, her tall leather boots quiet on the wood steps leading down from the house. Her name was Suzanna Holmes and Hanna had learned she and her husband bought the place five years ago. Her husband was a doctor in Georgetown.

"Good morning, ladies," their host said with a gracious smile. "Welcome to *Tanglewood*."

Hanna and Grace introduced themselves and then Hanna said, "It's so nice of you to have us up today. I hope it's not too much of a bother."

"No, of course not. It gets a little quiet out here and I enjoy the company."

"Well, thank you for having us," Grace said. "My friend has been an excited mess ever since you invited us to come."

"Welcome home, I guess I should say, Hanna," said the new young matron of *Tanglewood*. "I have something to show you inside. I found it in a box in one of the old storage buildings when we first bought the place." She gestured out beyond the barn down the hill to their left. "Come on in!"

Hanna followed the woman up the stairs and through the large black door, framed on both sides with glass sidelights. As her eyes adjusted, she saw rich pine floor planks leading ahead down a wide hallway. To her left, a drawing room was furnished with what looked like original period furniture and to the right, an office with a dark mahogany desk and antique chair with a wall behind it filled with books. She was startled when their host took her hand and led her into the den. Grace followed them in.

They stopped in front of a framed black and white photograph, clearly taken many years earlier. Hanna felt her chest tighten as she moved closer to look at the picture of a large family assembled on the front porch of the house above the steps they had just walked up. She knew immediately it was the Paltierres, with mother and father in the middle, their three sons to the left, all dressed in Confederate officer's uniforms, one with a young woman at his side. To the right, Hanna saw another man and woman holding hands. The man was also dressed in his military uniform and he held his hat in his free hand. The woman wore a long flowing white dress and held a bouquet of cut flowers.

Hanna heard her host say, "That's Amanda, your great-grandmother and her husband, Captain Jeremy Atwell."

"Oh, honey," she heard her friend say as Grace pushed in closer as well to get a better look. "She was beautiful!"

Hanna couldn't take her eyes away from the old photo. Though faded some, the face of her many-times great-grandmother was as clear as if the photo had been taken today. It seemed as if the woman's stare held her own. It was a sad face for such an obviously bright day at the old house and it then occurred to Hanna this may have been a farewell photo with the men soon off to the war.

As Suzanna Holmes led them on a tour of the rest of the house, Hanna couldn't get the face of her distant relative out of her thoughts. When the tour was completed, they all sat at a long wooden dining table next to the kitchen and their host poured coffee and offered a plate filled with croissants and pastries.

"We'll take a walk through the property," Suzanna said, "but let's sit for a minute." She finished serving and then walked over to a flat package laying on the counter, wrapped in brown paper. She brought it back over to the table and handed it to Hanna. "I thought you would like this."

"Really!" Hanna said. "You didn't need to do anything special. Just taking time to show us around has been such a gift."

"Open it," their young host said, the excitement clear in her voice.

Hanna turned the package over and pulled off the tape holding the paper. She gasped as she looked at a replica of the framed family photo they had seen in the office when they first arrived.

"This is actually the original," Suzanna said. "We thought it only right it be returned to the Paltierre family."

"Oh, my goodness!" was all Hanna could say at first. She looked again into the sad eyes of her many generations great-grandmother and then across the gathering of her family so many years earlier.

"There is a note penciled on the back of the photo," she heard the woman say. "It lists the names of all the family members and is dated 1861."

"How can I possibly thank you?" Hanna said. "This is really so kind of you."

"I spoke with my husband and we both agreed the original needed to be returned to the family."

As they walked the grounds of the property later that morning, Hanna remembered feeling as if the ghosts of her past family members were with her that day. They were making their way back up the hill to the house to leave and she tried to imagine all her family coming together on the long porch for the old photo. She also could sense the tearful farewells as the brothers and Jeremy Atwell said goodbye to their family and loved ones. She knew her great-grandmother's sad eyes in the old picture would haunt her forever.

As Hanna sat in the musty old attic at the beach house, she reached for the faded letter again. It was a note to Amanda from her husband, Captain Atwell, during the war, promising to be home soon. From the early part of Amanda's diary, she knew that Jeremy Atwell never made it back to South Carolina.

Chapter Fourteen

Amanda

Georgetown, South Carolina 1865

Amanda sat with her father-in-law and man named Heyward on the front porch of the Atwell house, the sky dark now and filled with bright stars. A sliver of moon was barely visible through the canopy of live oak. Following dinner and the drunken departure of Jackson Atwell, the men had moved outside for a drink to continue their discussion about the battle that had taken Jeremy Atwell's life. They had found Amanda sitting on the porch, staring off down the street. The two men had pulled chairs up near her.

"How many men were there?" Atwell asked.

Their guest took a sip from his drink and then said, "The Union forces numbered about five hundred or so, nearly half were from the 62nd Colored Troops under the direct command of this man Barnett who ordered the attack on Brownsville."

"And on our side?" Amanda asked.

"Your husband was the first to encounter Barnett's forces," Heyward said. "He had been sent out to the east of

Brownsville with a small cavalry company of about fifty or sixty men."

Orlando Atwell rose up in his seat and slammed his glass down on the small table at his side. "Only sixty men up against five hundred!" he said.

"My God," Amanda cried out. "They never had a chance."

Heyward continued. "That first day, only half the Union force had arrived."

Orlando said, "Still, only sixty men with Jeremy?"

"Yes sir. Your son was very brave and a good fighter. He was able to hold off the Federals throughout the day with sudden attacks from heavy brush and cover," Heyward said. "He was even able to force the Union commander to order a withdrawal back to another small ranch to the east at the end of the day. Reinforcements for the Southern troops from Fort Brown didn't arrive until the next day".

Amanda asked, "And the Federals attacked again?"

"Yes, ma'am. This Colonel Barnett I mentioned also came the next morning with more Union troops and he was damned determined to reverse the previous day's defeat and get on to Brownsville."

Amanda stood and walked to the railing of the porch, looking out across the small yard. "And Jeremy was killed on the second day?" she asked. She turned to look at Heyward.

"That's right, ma'am," he said quietly. She stared at her guest, trying to imagine the scene that final day of the battle. She suddenly felt light-headed and had to hold on to the rail to catch herself from falling. Heyward stood quickly and moved across the space between them, reaching for her arm to help steady her.

"I'm sorry, Miss Atwell. I know this must be very hard. I didn't mean to trouble you this much."

"And I've had too much wine, sir, which certainly isn't helping," Amanda said. "I should turn in."

"Good night then, ma'am," Heyward said, stepping back.

Her father-in-law also rose and said, "Mr. Heyward, thank you for coming tonight and for the news of Jeremy. There is some small comfort in knowing of his brave actions."

"You're welcome, sir," Heyward said, bowing slightly.

Amanda said, "Yes, thank you. Thank you for coming all this way." Her voice was weak and soft. She still held the rail for support. "And will you be leaving now? Back to Texas?"

"Soon, ma'am. I have a room here in town for a few days. My horse and I both need a rest before we start back."

"Of course," said Orlando Atwell. "Do stop by my office down in the village before you leave town."

"I'll do that, sir." Heyward reached for his hat next to the chair he'd been sitting in. "Good night, then." He stood and walked down the steps and across the lawn into the dark.

Amanda lay awake in the small bed in the guest room of her father-in-law's house. Tulia and Atticus were staying outside in the servant's cabin at the back of the property. Her mind was troubled with the details of the last battle that had taken her husband. She was still finding it nearly impossible to accept his needless death. So many in her life were gone now.

She thought of her parents and the devastating loss of her mother over a year ago. The steady decline of their livelihood had certainly taken its toll, but her mother was a strong woman and tried to keep a bright attitude in the face of so much difficulty and loss. A long, cold winter added to her decline when a fever and then pneumonia set-in. The woman was bedridden for weeks as she fought to battle the illness. Amanda and Tulia had sat at her side for much of the time, trying to keep her cool from the fever and to feed her on occasion when she felt able.

Amanda recalled sitting with her mother that last day in the darkened bedroom at *Tanglewood*. Her father had been in earlier and sat with his wife as well, trying to lift her mood with stories of the farm and the few animals they had left, though his wife lay still and mostly unresponsive. Louis Paltierre had finally stood and leaned over to kiss his wife on the forehead, as he did each time he visited her room, but this time he lingered, his lips quivering. It was as if he knew this was their final time. When he rose, Amanda saw the tears on his face, the first time she had ever seen her father cry. She watched him walk out of the room unsteadily and then quietly close the door behind him.

Amanda looked back to her mother. Her eyes were closed, and her breath was coming in heavy rasping gasps. She held her mother's hand as her breaths came less frequently until there was one long final sigh before she grew still. Tulia was beside her and Amanda felt her hand on her back as they both watched Miranda Paltierre pass on.

Amanda stayed on in the room with her face on her mother's chest, quiet in death. It was near dark when she was able to stand and leave. Tulia met her in the kitchen and offered tea. Amanda asked of her father and Tulia told her he had ridden off on one of the horses.

The next morning, Amanda had stood on the porch as the undertaker's wagon started off down the drive with her mother's remains. Tulia came out to join her and held Amanda around the waist from behind. She said, "I'm so sorry, child."

Amanda said, "I know you loved her like your own daughter."

Tulia didn't answer.

They heard the door behind them, and Amanda turned to see her father coming out. He looked as if he hadn't slept and he stumbled as he came toward them, catching himself on a post at the porch railing. She went to him and took him in her arms, holding him close, his face a vacant stare looking down the drive as his wife was taken away.

Then, Amanda felt the slightest tremble in her father's embrace. She pulled back and started to speak when he suddenly crumbled in her arms and fell lifelessly to the porch deck. She gasped and fell to his side, seeing his eyes open, but lifeless and distant. "Papa, Papa!" she screamed out.

Tulia came down beside her and wiped at the man's brow. They could see his chest still rising and falling, but he remained unresponsive. Tulia left to find Atticus.

When Atticus came up from the fields, they were able to get her father up the stairs and into his bed. Atticus rode to town to bring a doctor. Later that night, her father had regained some consciousness and was able to at least acknowledge their presence at his bedside, if not physically speak. The doctor seemed sure the man had suffered a severe seizure, likely sparked by the grief at losing his wife the previous day.

Indeed, the episode had taken a terrible toll on the man as he recovered slowly over the coming weeks. Eventually, he was able to speak in halting sentences, though his mind seemed infirm and unsure. Physically, he was eventually able to walk again, though with a pronounced limp and need of a cane. The right side of his face drooped, and his right arm hung limp at his side.

As Amanda lay in bed at Orlando Atwell's house, she remembered how her father would sit out in one of the chairs on the front porch of *Tanglewood*, looking out across all that used to be the livelihood of his family.

Chapter Fifteen

Jeremy

Palmetto Ranch, Texas May 13, 1865

Atwell took a deep breath to gather himself and control his anger. The unexpected attack by the Union forces out of Brazos Island the previous day still infuriated him and even his own small victory in the late afternoon, forcing the Federals back from Palmetto Ranch, was little consolation. He could not make sense of the Union commander in charge and what he was trying to accomplish. *The damn war was over! Local commanders on both sides had already agreed to discontinue armed conflict weeks ago.*

He woke at daybreak to the sounds of his men moving around in the small camp to the west of Palmetto Ranch. He came out of his tent to see several small cook fires, men tending to a long picket of horses tied up along a row of chaparral bushes, the smell of meat frying and coffee drifting on the air. The sky was clear with the sun just coming up over the eastern horizon toward White's Ranch where his enemy had made camp for the night.

A messenger from Brownsville had arrived late the previous night with word from Colonel Rip Ford. The commander of the garrison at Fort Brown had sent word to other outposts across the countryside to round-up all remaining Confederate soldiers in the area. They would be assembled to move by late morning and Jeremy estimated they would arrive sometime mid-afternoon. A note from the Colonel had encouraged and challenged him to continue to hold off and delay the progress of the Yankees as long as possible. Ford would be bringing additional cavalry units as well as a company of artillery.

Jeremy stood looking across the early scene of his men preparing for another day of battle. He was encouraged in knowing they had done well yesterday and that Ford would soon even the numbers with reinforcements to allow them to push the damn Yankees the hell out of Texas!

One of his men came up and informed him the Federals were advancing on Palmetto Ranch again. He checked his pocket watch and saw it was a little after 9 o'clock. He considered his options as he waited for his commander to arrive later in the day. There was little to be gained in trying to hold the charred ruins of Palmetto Ranch, but he would do his best to keep them there until Ford arrived.

He had noticed the previous day that a sizable number of the enemy were sent south of the ranch to the higher ground of what was known as Palmetto Hill. Tactically, it may have made sense to hold the high ground above the Confederate skirmishers, but Jeremy also thought about how vulnerable the enemy would be if they repeated this. The hill sat on an isolated bend in the river that could easily be cut off from the north to halt another retreat and the river was much too wide and deep to offer an alternate escape. Plus, Jeremy knew the border across the river was heavily guarded by hostile Mexican troops and French forces who had sided with them. There would be a harsh reception for anyone trying to escape into Mexico. If he and his small force could continue to draw the

Yankees into this exposed position, it could be a very bad day for the Union Army.

He also knew his commander, "Old Rip Ford", would show little mercy for this band of rogue Federals, now violating all treaties and agreements between the two forces.

Jeremy called his officers together around one of the fires at the edge of the camp. After conferring with the men and getting their feedback on the current situation, he ordered half his troops to engage the advance position of the Yankees and harass them as they had the prior day with scattered quick attacks from the cover of low bayous and brush. He also ordered they keep the pressure from the north and west to encourage the enemy again to move south to the vulnerable high ground of Palmetto Hill at the bend of the river.

He then ordered the remaining members of his small force back to the west to another small ranch called San Martin to wait for the arrival of Colonel Ford, before he mounted his horse to join the advance attack parties.

He had lain awake most of the night thinking about the battle and how to attack the enemy again in the coming day. He also found his thoughts drifting to home and his wife, Amanda.

As he checked his weapons, he placed the strap of his leather satchel over his shoulder and thought of the unsent letter to his wife that rested inside. *I promised I'd be coming back Amanda. I swear I'll be home soon.*

Chapter Sixteen

Hanna

Pawleys Island, South Carolina *Present Day*

Grace climbed the stairs and poked her head through the door to the attic. She looked around for her friend, as she also kept an eye on the old wood rafters in the ceiling for any further sign of bats. "Hanna, it's late. Are you close to finishing up?"

Hanna peered out from behind some cardboard boxes. "Finished?" Hanna replied. "Oh, I've barely made a dent. Found an old family diary." She held it up for Grace to see in the dim light. "You remember our trip out to the old plantation a few years ago?"

"Of course, I remember. Honey, can you come down from here? These bats are really creeping me out!"

Hanna struggled to her feet as her legs and back were stiff from sitting against the old trunk for so long. She came over to the door and turned out the lights and then followed her friend down the stairs.

"I put a pot of coffee on a while ago," Grace said. "I couldn't stay awake."

"Thank you for being here with me," Hanna said and then she gave Grace a long hug. They continued down to the kitchen and poured two cups of coffee.

"You're not going to believe what I found up there," Hanna said.

"Besides the bats?"

"So, you remember our trip out to *Tanglewood*, the old family plantation?"

"Yes, dear. It was incredible."

Hanna put the worn diary down on the island counter-top. "This is the diary of my many-times great-grandmother, Amanda Atwell," she said as she patted the worn black cover. "She was in the picture the woman gave me that day. It's her recollections of the years they all spent during the Civil War."

"Really?" Grace said, reaching for the book.

"Be careful. It's in really tough shape."

Grace opened the diary to the page that still held the letter Hanna had discovered earlier. "What's this?" she said as she carefully unfolded the paper.

"It's a note home from her husband during the war."

Grace read the brief note quietly and then looked up. "This is amazing."

"He never made it home."

"What?" Grace asked. "He says he'll be home soon."

"In the diary," Hanna said. "It's so sad. Amanda wrote that her husband was killed at the end of the war."

"After he wrote this letter, obviously," Grace said, placing it back in the diary.

"I haven't finished her diary yet, but apparently, the letter was delivered sometime after she was informed of her husband's death."

"Can you imagine?" Grace said. Hanna noticed her friend's eyes were growing moist with tears. "I'm sorry, honey. This is the last thing you need right now while we're trying to deal with ...," she paused. "Well, with Ben's passing and all this with the houses."

"I'll be okay," Hanna said and then pushed the diary to the side. "How'd you do on that pantry? I haven't cleaned it out in years. You probably found some interesting stuff?"

"I threw out most of the food but kept a few kitchen items and other things I thought you should look at before we pitch them."

Hanna sipped from her coffee cup and said, "Let's do it in the morning. I'm beat. I know I need to get this place cleaned up for the new buyers coming in tomorrow afternoon, but I just can't get my heart into it."

"Of course not," Grace said. "You should think about hiring someone to sort this all out for you, honey."

"I'm not hiring anybody these days," Hanna said, trying to smile. "I had to mow our damn lawn in Charleston last week when my son was out of town."

"Hanna, I've told you, Phillip and I are not going to let you starve. If you need some money to get through this rough patch, you just need to say so."

"Thank you, but I can't take your money."

"Is your legal clinic bringing in any money at all?"

Hanna looked up. "It's a *free* clinic, dear. At this point, I can't even afford to pay the light bill to keep the doors open. The two kids doing pro bono work for me from other firms even offered to help me with the office expenses, but I can't do that. They're already doing so much."

"You need to let us help you," Grace said again.

"You're doing enough, and I'll never be able to repay Phillip for all the legal work he's doing for me."

"You don't need to worry about that," Grace said and then looked down at her coffee. "You got anything stronger to mix in? A little whiskey?"

Hanna went to a cabinet and brought back a bottle of Bulleitt bourbon. She watched as Grace poured a generous amount in her coffee cup and then offered her some.

"No, thanks," Hanna said.

"Oh, I forgot. Phillip called just a while ago. He spoke with the FBI office in Charleston. They want to come up tomorrow morning to speak with you."

"Just great!" Hanna said and then had second thoughts and reached for the whiskey.

"Phillip's coming up, too. He'll be here with you."

Hanna took a long drink. "I'll be honest, this FBI thing is scaring the crap out of me."

"I know, honey. I know."

Chapter Seventeen

Amanda

Pawleys Island, South Carolina 1866

Amanda asked Atticus to drive her back to the island from Georgetown the next morning. They arrived at the beach house shortly before noon after a long ride on old roads that threaded through the Low Country marshes. The summer heat continued to build through the morning and with clear blue skies, the sun beat down hard as they made their way slowly behind the old horses. Atticus helped Amanda down from the carriage and he and Tulia went to get their bags to help carry them inside.

She left him there and walked out around the side of the house toward the beach. A cooler wind blew up from the ocean and she opened the neck of her dress to feel more of the refreshing breeze on her skin. The east wind pushed up large rolling swells onto the beach and the roar of each wave coming ashore echoed off the side of the house. The midday sun cast shimmering blue and green colors across the wide expanse of ocean.

Amanda would usually find some comfort in the beauty of this place but was barely aware of her surroundings. She just wanted to walk and be alone, and to think about all she'd learned from the stranger, Heyward. She'd thought of little else on the long journey back to the island.

She walked down the narrow sand path in front of the house, across the dunes and then on to the long stretch of sand and water stretching out in both directions. A lone dog, scraggly and brown, ran by chasing and barking at a flock of seagulls that kept trying to land on the beach. It wasn't long before the dog's yelping was drowned out by the rumble of the sea crashing ashore. The heels of her boots were digging into the loose sand making it difficult to walk. She sat down and began unlacing them and then left them to the side with her stockings as she got up to continue south down the beach.

When she was close enough to the water, she let the cool push of the waves wash up over her feet, holding her long dress up to her knees. Her thoughts returned to Heyward and his description of the battle in Texas that had taken Jeremy. *Only sixty men*, she thought. *How could he have possibly survived against so many Yankees?*

She hadn't asked how many others had died. Heyward had told her earlier it was just too damned many.

The slow burn of anger she'd felt since the day the courier had told her of her husband's death, could not be quelled. The letter delivered by Heyward had only brought it to a renewed boil. She thought of whether there was any accountability for the unwarranted and unnecessary attack on Brownsville for the Union commander... *Barnett was his name.*

Chapter Eighteen

Jeremy

Palmetto Ranch, Texas May 13, 1865

Atwell ducked behind the tree trunk where he held his horse as enemy rounds came into the thicket where he and his men were staging their latest assault. It was mid-morning and there was still no update on when reinforcements with Colonel Ford might arrive from Fort Brown. Throughout the morning, he had ordered his men to continue the sporadic attacks on the invading Union forces, guerrilla-style with quick bursts of aggression to keep the enemy off guard and then retreats to cover to regroup and attack again. They had abandoned Palmetto Ranch for the second time earlier in the morning, seeing no strategic value in the burned and decimated ground, but Jeremy was determined to slow any further advance of the Yankees toward Brownsville until Ford arrived.

A scout came into the low cover to tell him a unit of the Union forces was pushing around them to the south, possibly trying to flank them. He sent word down the line to his men to be ready to move quickly. The return fire from the Federals slowed and then went silent. He listened to the wind for any sign of their intentions.

He pulled his horse back from the brush of the tree and mounted, motioning for one of his men to come with him. He rode quickly north, keeping low in the saddle and using as much cover as he could from the trees and ravines. The leather satchel he always carried with him hung over his shoulder and bounced at his side as the horse galloped on. He reached an end to the cover and pulled the horse up, looking out over a long expanse of open prairie to the high ground of Palmetto Hill beyond. He could see Union troops set in among the little cover the hillside provided and then to the north, a double column of Union soldiers marching out of the brush under the watch of three officers on horseback. The men broke formation at the shouts from the officers and ran out to set a skirmish line along the open field in front of the long hill. It looked to be about fifty men.

What the hell? Jeremy thought. He conferred with the sergeant who had accompanied him. They agreed the Yankee troops would be highly vulnerable to a coordinated attack from the cover provided to the west and north of their skirmish line.

And then Jeremy heard a rifle shot to the south to break the stillness of the temporary lull. He listened for a moment and then more shots followed. In front of him, the Union troops continued to dig in to their exposed position. He turned when he heard a horse approaching quickly.

"Captain Atwell," one of his trusted lieutenants said as he slowed his horse. "The Yankees are trying to flank us!"

Now, clearly seeing the trap the Yankees were trying to set, Jeremy quickly sent word to his small force to focus on the enemy approaching from the south. Under dense cover, his men began to pour heavy fire in the enemy's approaching position. For several minutes there was an intense exchange from both sides. When he was confident they had stopped the Union flanking advance, Jeremy sent orders to withdraw immediately to the northwest, out of range.

He looked across the small barren field where the Federal skirmish line was assembling as bait for the Union trap and then up the slope where blue uniforms were clearly visible, trying to build cover for the next attack. He could also see a group of officers on horseback conferring and shouting out orders.

As he turned to follow his men back to safety, he thought, *where in the hell is old Rip?*

Chapter Nineteen

Hanna

Pawleys Island, South Carolina *Present Day*

Hanna woke early and made coffee, taking a cup with her down to the beach. Grace had still been sleeping and she didn't want to wake her this early after their late night and a bit too much wine and whiskey.

A heavy cloud cover had blown in overnight leaving the ocean in dark shades of gray and blue in the early morning light. Just a breath of wind pushed in from the south allowing the water to calm. She waded out into the shallows and let the cool water wash over her bare legs. She turned back towards the old house, framed behind the low dunes and beach scrub and grasses. *How many years has my family been down here?* she thought. *And after all this time, I'm the one who has to give it away.*

She didn't want to start crying again, so she turned away and looked down the long expanse of beach and homes along the shore to the south. Many of the homes were occupied by long-time friends of the family. Word had surely been spreading about the sale of the Walsh property and the scandal that surrounded it, for many decades known as the Paltierre House for her late ancestors.

Hanna thought of her distant grandmother, Amanda, and the times she had likely stood on this same spot and enjoyed this house with her own family. The images sent a chilling shiver through her and she sipped at her coffee for warmth. She sensed a movement up at the house and turned to see Grace walking out on the deck, waving as she tried to smooth her morning hair and wipe sleep from her eyes.

Hanna waved back and started wading to shore and then walked up the beach to the house. The FBI and Grace's husband Phillip would be here in a few hours and she was dreading the thought of the encounter. *What more would she learn about her husband's illegal and disastrous business affairs? God knows!*

When she reached the path through the dunes below the stairs up to the deck, Grace whispered as if she might wake the neighbors in adjacent houses that were actually quite distant, "Good morning, dear."

Hanna just nodded and made her way slowly up the steps. When she reached her friend, she held up her cup. "The coffee's on."

"I'm trying to let the latest dose of aspirin kick in for this head of mine," Grace said as she rubbed her temples. "Whose idea was it to pull out the whiskey?"

Hanna smiled and said, "You've never been a good influence."

"What a dreadful morning," Grace said, looking out over the gray clouds and water.

"Dreadful is right," Hanna replied. "Your husband will be here at ten with the Feds, for God's sake."

"I know, honey." Grace took Hanna's coffee cup and savored a long drink of the caffeine. "Phillip will help you through it. They're not here to arrest you, silly."

"There's nothing silly about any of this!"
I'm sorry," Grace said, handing the coffee cup back.
"Let's see what we can scare up for breakfast and then would you help me tidy up the place a bit more for this showing I have this afternoon with the couple from Atlanta?"

"Of course. Of course." Grace looped her arm in Hanna's and led her back into the house.

The doorbell rang at a few minutes past ten and Hanna could see two men and a woman on the front porch through the glass in the door. As she opened the door to greet them, Phillip Holloway stood there dressed in khakis and a white dress shirt under a smart blue sport coat. He was ten years older than his wife, Grace, who had gone into town to give them some privacy. The gray at the temples of his hair was quickly spreading. His face was tanned and clean-shaven, edged with wrinkles at the corners of his eyes. He was "Old Charleston" and his graceful Southern accent captured all its sense of privilege and elitism. He spread his arms to give Hanna a hug. She saw the two people from the FBI standing behind him as she let Phillip encircle her in a firm embrace.

They were both surprisingly young, Hanna thought. The man was dressed casually, which again surprised Hanna, who had been expecting gray suits or blue windbreakers with yellow "FBI" stenciled on the back as she'd seen so often on TV. The woman was also in casual attire, an attractive young woman with blond hair cut short.

Phillip made the introductions with Special Agents Will Foster and Sharron Fairfield. After brief formalities on the porch, Hanna stood aside to invite them in. She had coffee and cups waiting on a tray by the fireplace in the big living room across the back of the house. The gray ocean and sky were framed through the many windows.

As they all sat in a grouping of chairs and couches around the table with the coffee, agent Will Foster said, "You have a beautiful home, Hanna."

"Thank you. It's been in the family for many generations."

"I've never been up to Pawleys Island," the female agent named Fairfield said. "It's breathtaking!"

"It's a special place," said the lawyer, Phillip Holloway, moving as always to take control of the situation and get the discussion going. "Hanna, I've spent some time with our guests here from the Bureau and understand they have a few questions they want to discuss with you. Be clear that you have every right to confer with me privately before answering any of their questions."

"Phillip, I've told you. I have nothing to hide," Hanna said, trying to quell the panic that was rising again. "They can ask me anything they want."

Holloway quickly said, "Just the same, you have the right to confer with your attorney at any time, okay.?"

"Yes, of course, Phillip."

Will Foster said, "Hanna, we know you're aware of the failure of the land deal your husband was involved with."

Hanna groaned and said, "Oh, trust me. I'm well aware."

Agent Fairfield, the blond woman said, "How closely were you involved with these dealings with your husband, Hanna?"

Hanna tried hard to control her rising anger. She reached for her coffee and took a sip from the hot steaming cup. Finally, she said, "I had very little involvement in my husband's business. He had many clients and many investments and deals." She paused, thinking back on how this had all come as such a surprise after his death. "I trusted my husband, Ms. Fairfield. I never had reason to intervene or feel I needed to be involved in his work."

"Of course," Fairfield said. "But, your husband never shared any information on the Osprey Dunes project?"

Hanna hesitated and then continued, "A few weeks before Ben's death..." She paused again, trying to gather herself. "A few weeks before was the first time I remember Ben telling me there were some issues with this real estate project and he would have to be away for a few days to deal with it."

"What issues?" Agent Foster asked.

"He didn't tell me, and I didn't ask," Hanna said. "As I said, my husband was involved in many affairs and I never had cause to press him for details on his business."

Foster continued, "Did he ever mention any involvement with organized crime?

Hanna answered quickly. "I'd never heard that even being a possibility until the Charleston police detective mentioned it to me yesterday."

"Ms. Walsh..." Agent Fairfield began.

Hanna interrupted. "Look, I've told you and I've told Detective Frank, I had nothing to do with this project. I know nothing of the details. All I know is my husband got in a hell of a financial mess and now that he's gone, my son and I are going to lose everything, including this house that's been in my family forever."

Phillip Holloway reached across and placed his hand on Hanna's shoulder to comfort her.

"Hanna," Agent Fairfield said, "we're sorry for your loss, but if there is anything you remember your husband did share, we may be able to not only bring the people responsible to justice but also help with your situation."

Hanna looked up at the female investigator and asked, "What are you talking about?"

"It's a long shot, Hanna," Fairfield said, "but there may be an opportunity for some recovery on the losses you and your husband incurred if we can bring the facts out."

Phillip stood and walked behind the chair Hanna was sitting in, placing his hands on the backrest. "Hanna, even the smallest detail may help," he said.

Hanna was suddenly overcome with the whole situation. She leaned down and placed her face in her hands, thinking back on all that had transpired with her deceased husband in those final weeks. She remembered a comment from the detective from Charleston the previous day. "So, you think my husband was killed by these people?"

Agent Foster responded. "We have a growing amount of evidence that organized crime was involved in this transaction."

"Transaction!" Hanna blurted out.

"This business deal, Hanna," Fairfield said, trying to calm her down. "A prominent crime family from Florida with connections here in South Carolina was clearly involved in the land project. We have mounting evidence of bribes for permits, intimidation and threats in city and county approvals and more."

"Bribes?" Hanna said, looking at the two investigators. "Intimidation?" They didn't respond. "So how did it all go south?"

Foster quickly said, "We can't get into that at this point, Hanna."

"Why the hell not!" Hanna said.

"Please, Hanna," Sharron Fairfield said. "We know this is very difficult and we're only trying to help."

"Help with what?" Hanna said skeptically.

Fairfield continued, "Help with finding out who killed your husband and help with recovering any of the lost money that seemed to disappear in the land deal after your husband died."

Hanna couldn't hold back the tears any longer. Phillip Holloway handed her a handkerchief from the breast pocket of his sport coat. She dabbed at her eyes for a moment. Her thoughts began to clear and then she remembered a brief conversation with Ben over dinner one night, just a week or so before he was shot and killed. She looked up at the two Federal agents and said, "Ben and I were having dinner one night at the house in Charleston. He had a few glasses of wine and started complaining about some real estate executive who was interfering with a project he was working on."

"A real estate executive?" Agent Foster asked, perking up.

Hanna watched as Phillip Holloway spoke with the two FBI agents on the front porch before they turned to leave. He came back into the house, closing the door behind him. The heat and humidity out on the porch had left damp splotches across his shirt. He rubbed at his brow to wipe away some of the sweat gathering and about to drip off his nose.

"Damn, when will this heat ever break?" he said as he returned to the seat opposite Hanna. "Well, that was encouraging."

"Encouraging?" she said. "What are you talking about?"

"The lead you provided on the real estate guy that Ben mentioned he was concerned about," Holloway answered.

Hanna shook her head. "They didn't seem all that excited to me."

"That's just their way."

"They said there may be a chance for some type of financial recovery," Hanna said. "What are they talking about?"

"I'm not sure. That's what I was talking to them about out on the step."

"What are they going to do?"

"Well, they have a lot more work to do. It sounds like they're just getting started on all this."

"Just getting started?" Hanna said, her voice rising in frustration again. "It's been months since Ben was killed. How long will their investigation take?"

"Very hard to say, dear."

"So, they're going to try to find this real estate person Ben mentioned?"

"It appears so," he said. "They seem to have some idea of who Ben was referring to. They're keeping their cards pretty close to the vest, which I've found is typical with the Feds."

Hanna was shaking her head, looking out the window at the beach. The clouds had begun to break up and patches of sunlight dotted the ocean. "That warrant they pulled out took me by surprise," she finally said.

Holloway just nodded. The two FBI agents had produced a warrant allowing them to search the old beach house. Hanna had let them go through her husband's small office at the back of the house before they left. They had pulled some files from his desk they wanted to take with them and Hanna had agreed, signing a form for their release.

"Will they be coming out to the house in Charleston?" she asked. "With another warrant, I mean. Do they know we've totally moved out?"

"I'm not sure, but I suspect they'll want to get inside the house," he said. "And our offices, too."

"It's past noon," she said, looking down at her watch. "Can I make you something for lunch?"

"No, thank you. I need to get back to Charleston."

"Is there anything else we can do at this point to help these agents?"

"Just keep thinking about anything Ben may have said or done that could help them." He took a sip from his coffee cup, seeming to consider her question. "Are you sure you've found all of Ben's papers in his office at home?"

"Yes, I believe so."

"And you're certain he wouldn't have kept anything else here at the beach? Up in the attic or in the garage?"

"I'll look again, but I was just up in the attic last night and there's just a lot of old junk."

"They may want to come out here again," Phillip said.

"Whatever they need to do, but I may not have it for long. Some people are coming back again this afternoon to look at the house."

"I'm sorry, Hanna. I know how much this place means to you."

"Thank you, Phillip."

"I know Grace has offered, but is there any way we can help you, at least for a while with some money to see you through? Maybe buy some time to let the Feds work through their case in Miami."

Hanna hesitated and then stood up, stretching her back. "Phillip, thank you, but I just don't see how that will help with anything but delaying the inevitable. The taxes on this house are due in the next two months and the interest on the note Ben took out on the house here is due again next week. I still can't believe I let him talk me into that. He had already mortgaged the Charleston house to the hilt."

"I had no idea," Phillip said.

"I didn't know about the Charleston mortgage either," Hanna said. "The house had always been just in his name. I never questioned it when we bought the place. When Ben said he needed to use the Pawleys Island house as collateral for a loan to get him into the Charleston land deal, I really pushed back. He kept pressing me on it and assured me we'd be paid back within a year."

"Well, that won't happen," Holloway said. "Again, I'm sorry. Why won't you let us help you with the taxes and this next interest payment?"

"Thank you, Phillip, but I'm getting the feeling this investigation and any court action could take months if not years to sort out," she answered. "The court has already seized what little money we had left, except for a small stipend they approved to help me keep some food on the table and the lights on. If I don't sell this place, it's just a matter of time until the banks start foreclosure proceedings. They've already given me an initial warning."

"There are ways we can put the banks off."

"The two FBI agents didn't really seem that confident in finding any of the money and I think they regretted even bringing it up when I pressed them."

"You're probably right."

He stood and reached for his coat and bag with the documents he had brought along. Hanna followed him to the front door and walked out onto the porch with him. He turned to give her a hug before leaving. She was caught by surprise when he leaned in and kissed her lightly on the lips as he wrapped her in his arms. She returned his embrace tentatively as she tried to deal with the shock of his unexpected affection. They had always hugged as friends do and she could recall an occasional peck on the cheek, but this had never happened before.

He pulled back and returned her surprised look with a smile before he said, "We'll get through this, Hanna." He turned and walked down the steps, got in his white Porsche convertible and backed out of the drive. He waved as he shifted to drive away. She was too stunned to even respond and shook her head, thinking, *what in hell was that all about?*

Chapter Twenty

Amanda

Pawleys Island, South Carolina 1866

She woke to the sound of a low murmur of noises from the floor below. Amanda looked out the two windows along the front of the bedroom facing the ocean. Through the gauzy curtains she could see the sun already up several hours into the morning. An early wind from the southeast was pushing big swells, capping white as far as the eye could see.

Then she heard Tulia talking as she came up the stairs. Amanda had heard that voice in this house throughout her life growing up with their cherished servant and nanny. She pushed the covers aside and used her hands to brush her long red hair back from her face. She reached for the light cotton robe at the end of her bed. Walking barefoot along the cool pine floors, she made her way out to the hall. From downstairs she could smell the cook fire in the kitchen and oatmeal boiling.

"Tulia, close the windows up here to keep in some of the night chill for a while, will you please?"

"Surely, Miss Amanda."

The two women turned when they heard a horse ride up to the back of the house. Amanda walked across the hall into another bedroom with a view of the drive out to the road. She saw her brother-in-law, Jackson Atwell, dismounting from his gray horse. She frowned and watched from the side of the curtain as he took off his hat and smoothed his dark black hair back. Tulia came into the room.

Amanda turned to her and said, "Jeremy's brother, Jackson, is here. Please have Atticus get him some breakfast while I get some clothes on." From the look on the old woman's face, she knew Tulia shared her disdain for the younger Atwell brother.

Tulia nodded and hurried out of the room.

When Amanda came into the kitchen, Jackson was sitting at the counter with a mouthful of pancakes. He swallowed and then noticed Amanda and stood, pushing his chair back from the small table. He brushed his hair back again and said, "Good morning, Amanda. Hope I'm not intruding, coming in unannounced."

Amanda nodded her head as she considered the man's comment. "You don't need an invitation, Jackson, but what brings you all the way out here?"

"I need to speak with you on a couple things."

She walked over to the counter and took a plate Tulia had made for her. "What's on your mind?" she asked as she took a seat at the table. Tulia brought her a cup of coffee and set it beside her plate.

Jackson sat again and pushed his plate back. "I'd like to speak in private if we could."

Amanda sipped at her coffee and then said, "There are no secrets here, sir." She watched as the man squirmed in his chair.

"Amanda, please," Jackson said. "I just need a few minutes."

She turned to look at Atticus and Tulia working now over the sink. "Let's go outside, Jackson."

She stood and walked to the door out onto the porch along the beach side of the house. She heard the man rise and follow her and then the screen door closing behind her. The ocean breeze met her face like a cool caress. She stood at the rail looking out over the beach and water and let her hair blow back off her shoulders. Jackson came up beside her.

"Damn beautiful place," he said.

"It certainly is. Now tell me what's so important you had to ride all the way out here from Georgetown."

Atwell cleared his throat and hesitated before he said, "First, Amanda, I wanted to apologize for my behavior at dinner at my father's house..."

She interrupted, "You don't need to apologize."

"I was a little drunk and I'm sorry I wasn't more hospitable to your Mr. Heyward..."

"He's not *my* Mr. Heyward, Jackson!" she replied, again cutting him off.

"You know what I mean," Jackson said. "I do have to tell you, Amanda, I don't have a good feeling about this man's intentions."

Amanda was quickly growing more impatient with her brother-in-law. "Is this all you have to tell me?"

"No, it's just there's something not right about this fellow. Who would come all the way from Texas just to deliver a letter?"

"It's not just any letter," she said quickly. "He was there when Jeremy was killed. He found the letter and wanted to make sure I got it... and he wanted to make sure I knew what really happened out there at what was it called, Palmetto Ranch?"

"Just be careful, Amanda. We don't know what he wants."

"I don't think he wants anything, for Pete's sake," she said and turned to go back into the house.

He reached out and grabbed her arm and she turned defiantly.

"Let go of me, now!"

He released his grip. "I just need another minute."

Atticus stuck his head out of the door to the kitchen. "Everythin' okay, Miss Amanda?" the old man asked. He stared at Atwell.

Before Amanda could answer, Jackson said, "Tell your boy to get his ass back in the house!"

"You have no right to speak to him that way!" Amanda said.

Atwell took a moment to calm himself. "Atticus, everything is fine."

Atticus looked over at Amanda. When she nodded, he went back inside.

"Amanda, look, there is this thing I need you to understand."

"And what is that?"

"I know my daddy's spoken to you about the money," he said, "That you and your daddy are near tapped out."

"That's none of your business!" she snapped and started into the house again.

"Amanda, wait."

"This conversation is over. Now you need to get back to town."

"Amanda, I know some people who can help."

"Help with what?"

Atwell walked over to the rail and leaned back on one elbow. "Your family owes a lot of money to the bank and to my father. "I know your daddy's got no way to pay that back now, without sellin' the place."

Amanda said, "We owe money to your father?"

"Yes, ma'am."

"Why didn't he tell me that? I was just in his office going through the finances."

"He didn't want to have you worrying about it. He's been trying to help your daddy get by with the rice not comin' in."

"I need to go talk to Orlando again," she said.

"Won't do no good. Like I said, I have some people who can help. They're investors looking to buy land down here."

"Investors?" Amanda asked. "You mean damn carpetbaggers!"

"Amanda, hold on," he said, coming over to hold the door so she couldn't go inside.

"Get out of the way!"

"Amanda, listen to me. You don't have any choice in this. These men have means to pay back the money your daddy owes and a fair price beyond that for *Tanglewood* for you all to live out here at the island. You don't want the bank movin' in on that land, do you?"

Amanda was trying with all her will to keep from slapping the man. She attempted to calm herself before she said, "You need to leave. You need to go back to Georgetown and tell these friends of yours to leave us the hell alone!"

Atwell moved away from the door. "Like I said, you won't have much choice in this for too much longer. The bank will take the plantation and sell it off to get their money back and pay off the lien to my father. You'll be left with nothin'."

"I'm not going to say it again, Jackson. Get the hell out of here!"

"Amanda, just calm down." He moved closer to her and reached for her hand. She jerked it away. "Amanda, this would all be so much easier for you if you had a man in your life again. Jeremy's been gone a long time and..."

"Jackson, that's enough!" she yelled out.

Atticus pushed through the door and stood between the two of them.

Jackson said, "You better tell your boy he's lookin' for a lotta trouble crossing me."

Amanda rushed to get around Atticus and raised her hand to slap her brother-in-law. Atticus pulled her away and glared back at the younger Atwell brother who said, "I'm sorry this had to happen, Amanda. Me and daddy care about you and we want to help."

Amanda was trying to hold back tears. She didn't want this man to see her cry. "Just leave, now!"

Jackson turned and walked into the house. She could hear him muttering as he went out the back. She pulled herself away from Atticus and leaned over the rail of the porch, afraid she might be sick. Then, she gathered herself and said, "Atticus, go help Tulia with the kitchen."

"Yes, ma'am," the old man said.

He turned to go inside and didn't stop when Amanda said, "Thank you, Atticus."

It was late afternoon and Amanda sat at the kitchen table, looking out the windows to the beach. Tulia and Atticus were upstairs changing linens and cleaning. She was playing back the conversation with Jackson Atwell in her mind, trying to make sense of the situation. It infuriated her that her father-in-law had not shared the full extent of her family's financial troubles, particularly that he was loaning money to her father without telling her about it.

She couldn't imagine her father ever agreeing to give up *Tanglewood.* His father and his grandfather had worked that land forever, it seemed. She was also aware her father was in no condition to manage the property, even if they could get the rice crop back or look for some other revenue crop. Since her mother died and all three of her brothers had been lost in the war, her father had been a mere shell of his former strong self. It wasn't just his physical health, but she knew his mind was failing as well. He seemed distant and was always slow in response to any conversation. She wondered if he was beginning to lose his memory when there seemed times he didn't recognize her and others coming to visit. He sat most of his days out on the front porch of the old house, looking across the unkempt lawns and fields.

The plantation itself was in total disrepair. Most of the family's workers had left when the Emancipation was announced. She heard some of them were working small share crop plats over in the next county. In the last years of the war as the Yankees made their way south chasing the Confederate forces to the sea, they had left little behind of value and destroyed much of what they couldn't take with them. They had spared the main house from their torches, but many of the outbuildings had been burned and the house looted and badly damaged.

Amanda had hidden in the woods with Tulia on several occasions as the Yankees came through. She had heard the stories of rape and even murder. Her father always refused to come with them, staying with Atticus to do what he could to keep the Yankees from taking and destroying everything. She was always afraid she'd find him shot dead in the house when they came back from hiding.

As much as she wanted to ignore the proposition Jackson Atwell had shared that morning, she was growing increasingly pessimistic there were any other viable options. She saw her diary on the table and dated a new page. As she wrote of the challenges her family continued to face, she also hoped some new inspiration would come to help them through it all.

Chapter Twenty-one

Jeremy

Palmetto Ranch, Texas May 13, 1865

Atwell first got word that Colonel Ford and his reinforcements were near when one of the colonel's men came riding into the small clearing west of the ranch where they had pulled back after the Federal's failed trap earlier that morning. It was now close to three in the afternoon. Ford and his supporting force were just two miles out. Jeremy had sent a messenger back to Fort Brown shortly after daybreak to let Ford know of the arrival of close to three hundred more Federal troops. *They were all in for a hell of a day!*

Jeremy stood holding the reins to his horse and looked at the men resting around him. All of them had been moving and fighting for a second day in a row with little or no sleep and barely enough food and water. He felt like every muscle in his body was drained of all energy and will, yet he knew the worst of it lay ahead. When Ford arrived, all hell would break loose. The man was known for his decisive and ruthless style in battle. *These Yankees have no idea what they're about to run in to.*

He took several deep breaths and then drank from the last of the water in his canteen. He closed his eyes just for a moment and let his thoughts drift back to South Carolina and a woman who was waiting for him there. He tried to picture the face of Amanda in his mind. After so many months and years away, he was still finding it hard to believe he could be home soon.

A volley of gunfire to the south of them brought him back to the moment. It occurred to him that throughout this entire engagement, he had felt no sense of fear or danger, despite the close encounters and relentless assaults on the enemy. It was as if these many years of fighting and waiting to fight had numbed him to any feeling of danger or threats of getting back home safely.

And then he thought of his father and brother. He had received no word of his brother, Jackson, for over a year. The last he'd heard of him was from Virginia. He'd been in a lot of scraps but was *still on the right side of the dirt,* as he'd said in that last letter. Jeremy's father was another issue. There had been little news from Georgetown in his years away. Jeremy knew he had some serious issues with his father to deal with when he returned. At times, he'd hoped the old sonofabitch would be dead by then.

His horse had its head down, nibbling on some sparse grass. Jeremy rubbed the animal's withers and watched the sand and dust rise with every touch. The horses were as tired and worn as the men. The horse lifted its head and turned back, nuzzling Atwell's face, almost knocking his hat off. This horse, Babe, had been with him for over two years. He'd had his own horse from home shot out from under him and killed in his first action, not two months after leaving South Carolina. He'd had the horse since he was a boy and it was a tough day, not only in losing the animal he'd grown close to over the years, but also getting his first taste of battle. He'd come out with just a few scratches and a bad knee where the horse fell on him, but the site of so many men lying wounded or dead was something he never could have prepared for.

He had become close with another young lieutenant he'd met when his unit first assembled in Richmond. The man's name was Lauten. He had a wife and two kids back home in Chapel Hill. Jeremy had helped bury his friend after he took a musket ball to the face in that first charge that took Jeremy's horse.

Jeremy felt for the gold chain with the cross around his neck that Amanda had given him when he left her that day on Pawleys Island. He tried not to believe in good luck charms, but a quick kiss of the cross before another fight had kept him alive every time. *No reason to stop now.*

Chapter Twenty-two

Hanna

Pawleys Island, South Carolina *Present Day*

Grace had the sense to get Hanna out of the house before her real estate agent brought the prospective buyers from Atlanta through again that afternoon. She got her in the car with some considerable resistance and drove her down to the Island Bar, a local favorite with a massive outdoor seating area, wonderful hospitality and ice-cold beer. The manager greeted Hanna by name as they came in, which did little to soothe her foul mood. She knew there were people in her cherished home who may soon take it away and who would give no second thought to totally gutting and redesigning the home her family and ancestors had cherished for so many years.

The manager led them out to a shaded table on the deck and introduced their server. Drink and sandwich orders were placed, and the server sped away.

Grace started to speak, but Hanna interrupted, "Don't say anything about the house! Nothing you can say is going to make this any easier. Thank you for being here with me, but please, let's just have a drink and talk about something else."

Grace reached across the table and took one of Hanna's hands in both of hers. "When all of this is settled, honey, have you thought about what you want to do? I mean, what about the legal clinic? Can you make enough money to live on?"

"Grace, the clinic is free!" Hanna answered with clear exasperation. "Free means that nobody has to pay. I've been able to keep the doors open through a few donations and financial backers, but frankly, Ben's income at the firm allowed me to offer my legal services at no charge. There are a lot of people in Charleston in really tough situations but with no money to hire a decent lawyer."

"Maybe you need to think about moving on," Grace said, "maybe start a new firm or go to work for one of the other established firms in town. I've talked to Phillip about it and he's sure they could find a place for you there."

Hanna managed a quiet laugh and said, "I appreciate that, but I think there's too much history there."

The server brought their cold frosted mugs of beer and placed them on the table. "Your food should be out soon."

As the young girl walked away toward the kitchen, Grace said, "You are a great lawyer, Hanna Walsh. Anyone in town would hire you on the spot, for God's sake!"

Hanna looked at her friend for a moment and then said, "You're forgetting my husband put some serious doubt on the integrity of the Walsh family with his final escapades."

"People won't think you had anything to with that."

"Guilt by association, I'm afraid," Hanna said. She took a long drink from the beer. "I'm not sure I want to stay in Charleston. The house is gone. So much has changed. I doubt my son will ever be back. All he talks about is Colorado when he's finished with school."

"But, where would you go?"

"Well, it looks like Pawleys Island is not gonna be an option much longer."

Grace asked, "Is Thomas going to call you when the showing's done?"

The server returned with their food and asked if there was anything else.

"No, we're fine, thanks," Grace said. "That sandwich looks good, honey. You need to get some food in you."

"I need to get some alcohol in me," Hanna said and took another long drink. "He thought they might be a couple of hours... in the house I mean. They brought their decorator, so you know that will be a big production."

"That place doesn't need a damn decorator!" Grace said and tasted her own beer. It was some local craft brew the server had recommended. "This is good."

"It's cold and 6.0 ABV, is all I care," Hanna said, referring to the alcohol content for the beer she'd read on the menu.

"So, tell me what else you found in that old diary?" Grace asked, clearly trying to get her friend's mind off the loss of her house.

"You know, it's really interesting. "Since you and I were up at *Tanglewood* to see the old plantation, I can picture so much of what she's writing about, certainly about the house out here on the island, too."

"I saw you have the family picture the woman gave you hanging in the den," Grace said, pulling the bread off her sandwich to rearrange the lettuce and tomato. "It's a little haunting to see their faces and know they lived out here."

"I do feel like Amanda is around me when I'm in the house, as creepy as that sounds."

"I'm sure she's a kind spirit, dear."

"I was reading another later entry this morning," Hanna said. "Her family was dealing with a lot after the war, even losing the plantation. All three of her brothers were killed, her mother died, let alone her husband. This latest entry also talks about her father having a stroke and losing his mind and not being able to take care of the property, at least what was left of it after the Union forces came through. Makes my situation seem a bit mild in comparison"

"Hardly, dear," Grace said. "But, I'm so proud how strong you're holding up. I'd be a damn basket case by now."

"How do you know I'm not?"

"I know you well enough. I know how incredibly difficult this has all become. You've been so strong."

"I wish I felt strong. I feel like a pile of mush who can't take care of herself, let alone her own son."

They both took a bite from their sandwiches and then Grace said, "Jonathan will be fine. Your son is a rock. He's also going to have every coed in Chapel Hill chasing after him. He got all the best traits of both of you."

"Let's hope he got a little more common sense than his father," Hanna said.

The call from her friend and realtor, Thomas Dillon, came about an hour later. Hanna and Grace were on their third beer and Hanna's gloom had only deepened. Thomas confirmed the buyers were going to submit an offer later in the afternoon. He asked if he could bring it out to the house to review with her and maybe bring something to cook for dinner. She agreed and told him to bring enough for Grace who was staying with her another night.

The two women were back at the beach house, sitting on chairs on the deck and sipping at glasses of white wine when Hanna heard a knock at the back door. She yelled for Thomas to come in. The sun had set over an hour earlier and it was dark enough now for a canopy of stars and a bright half-moon to shine above them.

Thomas poked his head out of the kitchen door. "How about Chinese take-out? Too late to cook after all the time it took to get the contract offer together."

Hanna started to get up, but Thomas said, "No, you sit and relax. I'll bring everything out."

"Thank you. You're a dear," Hanna said. "I feel like we need a beach fire. We can eat down at the beach. I'll go down and get it started. Grace, would you help Thomas?"

"Sure, sweetie." Grace got up and went into the kitchen.

Soon, they were all sitting in the comfortable wood Adirondack chairs arranged around the stone fire pit that had been built-in to the dunes above the beach. There was a rumble of big waves still crashing up onto the shore. Sparse clouds had blown in overhead, obscuring some of the stars and occasionally crossing in front of the moon. Hanna had put a lot of wood on the fire and it was roaring and hot and lit their faces as they ate the Chinese and washed it down with the wine.

Finally, Thomas got down to business. "So, the offer," he said. "Do you mind if we talk about this with Grace here?"

"Of course not," Hanna said, a little too loud, the beer and wine starting to take their toll. "Grace is family."

Thomas continued. "The offer is good, Hanna."

"Thank God!" she responded, feeling just a small sense of optimism returning.

"I made sure their agent was aware of the comparable sales and true market value of the house." He pulled some papers from his bag resting against the chair in the sand. "They're offering $1.9 million, dear, which is pretty high in the range we discussed."

Hanna let the number sink in for a moment and tried to clear her thoughts on all the house sale needed to cover. "Thank you, Thomas, for all you've done. I think that's very fair." She paused and thought again about all the ramifications. "I'm afraid that will barely cover what we owe on this place after what I let Ben do with the mortgage, but that's my problem."

"We can certainly counter," the realtor said.

Grace said with more than a little slur in her enunciation, "Make them pay, honey, for chrissakes!"

Thomas said, "Hanna, I think we're really solid going back to them at $2 million even. There's a lot of support for that number in recent sales. I'm sure they'll counter, but we should be able to get you a bit more."

"Sounds good. Go ahead."

"I'll write it up for you to sign after dinner."

"How soon do they want to close?" Hanna asked.

"They're paying cash, so they want it quick."

"How quick?"

"End of the month. Of course, there will be surveys and inspections. We can draw it out a bit longer if you want."

"Yes, please, do what you can," Hanna said, her spirits falling. "I'm not sure I can get everything out of here." She thought about the decorator. "Do they want to keep anything?"

"There's a short list in the contract," Thomas said.

"Christ, the nerve!" Grace said, taking another long sip from her wine glass.

Thomas said, "Hanna, I know what's happened with your house in Charleston and now all this. I have the guesthouse at my place down the beach. I'm between renters. You're welcome to stay there as long as you like."

Hanna looked over at her long-time friend and for a brief time many years ago, a summer love. "Thomas, that is so kind, but you know I can't pay you. I don't want to impose my problems on you any more than I already have."

"The rent is not a problem," he said. "I keep it open in the good season months as much as I can for friends and family. And you're both, practically!"

Grace said with a bit of a slur, "Thomas, you are an angel."

Hanna, feeling the effects of the drink and a bit giddy at the possible solution to her homelessness, stood and moved over to Thomas's chair beside hers and sat down on his lap, spilling his drink and sending Chinese food in all directions. She threw her arms around him and kissed his cheek. "Somehow, I'll pay you back for all this, you dear man."

More than an hour had passed. Grace had staggered off to bed and Hanna had signed the addendum to the sales contract with the price counteroffer for her house before Thomas had left a short while earlier. She grabbed a cold bottle of water from the refrigerator and went back down to the beach to watch the fire die. Pulling the chair up closer to the fading flames, Hanna sat down and put her bare feet as close as she could to the hot rocks around the fire. She took a long drink from the water and leaned back into the beach chair, the stars above her now clear again in the night sky. She closed her eyes and thought about what was coming together for the sale of the beach house and the prospect of moving down to her friend's guest house, at least until she could get the rest of her life sorted out.

She sensed a motion beside her and turned to see a man taking a seat in the chair next to her by the fire. It startled her and she cried out, "What...?"

In the fading light she saw a man dressed all in black with the collar of his jacket turned up around his face, sunglasses on and a ball cap with a Florida State logo pulled down low over his face.

Hanna felt the panic race through her. She was about to stand and run when the man spoke in a low, calm voice, "Hello, Hanna."

She managed to say, "Who the hell are you?"

"Just be calm, Hanna," the man said.

"What?"

"I'm not going to hurt you."

Hanna thought of screaming for Grace, but she knew her friend was probably beyond consciousness by now. The neighbor's houses on both sides were dark. "Who are you?" she said again.

"That doesn't matter."

Hanna tried to focus on his face in the dim light of the fading fire, but there was nothing recognizable in his features. "What do you want?" she asked, trying to control her panic.

The man sat staring at her for a few moments and then said, "I work for some people who want me to give you a message. That's all."

Hanna calmed a bit and asked, "Who are these *people*?"

He ignored her question and said slowly with a deliberate cadence, "It will be in your best interest to not provide any more information to the police or the Feds."

"Information?" she said, a numbness coming over her entire body, the panic returning and every fear and flight impulse within her telling her to run away.

"Hanna," the man said with a maddening calmness that was sending Hanna deeper into distress, "we know you had nothing to do with your husband's business, so that's all you need to tell the authorities. No need to help them find anything more related to the problems you know your husband got himself into."

Hanna was beyond panic now and her whole body was trembling. She finally managed to say, "I just want this all to be over."

He turned in his chair and leaned close. "So, do we, Hanna, but we need your help with one other thing."

Hanna didn't answer.

"Your husband put away a significant amount of money from our little land deal."

Hanna was stunned. "What are you talking about!"

"Let's not play games, Hanna."

"Games?"

"This can all go away much faster if you lead us back to the money, particularly the escrow accounts."

Hanna shook her head in total shock. "You have to believe me. I don't know anything about any money."

"We knew you would say that," the stranger said.

"Why didn't I hear about this before?" Hanna was trying to control the panic in her voice. She could see her reflection from the firelight in the man's sunglasses. She watched as he stood and moved between her and the fire.

Looming over her, he said, "Trust me when I say this doesn't have to be a problem. We'll be back in touch and we expect your memory about this money will be clear by then." He turned and walked away toward the beach, out of the light of the fire and gone.

Chapter Twenty-three

Hanna

Charleston, South Carolina *Present Day*

Hanna unlocked the door to her law office in downtown Charleston and then locked it behind her. She had ridden back to town from the beach earlier in the day with Grace who had insisted she take an extra room in their house for a few days until she could sort out longer-term living arrangements in town. She wasn't particularly excited about staying in the same house with Grace's husband, Phillip, after the kiss on the front porch at the beach house. She also couldn't bring herself to stay in some dreary hotel room.

She turned on the light switches for the small suite of offices that took the first floor of an historic old house that had been sparsely renovated years ago for business space. The house was on the fringe of the city's yet to be gentrified neighborhoods and proved more convenient for Hanna's lower-income clientele. There was a small reception area with a desk that one of her intern volunteers usually sat at, a row of six chairs for clients along the front wall of windows and a hall that led back to three private offices and a conference room, a small kitchen and bathroom. Her office was the first on the left.

Hanna turned on the light and walked over to her desk, piled high with files she had been dreading getting back into. She felt guilty about being away these past few days but knew she had to take care of the house issues out at the island. She left the blinds drawn and sat behind the old oak desk she had bought at a consignment shop a couple of years ago. She opened her purse and rummaged through the clutter until she felt the hard grip of the .45 caliber handgun she had brought back from her deceased husband's office out on the island.

The visit the past night from the stranger on the beach still had her on edge and she had slept fitfully all night remembering the chilling encounter. She was struggling with whether to call the Charleston PD detective, Alex Frank, but the stranger had made it very clear that any further cooperation with the authorities would lead to *unpleasant* outcomes. She still couldn't believe she was being threatened, she assumed, by the mob in Miami who had apparently swindled and killed her husband. And what money were they talking about? *What in God's name has Ben got me into!*

She placed the gun in the top drawer of her desk and couldn't stop her hands from shaking as she pushed the drawer closed. She had never felt the need for a firearm at her offices, even though the neighborhood was still a bit sketchy and her clientele occasionally presented some questionable visitors.

It was Sunday and she wasn't expecting any of her staff or clients. It was a day she could try to get caught up on the cases sitting on the desk in front of her. She could also sort through the financial issues she was dealing with including how long until she would have to close the doors to the clinic as expenses continued to go unpaid. Then, there was also the next visit from the stranger at the beach to consider.

The shrill ring of her office phone broke the silence and startled her. She looked down at the display and saw it was her private line and an unknown number. It was the number she gave to certain clients and others she didn't want to have her personal cell number. She debated on answering, but then picked up after the fourth ring.

"Hello, this is Hanna."

A female voice said, "Oh, Ms. Walsh. I thought I'd get your machine, so I could leave a message."

"Who is this?" Hanna asked.

"It's Megan Trumball. I spoke with you a couple of weeks ago about volunteering at the clinic. You gave me this number."

Hanna remembered the conversation. The woman worked at Ben's old firm but had called about doing some pro bono work for her at the free clinic. "Good morning, Megan."

"I wanted to schedule some time this week to stop over to see you," the young lawyer said. "I need to speak with you about something."

Hanna said, "I'm not sure I'll be taking on any new volunteers, Megan. With all that's going on right now, I may be cutting back on our caseload."

"No, it's not about that," Megan said.

"What is it?"

"I'd rather not discuss it on the phone. I need to meet with you."

"Sounds a bit *mysterious*," Hanna said. "I'm here at the offices all day if you would like to come over. Just ring the bell."

The woman said she could be over in an hour and they ended the call.

Hanna had her head down in a particularly difficult case file with an armed robbery charge against a single father supporting four children when the sound of the front door buzzer surprised her. She walked out to the reception area and saw Megan Trumball through the window in the door, standing on the front porch. The woman looked to be in her late twenties, a tall thin frame inside workout clothes and an Atlanta Braves baseball cap. Hanna unlocked the door to let her in.

"Hello, Megan."

"Thank you for seeing me so quickly," the young lawyer said.

Hanna stood to the side and gestured to the back of the office, "Come in."

She led Megan Trumball back to her office and offered her coffee, but she declined.

They both sat at a small conference table.

"I've heard you do terrific work here," Megan said.

Hanna frowned and said, "I wish we could do more and unfortunately, we may be forced to close the doors soon."

Her visitor didn't respond and reached into the leather bag she held on her lap to pull out some papers. "I could get fired for this," Megan finally said, "or worse."

"What are you talking about?"

"I'm sure the firm could have me up on charges and probably disbarred." She sorted through the documents in front of her and selected what looked like a memo on the letterhead of Ben's law practice. "A few weeks ago," Megan continued, "I was working on a new case and had to pull some information on work your husband was involved in that I thought was related."

"You have access to Ben's old files?" Hanna asked.

"This was information in the main office files of the firm," Megan said.

"What are we talking about?"

127

Megan hesitated, looking down at the papers in front of her. She looked up at Hanna and said. "I'm sorry if this will be difficult for you."

"Please, what do you have?"

"When your husband was killed, Hanna, and the real estate deal he was involved with came to light, we were all led to believe he was acting independently and outside the knowledge and approval of the firm. The senior partners tried to distance themselves completely from any of it."

"That's what we were all told," Hanna said.

"I'm not sure why this file was not pulled or destroyed, but it's clear the firm had very clear knowledge of what your husband was involved with."

"What!"

"All I can think is that your husband stored this information as backup in an unrelated file subject," Megan said.

"Just tell me what you've got," Hanna demanded.

Megan Trumball slid the first document across the table to Hanna. "This is a note to your husband from one of the firm's partners, Phillip Holloway. It's very clear Mr. Holloway was not only well aware of the Osprey Dunes real estate deal but was intimately involved in the project."

Hanna felt her stomach turn as she started to read the internal memo. She looked up at her visitor. "Why would they hide this from everyone?"

Megan said, "If you read through all this correspondence and the personal notes from your husband, it becomes pretty clear the firm was initially all-in for providing legal representation for the developers of this land deal. But, along the way, some of the partners began to push back. Your husband and Mr. Holloway apparently decided to continue on their own, it seems without the blessing of the firm."

Hanna's mind was racing back through several encounters with Phillip Holloway and other senior partners of Ben's firm. All of them had consistently claimed shock and surprise at Ben's involvement in this deal. Phillip had always feigned ignorance and even disdain for her husband's dubious judgment in getting involved. She looked across the table at Megan Trumball. "If this is all true, I can see why the firm would want to distance themselves from any connection to Osprey Dunes, but why would they be so sloppy in letting any of this correspondence survive if they had anything to hide or cover up?" she asked.

"Like I said, it appears your husband copied this file and placed it where he would be the only one who would know to look for it there, rather than in his own personal or client files."

"And you just happened upon it?"

"I was looking for something else related to a case your husband was involved with several years earlier," Megan said. "I was going through a lot of old information and just happened to pull this and look through some of the documents. I suspect your husband had only placed all of this temporarily and then..." she paused.

"Go on," Hanna said.

"Before he was killed, he had never recovered the documents."

"None of this was found in his personal files at work, I assume?"

"Not that I'm aware of," Megan said. She sorted through the papers and pulled another document which looked to be a copy of personal notes on legal pad paper. "I believe these are notes your husband made about the land deal. He seems to be summarizing some particularly troubling developments and laying out steps to be taken to confront the developers on certain issues."

Hanna started reading through the notes, immediately recognizing her husband's handwriting. It didn't take long to see Phillip Holloway was clearly an active partner in the Osprey Dunes project. She finally looked up at Megan Trumball and asked, "Why would you bring this to me now?"

"There's a lot of quiet talk around the firm that your husband and his involvement with this deal is still being investigated, even by the FBI," she said. "When I came across the information in this file, I was shocked at how deceptive some members of our firm have been about their lack of knowledge or involvement. Something is not right."

"But, why bring it to me?" Hanna asked.

"I can't go to the Management Committee or even my boss, frankly, who is one of the senior partners," she said. "I'm considering getting all of this to the police, but I wanted to speak with you first."

Hanna took a deep breath and tried to calm the sense of panic rising inside her. She thought again about the stranger who had confronted her on the beach the previous night. *No further cooperation...*

She heard the young woman ask, "Hanna, what is it?"

Hanna looked across the table at Megan Trumball, her mind running through all the questions she had. Finally, she said, "Megan, thank you for bringing this to me. I would strongly encourage you to keep this to yourself, at least for now."

The woman started to protest, but Hanna said, "Trust me. You don't want to get any more involved in this." Hanna could see the skepticism on the young girl's face. Hanna continued, "I'm as surprised about all of this as you, Megan, but I need to sort this all out. It just doesn't make any sense. I was just with Phillip Holloway yesterday *and* the FBI. None of this came up."

"So, the Feds are involved?" Megan asked.

"Oh, trust me, they're very involved."

"And Holloway, too?" Hanna asked. "He's helping me with all this, the financial issues after Ben's death and now the further investigation into the land deal." She was growing more and more angry as she thought about Phillip Holloway and his apparent deceptions. "He's given me no indication he had anything to do with this."

"Obviously, that's not the case," Megan said. "Don't you think we need to share this with the investigators?"

Hanna answered quickly, "No, not yet!"

"But..."

"I need some time," Hanna said.

Chapter Twenty-four

Amanda

Pawleys Island, South Carolina 1866

Amanda had been working through the afternoon with Atticus to clean brush away from the grounds around the beach house and the outbuildings. There was a cabin for the servants, a storage shed and a small barn for the horses and carriage. All the structures were made of rough timber with cedar wood roofs, aged gray over the years from the hot sun and weather. Heavy winds the past week had left palm fronds and broken branches from the live oak scattered across the sandy property. They were making a pile out by the road to burn. Amanda had been helping more with work around the houses in the past months with the difficult times they all faced.

Her father would not come out to the island with her anymore. Worry and declining health compelled him to stay at *Tanglewood*, particularly when the Yankees were coming through later in the war. He stayed alone there now, rarely leaving the front porch except to sleep and occasionally look for some food in the kitchen. Amanda felt she could stay away at the island only for a few days, concerned her father was becoming less able to care for himself alone.

She was pulling another load of debris around the house to add to the burn pile when she saw the man named Heyward riding up the crushed-shell drive on his brown horse. Atticus came up beside her. "It's okay," she said, and the old man walked back to the work he was doing.

Heyward pulled up his horse and tipped his hat. "Afternoon, Amanda." He pulled his leg over the saddle and dismounted, holding the reins for the horse in one hand, his hat in the other. His long brown hair was matted and wet from the day's heat and sweat had soaked through his shirt and pants.

Amanda looked down at herself for a moment and realized what a mess she must look in an old dress and dusty boots. Her hands and arms were dirty from the brush and her clothes stained from the work and the heat. She brushed at her hair and wiped some of the sweat from her forehead. "Hello, Mr. Heyward," she replied. "What brings you out so far from town?"

Heyward walked his horse over to a hitch rail beside the drive and tied the reins. He turned back to Amanda. "Is there somewhere we can talk?"

"Of course," she said, looking up at the house and then back to Heyward. She yelled over to Atticus, "Can you saddle one of the horses, Atticus? We want to go for a ride." The man nodded and started off to the barn. "You must need something to drink after that long ride," she said to her guest.

"Thank you," Heyward said. "I don't want to be a bother."

"Nonsense." She led him into the house and to the kitchen where she poured some tea she had made earlier. "Please take a seat," she said, motioning to the small dining table and chairs next to the kitchen.

Heyward set his hat on the table and pulled out a chair, waiting for Amanda to find her seat first. He helped her with her chair and then sat down.

"So, what is it you need to discuss, Mr. Heyward?" Amanda asked. "You've come a long way on a very hot day." She was struck by the man's determined face. He seemed on a mission of some sort. She realized she had never seen him smile. His demeanor had always been so serious. From that first day she had seen him here on the beach and later in the bar down in Georgetown, she had been fascinated, confused and even attracted in some manner with his mysterious way. His face seemed aged far beyond his years with deep lines etched into his forehead and along the edges of his eyes.

They had finished their tea and kept busy in the house with small talk about his ride out to the island. They were both mounted on their horses now, walking slowly out the long drive to the road. Amanda loved to ride and tried to find time each day to take one of the two horses they had managed to keep from the war. The afternoon winds across the marshes helped to cool the air and scattered clouds blocked the sun at times to help as well. They turned south on to the main sand and mud road along the beach.

Amanda said, "There's a path up ahead where we can get down to the beach. Bertie here loves to walk along the water," she said, patting the mane of the old black horse.

"That would be nice," Heyward said.

A hundred yards down from the house, she turned her horse left down a narrow sand trail through the dunes and scrub, sea oats swaying in the breeze and gulls screeching up ahead along the water. The west wind pushed out from the shore keeping the surface calm with only occasional swirls of wind scurrying out across the blue and green ocean. Heyward followed her along the path, and they came down onto the flat beach that grew firmer as they approached the water. Heyward guided his horse up alongside Amanda as they continued south along the shoreline. No one was in sight ahead.

"I used to take this ride with my brothers and later with my husband," Amanda said, "back before they all left."

Heyward didn't respond.

"Who did you leave behind?" she asked the man.

Heyward looked over at her, then took off his hat to rub some of the sweat from his brow. "I had a brother, too." He paused. "He didn't make it back either."

"I'm sorry..."

"No, it's okay," Heyward said. "We got word he was lost at Gettysburg."

Amanda looked over and said, "So, there was no one else?"

"A woman, you mean?"

She nodded.

"Yes, there was a girl I knew from our small town back home. A letter found me a couple years into the fighting. She had left to go west with another man who wanted to settle in Colorado. Guess she got tired of waiting."

Amanda didn't respond this time.

"When did you hear about your husband... about his passing?"

"The War Department sent a courier down from Richmond. It was months after the War had ended."

"They didn't tell you anything more about the fighting in Texas?" he asked.

"No, only that he was gone."

They rode in silence for a while, then Heyward said, "The man who shot your husband..."

"What?" she said, suddenly startled.

Heyward continued. "The Union officer who shot your husband was brought up on charges after the war."

"On charges?" she asked, totally confused.

Heyward took his hat and swatted at some flies that were buzzing around the head of his horse. "Yes, the man's name was Morgan, a Lieutenant Colonel who led one of the Union companies."

"What were the charges? I thought you said this Colonel Barnett fellow was to blame."

"Yes, Barnett was responsible for the entire mess but blamed Morgan for the defeat and forced withdrawal. Barnett had Morgan court-martialed. The man was eventually exonerated, but the damage was done to his reputation and career."

"And what of Barnett?" Amanda asked.

"We heard there was a lot of negative sentiment about Barnett and how he handled the whole situation brought up during the trial, but in the end, there were no charges filed against the man and he went home with no marks against his record. I suspect the U.S. Army just wanted to put the whole mess behind them."

Amanda felt her face flush with anger. "Where did you hear all this?"

"Many of us stayed on after the war to help with decommissioning the fort at Brownsville. The trial was held there."

They rode on for a while in silence, Amanda considering all she had just heard. The sun was pressing down low now behind the dunes and long shadows pushed out across the beach. Finally, she looked over at Heyward and said, "Why are you telling me all this?"

"I just thought you should know."

Amanda's anger burned deeper. "What, that the man responsible for my husband's death tried to blame it on another and then walked away with no repercussions?"

Heyward just nodded back.

Amanda pulled up her horse and Heyward stopped beside her. She was looking out over the ocean, thinking about all the man had just revealed. "What do you know of this man, Barnett?"

Heyward hesitated a moment. "What I've told you."

Amanda pressed, "No! Where did he go? What does he do now?"

Heyward said, "I heard he's back east, Philadelphia, I believe."

"Is he still in the Army?"

"I don't know."

Amanda kicked her horse to start again along the shore and Heyward followed. The low sun dulled the surface of the Atlantic to shades of gray. The wind had died to near calm and the water was glassy and reflected the high clouds above. They rode on to the end of the island and then back up through the dunes to return on the beach road. Amanda could only think of a man named Barnett, living well in Philadelphia, oblivious to her husband's needless death.

They arrived at the entrance to the Paltierre house and pulled up their horses. The sun was down now beyond the far horizon across the marshes. Dark clouds were pushing in and distant thunder could be heard to the west.

Amanda said, "It's late and it's a long journey back to Georgetown. There looks to be a storm coming in. You are welcome to stay in the barn tonight."

"Thank you," Heyward said.

"We have rooms in the house, but..."

Heyward stopped her. "No, it wouldn't be right, but thank you. I'll be fine in the barn."

"I'll have Tulia bring some dinner out.

"Please don't go to any fuss," he said.

"We don't have much," Amanda said, managing a smile.

They came up to the barn and Amanda got off the old horse and tied her reins to a post next to the barn. Heyward dismounted and stood holding the reins to his horse. Amanda came up to him and said, "I must thank you for coming all the way out here to share this news."

"I wish there was something more comforting."

Amanda looked down, shaking her head, still trying to quell the fury she felt for this man named Barnett. Without thinking, she leaned in and kissed Heyward on the cheek.

He didn't seem to react and just stood with his horse as she finally stepped back.

Amanda looked at him for a moment, then said, "Good night, Mister... Heyward. Good night and thank you." She turned and walked away up the drive, candles shining through the windows of the old house, Tulia looking out from the kitchen. She could feel the man's eyes on her as she walked up the steps and into the house.

Chapter Twenty-five

Hanna

Charleston, South Carolina *Present Day*

Hanna heard her friend come through the French door of the Holloway's house in the old historic district of downtown Charleston. Grace carried a tray of glasses and a pitcher of iced tea. Hanna was sitting in a grouping of comfortable wicker porch furniture on the back deck of the house, the setting surrounded by dense plantings of flowering shrubs and trees that blocked the view of any neighboring houses. She had left the legal clinic an hour ago to come back to Grace's, bringing a small suitcase of clothes and necessities for a stay she hoped would be no more than a couple of days.

She had brought along the old diary from her ancestor, Amanda Paltierre Atwell, and had been reading through more of the later entries. She placed the book beside her on a small table as Grace sat down and poured the tea. The sun was still high in the sky, burning down through the tree canopy. Both women were dressed in shorts and light blouses and Hanna had her hair pulled back from her face with a silk scarf.

"I have Sophie brew this tea every week," Grace said, referring to her full-time housekeeper and cook. "It's really the best."

Hanna took a glass and sipped the cool tea, nodding to her friend about the quality of the brew.

"You stay here, honey," Grace said. "Make yourself comfortable. Sophie and I are pulling together something for dinner."

"Oh, please don't go to any trouble."

"You need to eat, dear!" Grace got up and scurried back into the big house, the door slamming quickly behind her to keep in the air-conditioning.

Hanna picked up the diary again and continued reading Amanda's writing about a visit from her brother-in-law, Jackson Atwell, and troubling news he had shared about their plantation property. Amanda's father had apparently placed the family's holdings in a precarious situation with a local bank and Jeremy's father, as the war progressed and the Paltierre's financial situation continued to decline.

The back door opened again, and Hanna looked up to see Phillip Holloway coming out onto the back deck. He was dressed in golf clothes and held a glass of whiskey on ice to the side of his face to cool himself against the blast of the late afternoon heat. Hanna tried to calm her response as the man came over to sit beside her.

"Hanna," he said, placing his free hand on her knee, "so glad you'll be able to stay with us for a few days."

Hanna flinched and pulled her leg back out of his reach. She couldn't find words to respond and reached over to place the diary back on the side table.

"What's wrong?" he asked, his facing scrunching up in surprise.

Hanna wasn't ready to confront him on the information Megan Trumball had shared earlier in the afternoon. Her mind was still swirling with anxiety and the implications of what she'd learned. She was also more than stressed over the visit from the man who threatened her at the beach fire out at the island.

"Hanna?" Phillip asked again.

"Hello, Phillip."

"Are you okay?"

"I've been better, frankly," she finally said.

"Of course, I'm sure this is all a bit much."

"All of what?" Hanna asked, her anger growing.

He took a sip from his drink and placed it on the center table in front of them. "The houses and this damned investigation into Ben's situation."

Hanna looked away, trying with all her will not to slap the man across his smug face.

He changed the subject. "Grace was having Sophie pull some dinner together, but I suggested we go back to the club. They have a great redfish special tonight."

"You two go," Hanna said. "I'm not really up to going out."

"Well, we're not going to leave you alone." He stood to go back in the house. "I'll tell Sophie we'll eat here." He took a drink from his whiskey and his gaze lingered an uncomfortably long time on Hanna before he said, "Is that okay?"

"Of course, thank you," Hanna said slowly. She wanted so badly to come right out and confront the man on his deception in her husband's affairs but cautioned herself to wait until she was sure of the new revelations from the young attorney she'd met with earlier that afternoon.

Holloway disappeared back into the house and Hanna was alone again with her thoughts. *Why would Phillip lie about all this?*

She looked down and saw the old diary on the table beside her. She picked it up and continued reading. She was struck by the similarities of what she was dealing with and the difficulties her ancestor, Amanda, had faced so many years earlier. *Who can we trust?*

Chapter Twenty-six

Amanda

Pawleys Island, South Carolina 1866

Amanda had a pot of hot coffee and two cups as she walked down the sandy drive toward the barn where Heyward had spent the night.

She had been awake since dawn and laid in her bed thinking about the stranger out in her barn. She had to admit to herself she was drawn to the man. He was attractive in a rough way and strong in character, yet there was something unsettling in his manner that she couldn't quite get over. She felt guilty about her feelings for another man. She had been grieving the loss of her dear Jeremy ... *but he had been gone so long.*

Tulia had heard her stirring and looked in on her. She helped her get dressed and then met her down in the kitchen to put the coffee on.

Amanda continued down the walk to the barn. She sidestepped puddles in the drive from the storm the previous night. She knocked on the old wood door of the barn and then pressed it open. She saw Heyward in one of the stalls, saddling his horse. "Good morning," she said as she walked in, dust and hay particles floating on the light from the early morning sun coming in from two small windows on the east wall.

Heyward said, "Well, hello. I'd hoped to be away before I woke you."

"Would you like some coffee before you go," she asked.

"Yes, thank you."

"Sorry about the accommodations," she said, looking around the barn.

He brushed away some hay on his pants. "Much drier here last night than out on that road back to Georgetown."

Amanda poured two cups of coffee and handed one to Heyward. He blew on the steam to cool it and then took a sip. "Thank you."

"So, you'll be headed back to Texas soon?"

Heyward hesitated and turned back to his horse. He cinched the strap tighter under the horse's belly and then checked the bridle fit. He looked back at her "Yes, I need to get started back."

Amanda walked around to the other side of the horse, patting its brown hindquarters. She could see Heyward across from her, still fussing with the saddle. "I think Orlando Atwell would like to see you before you go. Could you stay for dinner tonight?"

He looked back at her and smiled. "Yes, I'd like that. I'll be leaving in the morning to start back west."

"I'll have him join us at *Tanglewood*. I'd like you to see our farm before you go and I need to see Mr. Atwell on some other business."

He nodded. "Yes, thank you. What time should I come out?"

Amanda thought for a moment and then gave him a time and directions out to *Tanglewood* from Georgetown. "Plan to spend the night," she said. "Papa will be there, so you don't have to sleep in the barn." She smiled. "You can leave from there in the morning, if you like."

"Yes, that will be fine." He backed the horse out of the stall. "I'd better be going. I have to pull together supplies I need for the trip."

"Of course." She followed him out of the barn into the bright morning. He stopped, and she came up beside him. She thought of the kiss she had given him the previous night and she could tell he was unsure of what to say or do. Finally, she held out her hand and he took it and shook it gently. "I'm sure Orlando will enjoy seeing you tonight."

"Yes, Orlando," he said and smiled again and then he placed his boot in the stirrup and pulled himself up on the horse. He tipped his hat to her and then turned the horse and rode away down the drive.

Amanda watched until he was out of sight around the bend in the road. She couldn't help but think of another time, so many years ago, when she had stood in the same spot and watched her husband ride away, never to return.

Chapter Twenty-seven

Jackson and Orlando

Georgetown, South Carolina 1866

Jackson Atwell waited at the bar for the two men from the North, Westerman and Sullivan, to join him. They had met earlier in the day on a road outside the Paltierre plantation, *Tanglewood.* He was waiting to hear of their latest meeting with the old man, Paltierre, and probably the daughter, Amanda. He reached for the bottle on the bar and filled the small glass in front of him to the rim with the deep amber whiskey. He threw the drink back and let it burn deep into his gut. The bottle lay half empty in front of him.

He turned when he heard someone coming in. His two associates walked up and sat to his right, Westerman the closest. They both reached for glasses and poured drinks without speaking, then quickly threw the shots back. Westerman said, "Let's get a table over in the back where we can talk."

The three men walked slowly to the back of the small bar, their boots loud on the old wood floor. Only one other table was occupied, and the man had fallen asleep, his head buried in his arms. Jackson placed the bottle on the table and the three men sat.

Sullivan spoke first. "We have a bit of a problem."

Jackson took another sip from his drink. "And what would that be?"

Westerman said, "The old man went crazy on us. We were trying to explain again how we could help with his goddamned farm and he just lost it."

"What do you mean?" Jackson asked. "Was the daughter there?"

Westerman said, "No, we didn't see her."

"Good. Good."

"But, the old man is dead," Sullivan said and then took a long drink.

"What!" Atwell cried out and jumped up from the table. "What in hell happened?"

"Just sit down, you idiot," Westerman hissed. Jackson sat back on his chair.

Sullivan spoke softly. "We were standing on the porch talking to the old fool and he just went off crazy on us. Grabbed a rifle leaning against the wall next to him. I swear he was gonna shoot us. It was him or us."

"Oh, shit!" Jeremy could feel the bile rising in his throat as he began to panic. "You're sure no one saw you."

"Wasn't no one else around," Westerman said.

Sullivan continued, "We took the man's watch and gun so it might look like a robbery. Threw it all in a pond on the way back to town."

Atwell sat thinking for a few moments, his hands shaking on the glass of whiskey in front of him.

"So, we deal with the daughter," Westerman said. "It's not a problem. She'll be even more ready to get rid of the place. No way a woman can take care of all that needs attention out there."

Jackson sipped again from his drink. "You two need to get out..." He stopped when he heard someone coming up from behind him. The bartender asked, "Mr. Atwell, get you anything else, sir?"

Jackson turned and said, "No, Billy. We're fine for now." The man walked back to the bar. Jackson tried to get his clouded brain to focus on the events of the day. Again, he said, "I think you two boys need to get scarce."

"We're not going anywhere 'til our business is finished," said Westerman. "You know we're talking with two other farms."

Jackson looked at the two men for a moment. "And I'll be here to manage it all for you, but I think you all need to let things simmer down for a while."

Sullivan looked at his partner. "It will look worse if we disappear right after this happened. We all need to stay calm and this will pass."

Jackson looked down at the table and then at the half-filled glass in front of him. He reached for it and threw it back, holding the empty shot glass in front of his eyes, seeing the reflection of the dim lights from the bar. "Holy shit!" he finally said.

Orlando Atwell held his daughter-in-law in his arms. They were standing together in his office. Amanda had come in unexpectedly just a few minutes ago. Between gasping sobs, she had explained their servant, Atticus, had found her father shot dead on the front veranda of their house at *Tanglewood*. The man thought it might have been a robbery as some of Mr. Paltierre's personal belongings were missing.

He tried to comfort the widow of his deceased son. "Amanda, Amanda, dear," he whispered, holding her close. "I'm so sorry." He got her to sit down on a leather couch along the wall. "Let me get you something to drink." He walked from the office to the kitchen and brought back a glass of water.

Amanda sipped at the drink and tried to calm herself. "We need to speak to the sheriff."

"I'll send someone for him." He called his assistant into the room and asked him to run down to the sheriff's office, quickly.

Amanda took several deep breaths and sipped at the water. "Tulia and I left the island around noon today to go back to *Tanglewood*. I didn't want to leave Papa there alone any longer and I sent Atticus ahead earlier this morning. When we pulled the carriage up the drive, we saw Atticus carrying Papa inside the house. I thought he was asleep. When Atticus came back out to greet us, there was blood all over him. God, there was so much blood!" She put her face down in her hands.

Orlando sat beside her and put his arm around her shoulders to comfort her. "I'm really so sorry, dear. I can't imagine who would want to hurt an old man like that."

Amanda blew her nose on her handkerchief and cleared her throat. She said, "Orlando, now is not the best time, but I've been meaning to speak with you about Papa and *Tanglewood*."

"What is it, dear?"

"Jackson told me you're holding a note on the property. He said we owe money to you *and* the bank on the property."

The man sat back on the couch. "That's right, dear. Your father came to me over a year ago and asked for my help. He was desperate to keep current on the money he owed to the bank, so I was obliged to help."

"Why didn't you tell me this when we were talking about the money and accounts earlier?"

"Your father asked me to keep the transaction in confidence. I was honoring his wishes. He and I discussed a plan to let the markets settle after the war and sell off part of the property to an adjoining farm to get the debts current, if needed. We can still do that, dear."

Amanda stood and walked to a window on the far wall. She turned and looked at her father-in-law. "Jackson has been pressing me to sell the place to these two men in town from up north."

"I know who you're talking about," he said, shaking his head. "I'm afraid Jackson is in with a bad lot there. I've tried to convince him of that, but he's not listening."

"They've been out to *Tanglewood* to talk with Papa. I've had to chase them off."

"Dear, let's wait for the sheriff and tell him everything you know," Orlando said. "Then, we need to make arrangements for your father. I'll help with that. I'm really very sorry. He was a dear friend and a fine man. I know he was fading some these past years, but he was a fine man, Amanda."

He held out his arms to hug her again and she came to him. "And I'll talk with Jackson. He and his *friends* will leave you alone."

The old lawyer left her in the office to go check on the sheriff. She sat again on the couch, unable to fully comprehend that her father was gone, and she was alone now. Everyone was gone. In such a short time, everyone in her life was gone. She remembered her invitation to the man who called himself Heyward, for dinner that night at *Tanglewood*. She would have to find him or get word to him about what had happened.

Chapter Twenty-eight

Jeremy

Palmetto Ranch, Texas May 13, 1865

There was a sudden quiet lull across the field of battle. Atwell watched as his men herded the prisoners they'd just captured in their furious charge against the poorly defended Union position at the base of Palmetto Hill. Several of the enemy had been killed or badly wounded in the assault. He felt his heart beating hard as he tried to catch his breath and assess all his men had just accomplished and how they should continue to press the attack. His eyes and mouth were caked with sand and dust and the acrid smell of gunpowder was heavy in the air.

He heard horses coming up fast behind and saw Colonel Ford leading his small officer corps toward them. Ford pulled up in a cloud of sand and dust, a broad smile across his face. He took off his hat and wiped his brow. "Damn fine work, Captain!"

Atwell just nodded back, trying to fight off the exhaustion that was consuming his every breath.

Ford said, "I know your men need a rest, but we have to continue to press the attack on their rear." He looked north to the retreating columns of blue several hundred yards off. "We'll pinch them in from the north, but we have to take it to 'em there in the rear. Keep them busy as long as you can 'til we can flank them to the north."

"Yes sir! Give me a few minutes to gather my officers. We'll be ready to go as quick as we can."

Ford and his small contingent rode off in a thunder of hooves to the north. Atwell looked around him. The smoke from musket fire was clearing. He could see no casualties among his own men. The prisoners were being marched off under the watch of one of Jeremy's lieutenants and his men. Two medical officers rode up in a wagon to see to the wounded. The dead would be dealt with later.

Jeremy called to his sergeant to get word to the other officers to reassemble for further orders. The man rode off quickly. In his mind, Atwell knew Colonel Ford was right to continue to press the attack. His mind was also telling him his men and their horses were near collapse.

Chapter Twenty-nine

Hanna

Charleston, South Carolina *Present Day*

Hanna knew she needed to take a walk when Phillip made another inappropriate attempt to get close to her. They had been eating dinner on the back deck of the Holloway house as the sun set over the old neighborhood. Grace had gone back inside to bring out some dessert when her husband stood and came around the table. He stopped behind Hanna's chair and started rubbing both of her shoulders.

"Phillip, please don't!" she said, pushing back her chair and standing to confront the man.

He seemed completely surprised by her reaction. "Hanna, we just want you to know you have friends who will help you through all this."

Hanna tried to calm herself. "Phillip," she started and then paused, wanting to come out with all the questions she had about this man's role in her husband's calamities. Quickly she realized she wasn't ready for the confrontation. "Phillip, I need to take a walk. Would you tell Grace I'll be back shortly?"

He didn't answer. Hanna pushed by him and went down the back stairs of the porch and then around the house to the front walk. The neighborhood was dimly lit with old street lamps. The chirps of crickets and tree frogs echoed in the evening air. She was just a few blocks from her old house on the Battery and she knew the neighborhood well. Cars were parked close together down the length of the street. She walked quickly, fuming over the latest overly affectionate approach from Holloway. *Did he really think she had any interest in something physical with him?* She was not only furious at the man over his treachery regarding her husband's problems but also incredulous at the arrogance in his clumsy sexual advances, particularly with his wife just inside.

The headlights from an approaching car made her shield her eyes as she reached the corner of the block. To her left, she noticed the shadowed form of a man approaching on the sidewalk of the cross street in the darkness walking a large dog. She didn't notice the car beginning to slow or the door on the passenger side opening as it came through the intersection. She turned when she heard someone approaching through two parked cars beside her. Immediately, she recognized the dark features and dress of the stranger from the beach the previous night. She felt a chilling panic race through her and turned to run, but the man grabbed her by the arm.

"No!" she cried out as loudly as she could. "No!" She felt the man's tight grip around her lower arm, pulling her close.

He put his face close to her ear and said, "Hanna, you need to shut up or this is going to get much worse."

She heard someone calling from down the street.

It was the man with the dog.

"Hey, what're you doing?"

Hanna yelled out, "Help me!" The stranger pulled her hard toward the street and she fell to her knees as she tried to resist. She heard the dog start barking and then the sound of the other man's footfalls running toward her. She pulled away from the stranger's grasp as hard as she could and continued to scream out for help. She turned to see the man with the dog running toward her, the big dog still barking. Her assailant released his grip and turned to run back to the waiting car.

Hanna heard him yell out, "We warned you!" as he closed the door and the car sped off.

Her heart was racing. She felt the first pain from the scrapes on her knees as the man with the dog stopped beside her.

"Are you okay?" he asked, his dog sniffing her as he tried to pull it back.

She sat on the sidewalk, still stunned at the attack from the man from the beach. She didn't respond and watched as her rescuer pulled out his cell phone and began to punch in a number. "I'm calling 911," she heard him say.

Without thinking, she said, "Ask for Detective Frank."

Thirty minutes later, she was sitting on a deeply cushioned couch in the large living room of the Holloway house, a cup of coffee in her hands and Grace finishing her clumsy first aid of disinfectant and bandages on her bloody knees. Phillip and Detective Alex Frank sat across from her in two chairs pulled up close to the antique ottoman between them. Hanna was still stunned over the sudden attack on the street, and she struggled to sip from the coffee without spilling on her friend's expensive rug.

She heard the detective ask, "And this was the same man who approached you last night at the beach?"

Hanna looked across at the policeman and then at Phillip, who seemed deeply disturbed. Frank asked her the same question again and she struggled to compose herself to answer. "Yes, it was the same man."

"Do you remember anything about the car?" Frank asked.

"No, it was dark, and I couldn't see around the cars parked on the street."

"You didn't notice a color or type of car?" Frank asked.

Hanna tried to remember anything more from the encounter with the stranger but could only see the same dark cloaked face. She shook her head.

Frank said, "We spoke with the man who helped you and he didn't get a very good look either. He thinks it was a black SUV."

"I don't know," Hanna said. She had already gone through the previous night's run-in with the man at the beach and his threat of any further cooperation with the authorities. She was too scared now to follow the man's dire warning. She hadn't mentioned anything about the money her husband had supposedly secreted away from the land deal.

"Hanna, Jesus. You should have told us about this," Phillip said.

Grace said, "I can't believe this, honey. Why didn't you tell us?"

Hanna looked at her friend and struggled to respond.

Frank said, "Are you up to going through all this again? We need to get a full statement."

"Of course," Hanna said, hesitantly, the fear and adrenaline still coursing through her.

Hanna woke early the next morning, sleep coming reluctantly over the long night after seemingly hours of playing back the past day's events and the attempted attack or abduction the previous night. She was still having trouble placing all the loose ends together and finding it hard to believe her life had turned so suddenly down a dark and dangerous path.

She told Alex Frank as much as she could remember about her encounters with the man on the beach, and then again last night out on the street corner. He left without much reassurance her information would help. Most of the night she had been weighing the merits of telling even more of what she had recently learned from the lawyer at her husband's old firm, Megan Trumball ... and about the money the stranger was looking for.

Hanna pulled herself out from under the covers and found some clothes in her bag for the morning. She went quietly down the stairs and out the front door of the Holloway's house. When she was a few houses away down the sidewalk, she pulled her cell phone from her pocket and looked for the number of Alex Frank.

He met her an hour later at a coffee shop a few blocks away. They sat across from each other at a small table as Hanna relayed all she had learned from the young woman who had come to her office on Sunday afternoon. Frank made a few notes in a small book he carried but mostly just listened intently to her recollections of the conversation.

When she finished, he asked, "Are you sure you had no indication Holloway was involved in any of this?"

Hanna thought for a moment and took a sip from her hot coffee. "You would think the man lived on an entirely different planet from my husband, he seemed so removed from the whole mess."

"And he's been coming on to you?" the detective asked.

"He's been pretty clear about his intentions," Hanna said. "The man makes my skin crawl when I think about all this."

Frank looked out the window of the coffee shop, seeming to consider the information he had just learned. He turned back to Hanna. "First, we need to get you some protection. I'll have a patrol car keep a regular route past the Holloway house. I don't want you out walking alone anymore."

Hanna started to protest, but Frank continued, "Whoever this is who came after you last night may very well be aware you've called me and that we're here this morning."

"How would they know?" Hanna asked.

"They may have someone watching the house, following you... who knows. They've been pretty clear about trying to keep you away from talking to us or the Feds."

Hanna felt a rush of nausea as she thought about what may have happened last night if the man had been able to get her into their car. "Do you think Phillip has anything to do with these people?"

Frank returned her intense gaze for a moment. "I really don't know, but I'm sure as hell gonna find out."

Chapter Thirty

Amanda

Pawleys Island, South Carolina 1866

Amanda walked down the main street of Georgetown, her head in a fog of confusion and grief. She had left Orlando Atwell's office a few minutes ago. Tulia was waiting for her in the carriage out on the street. She told her to go to the Atwell house and wait for her. They'd be staying there for the night. The sheriff had come to her father-in-law's office earlier and she told him what little she knew of her father's death. She also told him of the two men who had been out to see her father about the property. The sheriff was going to ride out to *Tanglewood* to speak with Atticus and see what else he could learn about the murder.

People she knew greeted her as she passed on the walk, but she didn't respond, so overwhelmed in all that faced her now with her father gone. She came up to the front door of the old boarding house where Heyward said he'd been staying. She saw his horse tied up in front. Then, she heard her name called.

"Amanda!"

She turned and saw Heyward coming down the wooden walk with two large parcels in his arms.

"What are you doing here?"

Amanda stood silent as he came up to her.

"Amanda, what is it?

She wiped at the tears forming again and took a deep breath. "There's been..." She couldn't finish.

Heyward put his supplies down on a bench beside them. He moved closer and took her in his arms. She rested her cheek on the leather vest he wore.

She managed to get herself under control and quietly said, "My father is gone."

"Gone where?"

Amanda looked up at him and said, "Atticus found him out at the farm today. He'd been shot."

"Oh God!"

"He's gone," she said and put her face back on his chest. She could feel him tighten his arms around her and she held him close, searching for some comfort in all that was lost.

She heard him say, "What happened?"

She sighed deeply. "We don't know. The sheriff is on his way out there now.

"Is there anything I can do?"

She pulled away and looked up at the man. She saw the stain of her tears on his clothes. She shook her head. "No, but thank you. I needed to find you about dinner tonight. We won't be..."

"Of course."

"I need to get back to the Atwell's. Tulia is waiting for me and I want to be there when the sheriff returns."

"I'll walk you there," Heyward said.

"No... no, but thank you." Amanda turned to leave. "Would you come by this evening, later?"

He nodded. "Will you need help with anything out at the farm?"

She hesitated, trying to think through all that needed to be done. "I don't know. Let me... let me think it all through. Thank you, though." She left him there and turned to walk back to Orlando Atwell's house.

Amanda could hear her footsteps on the creaking old boards of the walk along the street, but her head was in a fog and her body felt dull and numb. She heard another noise and sensed someone ahead. She looked up to see Jackson Atwell stumbling out of the open door to the bar. She watched as he caught himself on one of the posts holding up the roof over the entry. When he noticed her coming up, he got a confused look on his face.

"Amanda..." he said, trying to steady himself against the post. "Amanda," he said again in a slurred mumble.

She stopped a few feet away. She could smell the man and the whiskey, even from so far away. She started down into the street to walk around him, in no mood to deal with his drunkenness.

Jackson stepped down from the walk and grabbed her arm. "Amanda, I heard about your father," he said, speaking slowly, trying carefully to enunciate each word.

Amanda turned to look at him, pulling her arm away. Her anger boiled. "And what do you know of that, Jackson?"

"I'm sorry, Amanda," he managed. "Word is spreading. What happened?"

Amanda shook her head in disgust. She flinched when he tried to grab her again and backed away.

He said, "You'll be needing some help out at the farm?"

"I don't need any help from you."

He lunged forward, almost falling, then catching himself as he grabbed both of her arms, his breath foul with the whiskey. "Let me help you..."

She struggled to pull away, but he tightened his grip on her arms. "Jackson! Let go of me!" She sensed a whirl of motion and then the man was pulled away. She watched in astonishment as Heyward turned the man and then threw a roundhouse punch that caught him on the side of the face. Jackson staggered back for a moment, trying to find his footing, then fell over backwards in the dirt. He lay there, breathing heavily, but not moving.

Heyward said, "Are you all right?"

She was so stunned by the whole encounter, she didn't answer.

"Let me walk you back to the Atwell's," she heard him say and didn't respond as he took her arm and led her away. She looked back. Jackson Atwell was still lying there, breathing heavily but not moving.

Amanda listened as the sheriff talked on about his trip out to *Tanglewood*. She was sitting around the dining table in Orlando Atwell's house with her father-in-law and Heyward listening to the Sheriff's account as well. He had spoken with Atticus and inspected the body. He apologized to Amanda when he provided details of the wounds her father had incurred, two bullets to the chest, one surely entering his heart.

Sheriff Connor said, "I'm sorry, Amanda. There wasn't much more to help us at this point. I looked around the property. There were many horse tracks to and from the house. With the rain last night, they were probably all fresh tracks. Hard to say who had been out to the farm since last night, but safe to say, there was probably more than one person involved in this."

Amanda thought about what she was hearing.

Connor said, "I've sent the undertaker out to..." He paused. "Well, he'll take care of the arrangements. You can go over to see him in the morning."

"Thank you, sir."

"Your man, Atticus, said he was staying out there for the night to keep an eye on the place," the sheriff said. "He's a good man."

Amanda nodded.

The sheriff said, "Well, I should get back." He stood and excused himself. Atwell walked him to the door and out onto the porch. Amanda couldn't hear what they were discussing. She turned to Heyward with a confused look.

"You should get some rest," Heyward said. He stood to leave. "I'll stop by in the morning... before I go."

Amanda looked up at him, feeling dazed and bewildered.

"Get some rest," he said and reached for his hat on the table. He walked out the door, closing it behind him.

Amanda lay half-awake on the bed in the guest room at the Atwell's, still in her clothes, only her boots lying on the floor. Tulia had checked on her some time ago. The room was dark now. Occasionally, she heard noises coming from downstairs. She kept her eyes closed, hoping sleep would come. She thought of her father, now lying alone down at Samson's Funeral Parlor. She felt a shudder rush through her, and she squeezed her eyes tighter shut.

She heard a squeaking on the floorboards outside in the hall, then the sound of the knob turning on the door to her room. She looked up to see a man's shadow standing in the open doorway in the light from the hallway. She sat up as the man came in and closed the door behind him. She could smell the drink on Jackson as he approached her bed. He was bare-chested and held something in his left hand. In the dim light from a window behind her, she sensed it was a bottle. She bolted up and stood beside the bed.

"Jackson, you need to get out of here now!" she said, backing up to the window.

He kept coming toward her, then said in a drunken slur, "Amanda... just wanted to check on you... you're okay?"

"Get out, now!" she screamed. She watched as he tried to place the bottle on the nightstand, but it fell over and broke on the floor.

He pressed her up against the window, his bare arms holding her shoulders. He said, "Amanda, dear... just want to share my condolences."

Amanda struggled to pull away, but he pushed her tight against the wall. She turned her head as he leaned his face in close. He tried to kiss her neck. With all her might, she kicked up with her knee and caught him full in his groin. She felt his grip release and he bent over, screaming out, "Damn, woman!"

She ran around him and out into the hall. She saw Orlando coming out of his room in his night clothes, a look of confusion and concern on his face.

Amanda rushed by him and down the stairs. She ran into the kitchen and found Tulia sitting at the small table with Orlando's house servant, Sadie. Tulia stood, and Amanda ran into her arms. The old woman held her tight and caressed her back. "What is it, child, what is it?"

Chapter Thirty-one

Jeremy

Palmetto Ranch, Texas May 13, 1865

He was satisfied his officers had their men assembled for the next assault. Atwell surveyed the field ahead, a rising strip of sand and scrub with the high Palmetto Hill off to the right. Thirty minutes ago, his force of nearly two hundred cavalry troops with the reinforcements from Fort Brown who arrived with Colonel Ford, had quickly overwhelmed the small rear guard the Yankees had left at the base of the hill to defend their retreat to the Gulf of Mexico.

His orders from the colonel had been clear...continue to press the attack on the enemy's rear and keep them distracted at all cost while the remainder of Ford's forces raced north to cut off the retreat. Atwell could see the Yankees forming a defensive position to the north of Palmetto Hill. Again, he was amazed at the small numbers left for this duty, perhaps no more than fifty again. Most were foot soldiers and they were now digging in across a long picket line with little natural cover. Two officers stood by their horses, yelling out orders.

Atwell knew they had the benefit of cover from the heavy mesquite and chaparral brush until the last hundred yards from the enemy. They needed to move quickly. His men knew to move on his signal, two quick shots from his revolver. He took a deep breath to gather himself for what he hoped was their final attack after two full days of relentless pursuit of the enemy.

He took his revolver from the holster at his side and held it in the air. With one more look each way at his mounted troops lined up in both directions behind the cover of low ground and dense underbrush, he fired off two quick shots. As he spurred his horse forward, he heard the loud yells from his men and the thunder of horses moving off quickly toward the enemy line.

He guided his horse fast through the heavy brush, other horses visible to each side. He held the reins with his left hand and his gun in the right, prepared to shoot. His brain pounded with the rush of adrenaline and chaos all around him. The sounds of return musket-fire intensified as they cleared the underbrush and rushed forward out into the open field. The Federal rear-guard line was now in clear view ahead and Atwell saw the smoke of firing muskets burst up and down the line. The Union officers were riding quickly now up and down behind the picket, shouting out encouragement to their men.

Atwell felt the power of his horse beneath him, rushing with seemingly no fear directly into the guns of the enemy. The sound of gunfire and men's screams was now deafening. He pressed his horse forward, leaning low over the right of its head, steering toward the center of the enemy line.

At that moment, he seemed to draw within himself. The noises all around him became filtered and the flurry of motion seemed to slow. A rider next to him yelled out in a muted scream and Jeremy turned to see the man rise up, then waiver and fall from his horse. The animal kept running with all the others, bearing down on the enemy position. In his mind, there was a quiet voice speaking to him. It was his wife, Amanda's voice. She was calling him home.

In the blur and frenzy of the scene ahead, now only yards from the enemy picket, Jeremy saw one of the Union officers on horseback pull up and turn in his direction. Jeremy began shooting now that he was almost on top of the enemy line. He saw the mounted officer raise his arm to fire, the glint of a gray revolver in his hand. Jeremy continued to pull the trigger on his own gun until the hammer clicked, but there was no further kick from a shell firing. He holstered the empty weapon and reached for the sword held at his side. He pulled it out across his body and held it skyward as he screamed out at the blue-clad enemy ahead.

Two men lay prone before him, their long muskets aimed at his approach, smoke now coming from the one on the right as the man fired. Jeremy felt his horse jump as they reached the enemy line. He saw the eyes of the mounted Union officer looking straight back at him, now only a few feet away. The man was yelling and trying to hold his horse in position. Jeremy steered his horse at the man, swinging his sword and screaming out into the din of the battle.

Jeremy saw the man's pistol kick up twice as he fired back.

There was only a brief awareness of pain as his senses went suddenly blank and dark and silent.

Chapter Thirty-two

Hanna

Charleston, South Carolina *Present Day*

Grace had dropped Hanna at her office early in the afternoon. She had been in meetings and on phone calls with clients for the past two hours. She tried to focus on the work and block out the events that were closing down on her like an impenetrable fog. She had just hung up the phone with a woman she was working with on a custody battle for her two children. She made a few notes in the file and then added a phone call she needed to make for the woman to the judge's office on her "to do" list.

There was a quiet knock on the closed door to her office and one of her volunteer assistants, Katherine, a second-year law student at the Charleston School of Law, leaned her head in. "Hanna, you have someone here to see you."

Hanna looked up from her work, distracted with the details of the case she was struggling with. "What's that?"

"They're from the FBI, Hanna," Katherine said, coming into the office and handing her two business cards.

She looked down at the simply designed white cards that indicated Special Agents Will Foster and Sharron Fairfield were waiting to speak with her. Hanna felt a rush of apprehension as she immediately thought about her attacker's warnings about any further cooperation with the authorities. She placed the cards down carefully on top of the file on her desk and then regained her composure.

She stood and thanked her assistant and walked with her out to the reception area. The two FBI agents were standing together by the front windows, Agent Fairfield holding a cell phone to her ear. She saw Hanna coming down the hall and concluded her call. Hanna was relieved to see they were wearing standard business apparel and not some high visibility FBI logo on their jackets that would have been a beacon to the people who were apparently watching her every move.

"Hello Hanna," the female agent said. "We're sorry to drop in without an appointment, but we have some additional information to discuss with you. Is now a good time?"

Hanna shook each of their hands. "Of course. Let's go back to my office." She turned to her assistant. "Katherine, can you hold my calls and try to get in touch with my next appointment to push it back to later this afternoon."

"Sure, Hanna."

She led the two FBI agents back to her office and they sat around the small round conference table.

Special Agent Will Foster spoke first. "Hanna, we understand you had an unpleasant encounter last night."

Hanna couldn't help but chuckle before saying, "I would say 'unpleasant' would be putting it mildly."

Foster said, "Detective Frank filled us in this morning. It sounds like you were very fortunate a passerby was there to help you."

"Very!" Hanna said.

"It appears the Charleston PD is taking sufficient steps to keep watch over you now," the other agent, Sharron Fairfield said.

"Yes, I feel a little better knowing someone's checking on me," Hanna said. "So, you know, these people threatened me to not cooperate with you?"

"Yes, Detective Frank shared that information with us," Foster said.

"What is it you wanted to discuss?"

Fairfield said, "We've come across some additional information we wanted to get your thoughts on."

"Okay."

Fairfield pulled a notepad from her jacket pocket and turned to a page in it. "We've come across a contact in your husband's cell phone records we thought was interesting."

"And who is that?"

Foster said, "I believe you know an individual named Thomas Dillon, a real estate agent out on Pawleys Island."

Hanna's shock was more than evident to the agents across the table from her. "Thomas!" she said.

"Yes, it appears Mr. Dillon was in frequent contact with your husband in the months leading up to his death."

Hanna tried to think back to that time period and why her friend would have any reason to be speaking with her husband even once, let alone on frequent occasions. "You'll have to forgive me," Hanna finally said. "That doesn't make any sense."

"And why is that, Hanna?" Foster asked.

"My husband certainly knows Thomas Dillon," Hanna said. "They've met on occasion out at the island at parties and I'm sure we've had Thomas over to the house, but I certainly didn't think they had any relationship beyond that."

"We understand he's helping you with the sale of your house up there," Fairfield said.

"Yes, he is, but the listing only began a few weeks ago, so that wouldn't have been the reason for their contacts before Ben's death."

Agent Fairfield was referring to some of the notes in her book. "You're not aware of any other business they may have had?"

Hanna thought for a moment and was unable to come up with any logical connections or reasons for their phone discussions. "No, I really can't imagine what that was all about."

Foster said, "We were up at Pawleys Island this morning and we spoke with Mr. Dillon.".

"You spoke with Thomas?" Hanna said, surprised they were moving so quickly. "What did he say?"

"He claims to have been consulting with your husband on the Osprey Dunes land deal."

Hanna couldn't believe what she'd just heard. She tried to think back on any conversation or indication Thomas had been working with Ben on any project, let alone the failed Osprey Dunes deal. Her surprise quickly turned to a growing anger as she realized her long-time friend had failed to ever mention his involvement in Ben's business.

Hanna was shaking her head, staring out a side window to the office when Foster said, "So, safe to say you had no idea of Dillon's involvement with your husband?"

"No, I'm shocked, really. What else did he tell you?"

"We can't get into all the details, but it's clear he was very involved in the transaction."

"You're kidding!" Hanna said, pushing her chair back and standing. She walked over behind her desk, trying to sort through what she was hearing. She leaned on both hands on the old wood desk, closing her eyes to focus her thoughts.

"Hanna?" she heard the female agent ask.

Hanna looked up. "You'll have to excuse me. Thomas is one of my closest friends. I can't imagine why he would keep this from me, let alone Ben never mentioning it."

Fairfield said, "It appears Mr. Dillon profited quite nicely from the deal before it went south, according to the financial records we've had a chance to review...acting as an advisor and related fees he charged the development."

Again, Hanna was absolutely dumbfounded. "You've got to be kidding me!" She walked over to the window. "This just doesn't make any sense."

The FBI agents turned the conversation back to the man who had confronted Hanna on the beach and then back in Charleston the previous night. Hanna shared all she could remember about the encounters, but really nothing new the agents hadn't already learned from the Charleston PD. She hesitated, then decided to mention the mysterious reference to lost money the man had made. They became quite interested in how the man had referred to the whole situation regarding the money and she shared what she could.

They thanked Hanna for her time and promised to keep her apprised of any additional developments.

Hanna didn't accompany them out to the front of the office, but instead, closed her office door and went back to sit behind her desk. She sat staring blankly at the far wall for a few moments and then put her head down in her hands, the conversation with the FBI agents racing through her brain.

Chapter Thirty-three

Amanda

Georgetown, South Carolina 1866

Amanda woke as the sun pressed in through the blinds, confused at first at where she was. Then, she remembered Tulia had brought her to the home of a friend in Georgetown the past night after Jackson Atwell had assaulted her. Jessica Samuels was her old childhood friend. Her family had lived here in Georgetown for many years. Jessica was still living here with her parents.

Amanda sat up on the bed and noticed she was still fully dressed. She had managed to get some sleep the previous night, but she woke frequently with images of a drunken Jackson Atwell pushing himself on her. There was a quiet knock on the door.

"Yes."

The door opened, and Jessica leaned her head into the room. "Ready for some company?"

Amanda nodded, and Jessica came in and sat beside her, putting one arm around her shoulders. When Amanda and Tulia had knocked on her door the night before, Mr. Samuels came to see who it was. He let them in, and Amanda had shared the night's events with her friend before turning in to try to get some rest.

Jessica said, "Again, dear, so sorry about your papa."

Amanda nodded, leaning into her friend. "Thank you for putting us up."

"You need to talk to the sheriff about that Jackson boy," Jessica said. "Sounds like you got a good kick in on him, anyway." She laughed and shook Amanda's shoulders, trying to brighten her mood. "Always knew that man was no good. Hard to believe he comes from the same family as your Jeremy."

Amanda said, "I don't know what would have happened if..." She paused.

"Don't you worry about that. You took care of yourself like you always do. You're welcome to stay here as long as you need."

"Thank you."

"We've got some breakfast on downstairs," Jessica said. "Come down and join us. We already got some food for Tulia." She stood to leave. "There's some cold water in the bowl there for you to wash your face." She patted Amanda on the shoulder and then went out the door.

Amanda looked around at the spare room, a crucifix with Jesus hung over the bed. She looked at it and said a silent prayer for her father and all that lay ahead.

Orlando Atwell came by the Samuels house later in the morning to check on Amanda. They sat together on a long bench on the front porch. Atwell said, "Amanda, I can't begin to say how sorry I am about Jackson's behavior..."

"Orlando, please, I don't want to talk about it."

"He's still sleeping off that terrible drunk, but..."

"Please don't try to make excuses for him," she said.

"I'm not. It's just that..." He paused, taking a big breath of air and shaking his head. "I've never been able to get through to that boy."

"I'm not going to press charges, but if you let that man anywhere near me again, I swear that..."

Orlando broke in, "You won't have to worry about him."

She looked at the man and could see he was dead serious.

"If you'd like, I'll go with you over to the funeral home to see to the arrangements for your father."

"Thank you, maybe this afternoon," Amanda said. "I'll come by your office."

He stood. "I'll see you then.

She watched him walk down the steps and on down the street toward his office. She heard a horse coming up from the other direction and turned to see Heyward riding up to the house. He stopped and dismounted, tying his horse up to the fence along the road. He came through the gate and up onto the porch. "Good morning."

"I thought you were leaving," Amanda said.

"I stopped by the Atwell's to see you and their woman, Sadie, told me you were here. Sounds like you had a tough night," he said, sitting down beside her. "When that bastard comes to, I'll..."

"You don't need to worry about that but thank you."

"Thought I'd stay around another couple of days, maybe give you a hand out at the farm until everything is settled with your father."

Amanda looked over at him. He sat with his hat in his lap, his dusty boots on the painted planks of the porch and several day's growth of beard on his face. She knew she didn't want him to leave, but hesitated for a moment, then said, "I would like that."

Later that afternoon, Amanda had finished her meeting with her father-in-law and the undertaker. She was riding in the carriage with Tulia on her way back to *Tanglewood*. Heyward rode his horse alongside on the sandy two-track road out to the plantation. They had been riding in silence since leaving town. Amanda was deep in thought, memories of the discussion with the undertaker too fresh in her mind, fanning her grief. She saw the gate to the drive up to their house up ahead. She said to Heyward, "This is our farm."

A white but worn and overgrown split-rail fence ran several hundred yards in each direction from the gate along the road and then up into the fields. A small painted sign at the gate had the name, *Tanglewood*.

They turned up the drive and after a couple of gentle turns, the low white house came into view, the outbuildings spread off to the west along the planting fields. The late afternoon sun burned through the tall live oak trees along the drive, brown Spanish Moss swaying slowly in a light breeze. Two big black and white magpies flew in low in front of the carriage and then up into the tree branches.

Atticus was waiting in front of the house and took the head of one of the carriage horses as they stopped. The old man nodded at Heyward as he dismounted.

Atticus said, "Welcome back, Miss Atwell. So sorry about your pappy."

"Thank you, Atticus. Everything is arranged in town. The funeral will be in two days on Saturday at the church."

He nodded back. Amanda and Tulia climbed down from the carriage. Atticus led the horses away toward the barn and Tulia scurried inside.

Amanda said to Heyward, "Let's get your horse down to the barn. I'll show you around."

Later, they came into the house. Heyward stopped in the front entry when he noticed a large family photo framed on the wall. Amanda came up beside him. "All the family, just before they all left..."

"And that's your husband?" he asked, pointing to the man who held her arm in the picture.

"Yes, that's Jeremy." She looked at him quizzically.

He noticed her gaze. "Yes, I see the likeness. He looked much older by the time I saw him in Texas."

They walked into the kitchen and Tulia was pulling some food together out of the pantry. "Don't have much for lunch, Miss Amanda."

"Whatever you can find, Tulia. Thank you. We'll be back. I want to take Mr. Heyward out to the north pasture to see the rice fields."

Tulia said, "You go ahead. Don't need to hurry."

Heyward followed Amanda out the back door and down the steps onto a sloping yard away from the house. The little grass left was brown and cluttered with weeds. The shade from the tall live oak covered their path as they walked off down the hill. Amanda stumbled and reached her arm through his. He looked at her as she smiled back.

"You're very sweet to come out with us," she said.

"I just want to make sure you're on your feet," he said. "I know this must all be hard for you."

They continued down through the trees. Ahead, a broad expanse of rice fields framed in low grassy levies spread out before them. The fields were sparse and unkempt, clearly not tended or cultivated in the recent past.

They came to a stop on the first levy and Amanda said, "This used to be such a vibrant place, the rice growing, the workers in the field, my father and his crew keeping tabs on everything. It was a marvelous place to grow up."

Heyward said, "Your workers were slaves then?"

Amanda looked at him and let his hand go. She hesitated, then said, "Yes, they were bought and cared for by my family. Over the generations, their families grew here, too. My father was good to them. I never saw them mistreated. Atticus and Tulia decided to stay with us after the war. They had their freedom and my father offered to give them some land out on the edge of the property, but they wanted to stay."

"I didn't mean any offense," Heyward said. "I know it was the way here."

Amanda didn't answer. She took her arm away and started to walk back. "I want to show you something."

They came upon a trail that led around the levy and then off into a stand of heavy cypress and swamp, the elevated trail just above the level of the dark water covered in lily pads and green slime. Up ahead, a small structure came into view. It was a small cabin set on a rise in the swamp that kept it dry. The cabin was made of rough logs and had a sod roof, much overgrown with trailing vines and weeds. There was no door on the entrance and Amanda ducked and led Heyward in. The light from the opening and two windows showed the sparse furnishing of an old wood table and two chairs. A wooden bed with a straw mattress was against the far wall. The room was dank and close, then a breeze blew up and some fresh air rushed through the windows.

"My father had this built for my brothers and me when we were young. We used to play out here."

Heyward looked around and then walked over to one of the windows. "What about the snakes?"

Amanda laughed. "Oh, we saw a Cottonmouth now and then. The boys liked to catch them."

"Rattlesnakes!" Heyward said.

"We'd see an alligator in the swamp here from time to time, too."

Heyward shook his head, turned back and smiled. "Heck of a place for little kids."

"We never knew any different."

Heyward came over and stood beside her, looking out one of the windows.

"When I came out from Texas, I never expected to meet someone like you." Amanda didn't respond. "You're a special woman, Amanda Atwell." She looked up into his face. "I know you're probably still grieving for your husband... and now your father..."

Amanda placed her fingers on his mouth to stop him and said, "We should get back."

Chapter Thirty-four

Hanna

Charleston, South Carolina *Present Day*

Alex Frank sat across from Hanna at a booth along the wall of a small neighborhood diner down the street from her office. It was just past six in the evening. There were only two other tables with customers in the place. Small ceiling fans pushed the air filled with the smells of grease fires and garlic. She had finally called the detective an hour after the FBI agents had left her office where they filled her in on the unexpected involvement of her friend, the Pawleys Island real estate agent, Thomas Dillon, in her husband's land deal debacle. She was still reeling from the new revelations of her friend's connection to the deal. Alex had agreed to meet her and get some dinner at the same time.

Hanna had just finished summarizing her discussions with the two FBI agents and the young lawyer from her husband's firm regarding the complicity and deception of both Phillip Holloway and Thomas Dillon in the Osprey Dunes real estate deal. She also shared the stranger's request for the return of missing money from the deal.

Alex took a drink from his water glass. He looked around the restaurant, seeming to consider these new developments. When he looked back at Hanna, his face was resolute and determined. "I would suggest you and I have a very serious discussion with both these gentlemen, sooner rather than later."

Hanna could feel her heart quicken as she considered the confrontations with the two men she had always felt she could trust, who had now apparently had deceived her and been more than casually involved in her husband's spiraling problems. She also tried to put the images of the stranger's recent threats and attempted abduction out of her mind. Finally, she nodded her head in agreement, a growing anger building inside. "I agree. I want to look these two in the eye and hear what in hell has been going on."

"Let's start with Holloway," the detective said. "We need to do this on our terms. He's a smart lawyer and we need to catch him off guard. I'm going to have him come into my office at the precinct first thing in the morning."

Phillip Holloway walked into the downtown precinct of the Charleston Police Department at 8:30 a.m. the next day. He was dressed in an impeccable gray summer suit, a starched blue shirt and bright patterned paisley tie. His leather loafers cost more than most police officers on duty would make in a week. He stood confidently at the front reception desk and asked for Detective Frank.

After a minute, he was directed back through a locked door the front desk sergeant opened for him and down a long hall to the room that housed the department's detective squad. He spotted Frank sitting at his desk against the far wall beneath a window that let in the bright morning sun. They made eye contact and Frank stood and came across the room. The two men shook hands.

Alex said, "Thanks for coming in on such short notice."

"Of course," Holloway answered. "You said you had some new information on Ben's case to share."

"Let's go down to a conference room where we can have some privacy."

He led the way down another dark hallway, doors with small windows along each side. He stopped at the last room on the left and pushed the door open to lead the way inside. When Holloway walked through the door, he stopped suddenly, a look of surprise finally replacing his smug and confident facial expression.

Hanna Walsh stood behind a small metal table.

"Hanna! What the hell is going on?"

"Let's all sit down," Frank said and directed Holloway to the nearest chair. He sat facing Hanna.

"What's this all about?"

"I think that's an excellent question for you, Phillip," Hanna said.

Holloway sat and listened intently as the detective shared the information they'd learned from Hanna's source who they declined to name. As Frank continued to lay out the revelations of Phillip's and his firm's involvement in the Osprey Dunes land deal, the man struggled to regain control. His face became impassive and expressionless as he listened without commenting.

When Frank had finished and looked up from the notes on the legal pad in front of him, Phillip looked over at Hanna and smiled. "Hanna, you've got the wrong idea about this."

"The wrong idea about what?" Hanna asked, trying to control her anger, gripping the coffee cup in front of her with both hands.

Phillip looked back at Alex Frank. "Where did you get this?" he said glancing down at the notes on the pad.

"From a very reliable source."

Hanna had finally had enough. "Phillip, after all this time, we find out you were actually involved in this mess! You've led me on to believe you were so shocked by Ben's scheme and that you were trying to help me, for God's sake!"

"Hanna, please."

"No, Phillip!" she interrupted. "No more lies!"

The man sat for a moment without responding and then he stood suddenly, pushing his chair back. "This little ambush is not going to work. You two have no idea what you're getting into here."

"Why don't you sit down and tell us," Frank said.

"I don't have to tell you anything." He started toward the door and then turned back to Hanna. "You need to know we're doing everything we can to protect you and help you through all this."

"Then why have you been lying to me!" Hanna yelled out. She stood and came around the table. Holloway continued backing toward the door and reached for the knob. "Damn it, Phillip! Tell me what in hell is going on!"

"Not here, Hanna," he said. "Not now."

Frank stood and said, "Are you refusing to discuss any of this?"

Holloway looked at the detective for a moment before saying, "Yeah, that's right. I have nothing to say to you after this ridiculous attempt to trap me."

"We're not trying to trap anyone," Frank said. "We just want to get to the truth."

Holloway finally began to lose his composure. "The truth is, Ben Walsh got himself involved with the wrong people in the wrong deal. We tried to help him, but he just kept digging a deeper goddamned hole. I don't know what you're trying to do here, but you are way off base."

He turned and walked out the door, slamming it behind him.

Hanna was back at her office an hour later when her cell phone rang. She looked at the number on the screen and saw it was Detective Frank. She pushed the "receive" button.

"Yes, Alex."

"I reached out to your friend on Pawleys Island, the real estate guy."

"Thomas Dillon," Hanna replied. "What did he have to say?"

"Seems he's left town on vacation... out of the country, apparently."

"Out of the country!" Hanna said. "I just saw him this weekend. He's helping me sell my house out there. He didn't say anything about a trip."

"I guess he had a sudden urge to see the Caribbean. He bought a plane ticket yesterday all the way down to St. Croix."

Hanna sat staring at the far wall of her office. Her anger returned as she tried to sort through the betrayal and lies from people she had always felt she could trust beyond any doubt.

"When is he coming back?" she asked.

"No return ticket."

"Are you kidding me! Can he just take off like that? The Feds are talking to him and he can just leave the country."

Alex said, "I'm sure our friends at the FBI are not going to be very happy about this."

"We have to get Phillip to tell us what is going on here."

"We're in the process of getting a warrant to search his home and office," Alex said. "We're also taking steps to get a sworn statement from him. The Feds will probably try to shut us down. They want control of this investigation, but I've got a murder in my city that we need some answers on."

Hanna couldn't respond. She was too stunned by the duplicity of her friends and the dead-ends they kept encountering.

"Hanna," she heard Alex say on her cell phone. "Hanna?"

"Alex, I don't know what to say," she finally responded. She thought for another moment about Thomas Dillon running off to the islands. "I have Dillon's cell phone. Can't we just call him?"

"I've already tried. He's not answering."

Chapter Thirty-five

Amanda

Tanglewood Plantation, South Carolina 1866

Heyward came in through the back door rubbing his hands on an old towel, his face and arms slick with sweat. The pipes from the water cistern out next to the house had rusted up and he'd been working through the morning with Atticus to free it up. Tulia was in the kitchen working on some sewing.

Heyward said, "You should have some water now, ma'am."

Tulia got up and went over to the sink. She pumped on the well handle several times until a trickle of rusty water started to come out. She kept pushing on the handle and soon there was a flow of clear water. "Thank you, Mr. Heyward. Looks fine now."

"Where is Amanda?"

"She's over in the vegetable garden, seein' if there's anythin' worth eatin' left." She pointed out to the side of the house.

Heyward nodded and went back out the door. He walked around the side of the house and saw the garden down below, about a hundred yards through the trees. There was a low wire fence around the plot of land that had about twenty rows laid out, remnants of a few plants still showing through the rough dirt. Amanda was on her knees digging under one of the plants, pulling up some potatoes and placing them in a basket at her side.

Heyward pulled a piece of the wire mesh aside that was fashioned as a gate and walked across the rows.

She looked up when she heard him coming. She held up a small potato and said, "Here's your dinner."

"Can't wait."

"Did you get the water running?"

"Clear as a stream," he said.

She stood and brushed at the dirt on the knees of her dress. "Atticus has a long list of projects he's been trying to catch up with."

Heyward said, "I'll help him for a few days."

"Thank you." She smiled and walked over to him, standing close. "I know you hadn't planned to stay. Don't you have to get back?"

"Texas will be there whenever I do get back."

She led him back toward the house. "Let's go get these potatoes peeled. Tulia can add them to whatever else she's found for dinner."

Later that afternoon, Amanda sat with Heyward in chairs side-by-side out on the front porch of the house. They were sipping at tea that Tulia had made, enjoying the shade of the porch and the lovely scene out to the rice fields. They both turned when they heard a horse coming up the drive from the road. The horse was obviously running fast and then it came into view around the last bend, Jackson Atwell astride, holding on to his hat.

Heyward said, "What the...".

Amanda stood and walked to the edge of the porch. Heyward joined her as Atwell pulled up his horse hard and jumped to the ground. Amanda noticed his face, black around his left eye where Heyward had hit him.

"You're not welcome here," Heyward said, starting down the steps, but Amanda held his arm.

Jackson placed his hat back on his head and brushed at the dust on his clothes. He looked up at the two of them on the porch and said, "Well, isn't this nice. See you're making yourself right at home, Heyward."

Amanda had to hold him with two hands. "Jackson, you need to leave now, or I *will* go to the sheriff after what you tried the other night."

Jackson took his hat off again and held it over his heart. He said, "Amanda, I'm here to apologize..."

"I don't want your apology!" Amanda said. "I want you to leave!"

Heyward said, "Get back on your damned horse and get the hell out of here."

Jackson backed away a few steps toward his horse, grazing now on some brown grass. "I have some news for Amanda. Just take a minute."

"Jackson..." Amanda started to say before Atwell cut in.

"I was down at the telegraph office yesterday. Sent a note up to an old friend at the War Office in Richmond a couple days ago. Still a few people working there, winding down the last details of the Army." He walked closer to the front porch, apparently emboldened with his news. He paused for another moment. "Quite odd, actually. Asked them to check the rosters for Confederate officers stationed out at Brownsville, Texas."

Amanda noticed Heyward step back onto the porch. She let go of his arm. He said, "Amanda, let me explain...".

Atwell interrupted, "Real curious. They checked those rosters and got a telegraph back to me this morning." The man paused again before saying, "Seems there was never a Confederate officer assigned to Fort Brown out in Texas with the name of *Heyward*."

She heard Heyward say, "Amanda...", but she held up her hand. "Jackson Atwell, I want you off our land now, or I swear I'll go inside and bring back the biggest gun I can find and ..."

Jackson smiled and backed up to grab the reins of his horse. "No need to do that. I'm leaving now." He mounted and the horse spun around in place until he reined it in. "You might want to ask who in hell this man is and how he got Jeremy's letter." He pulled the horse up and then jerked it around and kicked his spurs into its belly. The horse reared and then took off at a fast gallop.

Amanda watched the man ride off around the far bend. Her anger was near a boiling point now and she felt prickles all over her skin. She turned to Heyward and stared at the man. She watched as he looked away across the fields. "Do you care to explain?"

"Amanda..." he started.

"Just tell me the truth!" she said, clenching her fists.

He flinched and moved back a step, staring back at her, seeming to search for some way to respond.

Amanda came up to him and got close to his face. "I don't know who you are, but I do know you need to leave, now."

Again, he didn't respond.

"Get your horse and go!"

Heyward spoke softly. Amanda had to lean in to hear. "I'm sorry, I wanted you to have your husband's letter."

She looked back, trying to read the emotions on the man's face. "I have the letter. You need to go." She left him there on the porch and went into the house, slamming the door behind her. After a few minutes, she caught her breath and looked out one of the windows. She saw him walking away toward the barn. Later, she heard the muffled sound of his horse's hooves heading out the lane.

Chapter Thirty-six

Hanna

Charleston, South Carolina *Present Day*

Hanna had little interest in returning to the Holloway's home. The woman's husband had not only made inappropriate advances but had also been lying about his involvement in her own husband's financial calamities and possibly his tragic death. But, where was she to go? Her home in Charleston had been sold to help pay debts incurred by her husband. The beach house on Pawleys Island would soon be under contract to be sold. A friend she thought she could trust, her real estate agent, Thomas Dillon, had offered her his guest house out on the island but he too, appeared to have been hiding his role in her husband's failed real estate dealings and now was suddenly out of the country with no apparent return planned.

After confronting Holloway with Alex Frank down at the Charleston Police Department and ending up with more questions than answers, Hanna had returned to her office thoroughly befuddled about the betrayal of her supposed friends and the doubts and uncertainties concerning her husband's failed business dealings and murder on the streets of Charleston. She had tried to concentrate on her work and the clients she was representing, but her thoughts were overwhelmed by her personal issues.

Her cell phone buzzed on the desk beside her. She tried to ignore it but finally looked at the display. It was a local number she didn't recognize. She was about to touch the "decline" button when she changed her mind and accepted the call.

"Hello, this is Hanna."

There was a pause on the line with no response.

"Hello, can you hear me?"

She heard faint breathing on the other end.

"Who is this?" she demanded.

Finally, the caller responded. "Hanna, this is Phillip."

She considered hanging up immediately, but then her anger returned. "You have a lot of damn nerve calling after all that nonsense this morning down at the police department."

"Hanna," Holloway continued, "I really need to speak with you."

She took a deep breath and then said, "Go ahead. What do you have to say for yourself?"

"No, I need to see you," he said. "Where are you."

"It's none of your business where I am. I'm not meeting with you anywhere. Just tell me what you have to say."

"Are you at your office?" Holloway asked. "I can be there in ten minutes. I really need to explain about this morning and all this nonsense the police are dredging up."

Hanna considered his request. She needed to know what was really happening. She wasn't alone here at the office so having Holloway come down wouldn't pose any uncomfortable personal situations, or at least she hoped that was the case.

"Phillip, I'll agree to see you," she said. "But no more bullshit and lies!"

"Hanna, honestly, I need to explain. Are you at your office?"

"Yes."

"I'll be right over." The line went dead.

Holloway walked into Hanna's office and closed the door behind him. She started to protest, not wanting to be alone with the man behind closed doors but decided she could take care of herself if necessary. She was sitting behind her desk and didn't move to get up, motioning to a chair across from her. Holloway sat down, placing his leather case on her desk.

He was still dressed in his suit coat. He loosened his tie and said, "Hanna, I'm sorry for all the confusion about this. I understand why you're upset."

"I sure as hell am upset, Phillip!" She pushed her chair back and walked around the desk. "How many months have you been deceiving me about Ben's situation? I thought I could trust you and then I find you were involved from the beginning."

He stood and took off his jacket, folding it and hanging it over the arm of the chair. He grabbed his bag and walked over to the conference table. "Let's sit over here," he said. "Let me try to explain."

Hanna was tempted to throw him out of her office, but she knew she had to hear him out. She walked over and sat across from him. "Phillip, I swear to God, if you had anything to do with Ben's death..."

"Hanna, please listen. I need to take you through this whole crazy mess."

"Would you, please!"

"First of all, I couldn't get into this with you earlier."

"And why not?" she said, trying her best to keep her temper in check.

"We knew about Ben's involvement in this land project almost from the beginning. He came to the management committee of the firm to get our approval for his personal involvement representing this deal. He also wanted to bring in support from our Real Estate group, which we agreed to."

"And why couldn't you have told me this before?" Hanna asked, shaking her head in confusion.

"Very early into this deal it became apparent there were some questionable players involved. We confronted Ben with the legitimacy of the project when we found out who he was working with."

"The mob from Miami?" Hanna asked.

"Yes, it became very clear that organized crime elements were using this land development to launder money from some of their illegal operations."

"And what did Ben say when you took this to him?"

Phillip hesitated. "Well, at first, he got very angry and then he tried to rationalize the whole situation claiming the deal was legitimate and the people from Miami were totally aboveboard. He tried to tell us their share of the deal was a minority interest and the money was clean."

"And again, why in hell haven't you told me this before?"

When the firm found out who was involved, our managing partner... you know William Worthers?"

"Yes, of course," Hanna said.

"William practically had a coronary over this whole mess and the firm's involvement. He demanded everyone involved from the firm keep all details of the affair absolutely confidential and cease any further involvement in the project under threat of losing our jobs. The rest of the management committee backed him up."

"So, why did Ben continue to get so deep into this mess?" Hanna asked.

"We spoke with him on numerous occasions. He assured us he was dialing back his involvement and shutting down the firm's connections to the deal. What he didn't say was that he was personally invested in the project and much more deeply tangled up in this than any of us knew."

Hanna's pulse was racing, and she was doing all she could to keep her composure. "And you let him go right down the drain on this?"

"Hanna, no! We tried over and over to help Ben out of this. If he'd been straight with us we might have been able to do more."

"And what do you know about his murder you're not telling me?" she asked, her anger clear in her burning stare.

He shook his head. "I wish I did know what happened, Hanna."

"That's bullshit, Phillip!" she screamed, pounding her fist down on the table. "Why should I believe you when you've been lying to me about all of this."

"You have to believe me, Hanna. We really don't know any more than the authorities at this point. These guys from Miami are a bad lot. It's easy to assume they were behind Ben's murder, particularly if he was trying to get his money back out of the deal or threatening to go to the police, but there just isn't any hard evidence."

Hanna sat back, considering all she'd heard. "And obviously, you didn't tell Grace about any of this?"

"Of course not," Holloway said, emphatically.

Hanna took a deep breath. "So, what about Thomas Dillon?"

"Your real estate agent out on the island? What about him?"

Hanna glared at the man. "You honestly don't know Thomas was working with Ben on the project? No more lies Phillip!"

"Honestly, I had no idea."

Chapter Thirty-seven

Amanda

Georgetown, South Carolina 1866

The pastor offered words of comfort and peace as the small service for Amanda's father, Louis Paltierre, was coming to an end. Amanda sat with Jessica Samuels, holding her arm as they joined others on small chairs next to the open grave and the pine coffin that held her father.

"Ashes to ashes..." she heard the preacher say, but she was looking off into the trees and the dark clouds rushing by overhead. A cold chill had come in the night before and it had been spitting rain throughout the procession from the church out to the cemetery.

The service was apparently over as people around her started to stand and Jessica helped her up. Gathers waited in line to come by and give Amanda their final sympathies. She nodded in numb response as each person offered their thoughts on her father, not really listening to what they were saying. She looked back down to her father's coffin and the tears came again. She tried to remember back to the days when he was a younger, vibrant man.

The crowd was dispersed now. Jessica still stood with her. The preacher came up and paid his final respects and Amanda thanked him. She turned to Jessica. "Thank you. You've been a great help."

Jessica kissed her on the cheek.

Amanda said, "I'd like to stay a while."

"Sure," Jessica said. "You're staying in town with us tonight. Take as much time as you need."

Amanda saw Atticus and Tulia sitting in the carriage and motioned for them to come over. They joined her at the graveside and Tulia put her arm around Amanda's waist, pulling her close.

"He was a good man, child," she heard Tulia say. "He was always a good man."

She looked over and saw the family's oldest servant and former slave, Atticus, standing now with his hat in his hands looking down reverently at the casket. It struck her as so moving to see this man who had been owned as a slave by her father, now honoring his passing and paying his last respects.

Amanda had often questioned the humanity of slavery in her time, but she found some comfort in knowing her family and her father in particular, had always tried to treat Atticus and Tulia and the others with fairness and respect. Their freedom after the war had given her great relief and satisfaction. She would never bring herself to rationalize or accept the old ways. It was a time of shame for all to remember.

For so many to die in the war was a high price to pay, including her own Jeremy, but to see two of the closest people in her life now standing as free people after so many years, brought her some comfort on this terribly sad day.

Two cemetery workers were standing nearby with shovels. "A little more time please?" The two men laid their shovels down and wandered off into the trees. She sat back on the chair looking down at the grave site and her father's coffin.

Atticus and Tulia backed away to wait for her at the carriage.

There were no more tears, only an emptiness that chilled her. The time ahead seemed so overwhelming and now she was the last of the Paltierres. She would need to carry on, to find her own way, to try her best to save her family's place in the world.

She wasn't sure how long she had been sitting when she heard a sound behind her. She thought it was the gravediggers coming back, but when she turned, she saw the man who called himself Heyward walking up to her with his horse trailing behind. Two large packs were strapped behind the saddle.

Amanda felt her anger rise. She put up her hand, but he kept coming. She couldn't think of anything to say. She watched as he tied his horse to a tree and then came up to her, taking off his hat.

"I wanted to pay my respects."

Amanda said sternly, "You never knew the man!"

"I wanted to pay my respects to you... for your father and for your husband."

Again, Amanda couldn't find words.

"I also wanted you to know I *was* there the day your husband fell at Palmetto Ranch."

Amanda started to protest, "But Jackson Atwell..."

The man held up his hand to stop her. "Please let me finish. Can we sit?" he asked.

She looked at the chairs behind her next to the grave and reluctantly turned and sat down. He sat next to her, holding his hat on his knee.

"I told you your husband was a brave man."

Amanda stared back, resigned to listening to what the man had to say.

"For nearly two days he held off far larger numbers of the enemy until reinforcements finally arrived. On the second day, Colonel Ford got to Palmetto Ranch with significant forces of Confederate cavalry and cannon. Your Jeremy continued his assaults against the Union troops trapped in the peninsula along the Rio Grande River. Ford attacked along the northern flank and eventually the Union forces realized they were trapped with no hope of pressing on. The Union commander ordered a retreat to Brazos Island. Most made it out, though many were captured and some killed in the retreat."

"And tell me how you know of this."

He didn't answer for a moment and just stared back. Then, he said softly, "My name is Robert Morgan. Heyward is my middle name. I was there that day when your husband died at the battle of Palmetto Ranch. I am... I was a Lieutenant Colonel in the Union Army."

Amanda felt her breath grow short. She didn't know how to respond.

Morgan continued, "I told you about Colonel Barnett and his pathetic command of the Federal forces."

She nodded.

"All of that is true," he said. "In fact, I'm the man he had charges brought up against in the Union defeat those two days at Palmetto Ranch. I was sent before a military court and though cleared of any fault, was discharged from the Army. I've stayed on in Texas this past year through the trial and then trying to get my life in order."

"So how did you find Jeremy's letter? Why did you feel you needed to come all this way?"

Morgan looked away for a moment then turned back. "That last afternoon of the battle, your husband's cavalry unit rushed in again on our position We had been ordered to set up a rear-guard to defend the retreat. I was on horseback behind our picket line. There was gunfire everywhere and the Confederate commander, Ford, was starting to pour artillery in on our rear positions. Through the smoke of my men's muskets, I saw your husband riding fast at our line. He had his pistol up, firing, and then a sword." Morgan stopped for a moment, then said, "I had my own gun out. I pulled up my horse and fired all the rounds left in my revolver. I saw your husband lurch back, then fall."

Amanda gasped and then stood. "You killed him?"

Morgan tried to reach for her, but she pulled away.

"You killed Jeremy!" she shouted again.

Morgan stared back. She heard him say, "Before we started the retreat, there was a lull in the fighting. I saw the officer I had shot..." he paused. "I saw your Jeremy lying beside me behind our picket. He had a bag over his shoulder. I thought there might be some intelligence we could use if the battle continued. I went to him. He was already gone." He saw Amanda wiping at her tears, but he continued. "I took the bag from him and later found your letter."

Amanda was shaking now. The fury was burning inside, and it was all she could do to keep from sobbing in front of this man. She managed to speak, talking slowly and with clear purpose. "I swear, I should shoot you."

She turned abruptly, walking quickly away through the cemetery.

The man named Morgan stood there and watched her leave.

Chapter Thirty-eight

Hanna

Charleston, South Carolina *Present Day*

Hanna was walking to her car parked behind her office building. It was just past eight o'clock in the evening and the light was beginning to fade in the shadows of the houses and tall trees in the old Charleston neighborhood. As she approached the car, she reached into her purse feeling for her keys. The man, seeming to come from nowhere, the same man from the beach and the man who had tried to abduct her, was suddenly standing between her and the car's driver door.

Panic raced through her and she turned to run before the man reached out and grabbed her arm. He was dressed now in khaki pants and a white dress shirt, but still wore the old Florida State ball cap and his eyes were still hidden behind dark wrap-around sunglasses. Quietly and calmly, he said, "Hanna, please there's no need to be frightened. I'm not going to hurt you. Certainly not here in the middle of town behind your own office."

Hanna stopped pulling away and looked around for anyone she could call for help. The parking area was deserted.

She turned back to the man and managed to say, "What do you want?"

The man said, "Before you freaked out on the street last night, I just wanted to ask you a question again."

"What question?"

He said, "We believe your husband left you something that belongs to us."

"First of all," Hanna replied, "who in hell are you?"

"We've done some business with your husband in the past," the man said. "And it's not important you know who we are."

"And what has Ben supposedly left me?" Hanna asked.

"A great deal of money, Hanna.

Hanna had denied any knowledge of money left by her deceased husband for the third time when the man said, "We don't have time, Hanna, for you to screw with us. I'll be back to see you in the morning, and I expect you to have the money with you or information on how we can get it back."

"There is no money!" Hanna screamed. "Do you think I'd be selling everything I own if there was some secret stash of money?"

"How do we know you're not getting ready to leave the country?" the man said. "And with all of our cash."

Hanna tried to pull her arm free from the man's grasp, but he held her tight. "This doesn't have to get ugly," the man said.

"You killed my husband!" she cried out.

"No, we had nothing to do with that," he said. "Why would we kill a man who owed us so much money?"

"Then who did?" she demanded.

"Your friend, the cop, will have to help you with that," he said, pushing her up against the car and leaning his face in close to hers. "Let me be clear on one thing, Hanna. The people I work for have lost their patience. When they discovered your husband had diverted funds from their business deal, they made it very clear this needed to be cleaned up immediately."

"How many times do I have to tell you, Ben never told me anything about diverting money." She couldn't stop the tears building in her eyes. She wanted to scream out and fight to get away, but she couldn't muster the strength. She felt all will to resist slip away and she slumped against the car.

The man said, "I'll be back in the morning and you will have what we're looking for. If you don't, we have people up in North Carolina who know where your son lives. We don't want any harm to come to him, but that's entirely up to you."

Hanna screamed out, "You stay away from Jonathan!"

The man had left her as abruptly as he had appeared. Hanna had slipped to the ground and was now sitting with her back against the front wheel of the car. She tried to control the shaking that consumed her. Beside her, the leather purse she had dropped when the stranger grabbed her, lay on its side with contents strewn across the concrete parking surface. She saw her cell phone among the pile of clutter and reached over for it.

As she tried to sort out who to call, she thought back to the man's final warning before he disappeared again. Hanna had repeatedly denied any knowledge of money left by her deceased husband. She was terrified these people were now threatening her son. She tried to think back to any indication Ben may have given about money diverted from the Osprey Dunes land deal, but she couldn't think of a single comment or action. Their accountant had supposedly identified all assets and accounts held jointly or individually by her husband. There was virtually nothing left in any of them. She had already been to their safe deposit box months ago. It was filled with what she had expected, old documents and a few coins Ben had kept since he was a boy. There was nothing of real value there.

Was it possible he had some secret account held somewhere, even offshore? Certainly, it was possible, but she couldn't think of any way to even begin searching for it. *Wouldn't the FBI have already discovered anything like that?*

She thought again of her son, Jonathan. She brought his number up on her phone and pressed the call button. She had to warn him. The phone rang three times before he answered.

"Hi Mom," she heard him say.

Hanna tried to calm herself before she spoke.

"Mom, are you there?"

"Honey, I'm here," she finally managed to say, her voice quivering.

"Mom, what's wrong?"

"Where are you, honey?"

"I'm leaving for work in a few minutes," he answered. "What's going on?"

She struggled to think how to respond and how she could protect her son. Finally, she said, "I need you to go down to the nearest police station."

"Police station! What's going on!"

"This is important, Jonathan," she said. "I need you to go to the police immediately."

"Mom, what in the world is going on?"

She stared down at the cell phone in her hand. The man had again warned her of any further involvement with law enforcement. Would these people know if she reached out to the police or the FBI to help protect her son? They seemed to have eyes everywhere. She heard her son say, "Mom, are you there?"

She took a deep breath and decided it was best to first get her son out of danger in Chapel Hill. "Jonathan, I can't explain everything right now, but it's very important you get to a safe place. I think the people who killed your father may try to use you against me."

"What are your talking about?"

"Please, we don't have time, Jonathan."

"Mom, are you OK? Do I need to come down there?"

"I'm working with the police here in Charleston," she said. "Now please, get to the nearest police or sheriff's office. Tell them to call Detective Alex Frank at Charleston PD when you're safe there."

"Mom, this is crazy!"

"Honey, please," she pleaded, "just do what I've told you. I'm going out to the island tonight. Call me when you're safe. Please be careful so no one follows you."

Her son finally consented and they ended the call. She wasn't exactly sure why, but she knew she needed to check something at the house up at Pawley's Island.

On the drive out of Charleston and up the highway to the island, Hanna continued to sort through her emotions and doubts and the unanswered questions that kept running through her mind. She had taken as much precaution as she could to make sure no one was following her including several sudden turns and then stops to see if any cars were still behind her. Ten minutes earlier she had pulled into a gas station and sat in her car for a full five minutes to see what cars pulled in and who was driving. There were only two cars. The first was a mom and three kids in a Subaru station wagon. The last had been a teenage couple in a late model Mustang.

When she pulled back onto the highway, she watched her rear-view mirror to make sure there was no one else behind her. It was almost 10 p.m., and the road was empty as far back as she could see.

Later, as she approached the turn for the island, she wrestled again with the decision not to call anyone for help. She still hadn't heard from her son and was beginning to worry something had happened to him. She reached for her phone and dialed his cell number. After ten rings, the call went to voicemail. She left a message for him to call. Her panic rose again as she thought through all the reasons why he wouldn't answer. What if they had caught him trying to get to the police station. She was so distracted her car went off the edge of the road and the tires screamed along the rumble strips before she was able to turn back onto the blacktop.

She pulled over to the shoulder, coming to a quick stop. She rested her forehead on the steering wheel and then fought to control the panic.

"Damn you, Ben!" she screamed out. She thought of her dead husband and his deceptions and terrible decisions that had placed them all in financial ruin and now, even physical danger. She took several deep breaths trying to calm herself. She was startled by headlights coming up behind her and she watched closely as the car passed and turned onto the island road.

Suddenly, she knew she couldn't deal with this alone. Her phone was on the car seat beside her. She searched for the number and then pressed "call".

"This is Lieutenant Frank."

Just the sound of his voice was a great source of comfort. She said, "Alex, this is Hanna Walsh," the panic clear in her voice.

"Hanna, what is it?"

She quickly told him of the latest visit from the stranger and his threats to hurt her son if she didn't cooperate and bring them the money her husband had apparently taken from the failed land deal.

Alex let her get the full story out before he said, "I want you to go to the sheriff's office up there and wait for me. Don't go to your house."

"What about Jonathan?" she asked.

"I'm going to call the Chapel Hill PD and have them try to track him down."

Hanna quickly protested. "They'll know I've gone to the police! They warned me!"

"Hanna, listen," Alex said. "We'll find your son and make sure he's got protection. Give me his cell number and the Chapel Hill PD may be able to trace him. Keep trying to reach him by phone and let me know if you're able to connect. I should be able to get up there before midnight."

Hanna felt a small measure of relief start to take hold. She gave the detective her son's phone number. "Alex, thank you. Thank you for..."

"Hanna, just get to the sheriff's office and wait for me there."

"Alex, I have no idea about this money they're asking about," she said.

"I have to get going," he said, "but you need to think of any indication your husband gave you about what he might have done with this money."

Hanna had thought of little else and she still was coming up with nothing.

Chapter Thirty-nine

Hanna

Pawleys Island, South Carolina *Present Day*

Jonathan Walsh never made it to the Chapel Hill Police Department.

Ten minutes after Alex Frank met Hanna at the county Sheriff's Department, her cell phone rang. She saw her son's name and number on the caller ID.

"Jonathan! I've been so worried. Where are you?"

There was a silent pause.

"Jonathan?"

The voice on the other end of the line was familiar but not her son's.

"Hanna," the man said, "I told you earlier tonight not to go to the police for help."

"What have you done to Jonathan!"

She felt suddenly dizzy like she might fall, and she sat back on a chair in the sheriff's small office. She struggled to stay focused and calm, but her panic was overwhelming. She felt Alex's hand on her shoulder.

"He's safe, at the moment," the man said. "We know where you are and who you're with. I suggest you tell them everything will be fine if you just go home and get the money that belongs to us."

Hanna looked at Alex and then the local sheriff who had helped her when she came in earlier. Alex tried to reach for her phone, but she pulled away and said, "I've told you, there is no money. If I had it, I'd be there immediately to hand it over, but I don't.

There was silence on the other end of the call.

"Let me talk to my son!" Hanna said.

The man came back and said, "Eight o'clock tomorrow night, Hanna. No more excuses." The line went dead.

Hanna found some coffee in the pantry of the beach house and started a pot brewing. Alex Frank sat on a barstool across the kitchen island from her. After the man's call at the Sheriff's Department, Alex had called one of the FBI agents working on Hanna's case and filled him in on the latest developments. This whole affair now included kidnapping and the Feds were best qualified to respond. Agent Will Foster had a few more questions for Hanna and then promised to be out to the island early the coming morning. He was also going to alert the North Carolina FBI office and local police and have them begin a search for her son in Chapel Hill.

Hanna had called Grace Holloway back in Charleston to explain what was happening and why she hadn't come back to her house earlier in the night. She told her about Jonathan's abduction, but not about the money. For some reason she couldn't quite explain to herself, she didn't want Grace's husband, Phillip, to know. Grace had been shocked with the news and woke Phillip sleeping beside her.

"We'll come up right away, honey," Grace said.

"No, please don't," Hanna said. "There's nothing you can do here."

"But you shouldn't be alone," Grace said.

Hanna answered, "The Charleston police detective is here with me and the FBI will be here first thing in the morning."

"My God, Hanna," Grace said, "this can't really be happening."

Hanna said, "I'll let you know."

She poured two cups of coffee and sat unsteadily on a barstool at the kitchen island across from the Charleston policeman. She watched him sip at the hot coffee and look back at her. She searched for some measure of comfort in his gaze. He had remained calm and supportive through this entire nightmare from the time he had come to tell her of her husband's murder. She couldn't imagine how she would have made her way through these past months without his help.

Images of past trauma in her life came back to her as her desperation peaked again. Her mother and brother had been killed in an accident she and her father had managed to survive. Her father had recklessly piloted and crashed their family's private plane on a trip to the islands during questionable weather. She was in high school at the time.

In the days that followed that horrific event, she felt she would never find normalcy in her life again, but time has its way of softening the edges of despair. She still had issues with forgiving her father, but the pain of her loss was far more devastating and enduring.

When news of Ben's death came, the spiral of loss and grief returned in a rushing swell that left all the old wounds open. The thought now of anything happening to her son was more than she thought she could possibly deal with.

Alex's thin smile brought her back to the moment. When he spoke, she felt like he had been reading her mind.

"I know this sounds impossible, but you need to keep your head."

She started to protest, but he continued.

"We have some people coming in tomorrow who are trained to help us deal with this."

"I'm terrified these people will do anything. Look what's happened to Ben."

"They told you they weren't involved in that," he said.

"I don't know what to believe... who to believe!"

She stood and walked to the window looking out into the dark and the vast ocean beyond.

Chapter Forty

Amanda

Georgetown, South Carolina 1866

Amanda walked up to the fence along the front of Jessica Samuel's house. The row of white pickets had been freshly painted and stood in stark contrast to others along this street still in neglect and disrepair from the war. The Samuel house was a whitewashed low bungalow with a long gallery porch across the front and a port cochere pushing out from the right side for the horses and a carriage to pass through to a small stable behind. Two large live oak trees shaded the house.

She stood for a moment on the walk, staring up at the house, imaging the Samuel family inside, still together, alive together. The deep sadness she felt pressed on her soul as she thought of her father being lowered into the ground on this afternoon, the gravediggers shoveling the dirt. All her family was gone now.

And now this man, Heyward, whose real name was Robert Morgan, a man she had to admit she was beginning to have feelings for, had not only deceived her but killed her husband, Jeremy. He had lied to her, over and over.

Amanda reached for the latch on the gate. She saw Jessica coming out the front door to greet her. She walked up the stone path to the porch. Jessica came down and gave her a warm hug.

Jessica said, "You can stay as long as you wish."

Amanda squeezed her friend hard, comforted in knowing there would at least be a friend for her in these difficult days and months ahead. And what of Orlando Atwell, her father-in-law? She was finding it difficult to trust even this man after his deception with the debts on the family property. He claimed it was her father's wish, but...? *Who could she really trust anymore?*

As she thought again of her father's passing, she knew she would do whatever it took to preserve his love for the land his ancestors had called *Tanglewood*. There was no obstacle that she would not find a solution... the debts, the failing rice markets. Atticus and Tulia would be there with her. They would all make it work. They would survive.

She heard Jessica say, "Come inside. Let's get you something to drink."

Amanda stepped back and said, "Thank you, dear. I'd like to sit, just for a while."

They both walked up on the porch and Amanda sat on a long, cushioned bench against the wall. Jessica said, "We just made tea. I'll bring you a cup." She went inside.

Amanda looked out from the shade of the porch and tall trees. An old flatbed wagon pulled by two large dray horses rode slowly by, the man driving was slumped low, letting the horses have their way with loose reins. The wagon bed was loaded with rough lumber, likely from the nearby mill and headed off to some build site where families were attempting to repair the damages of a long war. She thought of the work needed at *Tanglewood*, certainly a new barn and broken windows on the house left by the Yankees, purely in spite.

They had missed a full season of the rice crop, her father in no condition to oversee the planting this past year and not enough workers even if he could.

Jessica brought out the drink and left Amanda to herself on the quiet porch. Amanda thanked her softly, then heard the door close. She sighed, trying to push away the heavy weight of sorrow that overwhelmed her. She knew in her heart she would be able to move beyond these dark days and dark thoughts, but it would take time. *But, how much time?*

Amanda was startled awake by the sound of the gate opening out by the street. She realized she must have dozed while sitting on the Samuel's porch. She flinched when she saw the man who now called himself Robert Morgan coming up the walk toward her. She stood quickly, dropping the cup she'd held in her lap while sleeping. It broke on the wooden floor of the gallery. She looked down at the broken pieces of china at her feet, then back at the man approaching. She said, "You need come no further," holding up her hand.

Morgan stopped about halfway to the porch. "Will you give me just a moment?"

Amanda looked down at Morgan, her anger rising again at his deception, his lies about her husband, the shots he fired that killed Jeremy Atwell. "There is nothing more to say."

"I just need a moment. I wanted to leave something with you at the cemetery, but you rushed away.

"I don't need anything from you!"

"Please," he said, "just a moment."

She didn't respond, but her hesitance gave him an opening to continue. He walked up and stood on the first step of the porch, just a few feet from her. He took off his hat and held it in both hands. "First, let me tell you... when I decided to come here to South Carolina to find you, I planned to tell you the truth right from the start. I knew you deserved to know how your husband died in Texas."

Amanda just stared back, her fists clenched in her lap.

Morgan said, "When I first met you, that day in the bar downtown..." He paused, trying to gather himself. "I couldn't bring myself to tell you it was me who killed Captain Atwell." He paused and then quietly said, "I couldn't find the courage."

Amanda stared at the man for a few moments and then finally said, "So you've told me. I want you to leave."

Morgan looked back at her and then reached into a pocket on the inside of his leather vest and pulled out a folded piece of paper. He held it for a moment, turning it in his hands. "I didn't tell you about this, either," holding up the piece of paper.

Amanda didn't say a word.

"Amanda, when I took your husband's satchel on the battlefield that day at Palmetto Ranch, there was more in that bag." He paused. "There was a second letter. It's a letter from your husband's father, Mr. Atwell."

"A second letter?" she asked. "And why have you kept this from me?"

Morgan hesitated, then said, "I always intended to share this with you before I left. I wanted to understand your relationship with Mr. Atwell, your father-in-law, I mean."

"My relationship?"

"It's clear to me now, you need to know the true intentions of the man," Morgan said. He walked up the steps and handed her the letter.

Amanda sat back and read through the short note and then looked up at Morgan, trying to understand what she had just read. Robert Morgan still stood on the steps to the porch, quietly watching as she read it again.

April 30, 1865

Jeremy,

I'm so heartened in knowing the war is finally winding down. While we all mourn the fall of our Confederacy, it is time to accept defeat and move on with our lives. We are all anxious to have you back with us soon.

You will find comfort in knowing I've been able to protect our financial position, unlike so many others around us. While I find no satisfaction in profiting on the challenges of others, one must do what is necessary to protect family and fortune.

You will find a comfortable position with our firm waiting for you on your return. You and Amanda will also be able to keep the plantation at Tanglewood far into the future, with our family's interest in the property greatly enhanced through the challenges the Paltierres have faced these past years.

Travel safe, son.
Orlando Atwell

Amanda let the letter fall to her lap. She sat stunned and motionless as she considered what she had just read. The treachery of her father-in-law did not surprise her. She had doubted the man's integrity and purpose for some time. The depth of his deception now seemed so much more threatening. Then, she remembered Morgan standing nearby. She looked up and stared hard for some sign of explanation or reason for his delay in delivering this second letter.

Slowly she said, "You found no courage in telling me of the true circumstance of my husband's death, and now you hold back this knowledge of the dealings of Jeremy's father." Morgan tried to stop her, but she continued, "Of course you came all this way from Texas, not to ease a widow's grief, but I'm sure now, to blackmail this man or threaten him in his duplicity."

"Amanda..." Morgan said.

Amanda stood quickly, holding the letter at her side. "I think you've done enough, sir!"

"No, that was not my purpose."

"And I don't believe anything you say!"

"I can only tell you I had no idea of the true circumstances you face with your family's property, or what role Mr. Atwell plays in all of that. I didn't want to plant some wedge in your family's affairs, " Morgan said. "With your father's passing, I knew you needed to see this." He looked at her for a moment, waiting to hear some response, but then turned at her silence and contempt and walked down the walk and out the gate.

Amanda watched as he untied his horse, mounted and rode off down the street to the west. She looked again at the written note in her hand, her anger seething now in the confirmation of the true intent of Orlando Atwell.

Chapter Forty-one

Hanna

Pawleys Island, South Carolina *Present Day*

Hanna woke to the sound of gulls screeching out in front of the beach house. She looked at the face of her cell phone. There were no messages from her son or the police. It was 8 a.m., and the sun was filtering through the curtains on the windows in her bedroom. She could hear the faint sound of the ocean waves spilling up onto the beach. She felt the dull ache in her brain from the stress of the past night, staying up late talking to the Charleston police detective, Alex Frank.

She remembered he had stayed over and was down the hall in one of the guest rooms. She pushed the covers back and walked into the bathroom to splash some water on her face and find some aspirin for her head. She didn't like what she saw in the mirror as dark circles spread beneath her eyes. Her skin look pallid and ashen. She didn't have the inclination or energy to try to cover it with anything.

A few minutes later she was down in the kitchen putting a pot of coffee together. She looked out the window to the ocean and saw the sun shining brightly above the deep green water with big white-capped swells pushing up onto the beach.

Then she heard Alex Frank coming down the stairs. She turned as he walked into the kitchen, his hair slightly askew and a look of too little sleep on his face, as well.

"Coffee's almost ready," she said. "Have you heard anything about Jonathan, yet?"

He put his cell phone down on the island and sat on one of the tall stools. "No, I just checked with both the Feds and Chapel Hill PD. Nothing yet."

Hanna said, "I was up half the night thinking about this money I'm supposed to know about. They want it by 8:00 tonight, Alex."

"Yes, we know. Our friends from the FBI will be here soon and I suspect they'll have a plan to deal with that," he said.

Hanna poured cups of coffee for both and stood across the kitchen island from him. She noticed his eyes looking back at her. "Thank you for staying here with me last night."

He just nodded and continued to look back at her.

"What?" she asked, growing uncomfortable at the intensity of his gaze.

He finally looked away, out the window toward the beach. He said, "I've been thinking about this local real estate guy, Dillon."

"What about him?"

"Safe to say he's neck-deep in this whole thing," Alex answered. "I'm also thinking if there was any money, it's with him now in some Caribbean bank."

"How do we get him back?" Hanna asked.

"We can get a warrant and start extradition efforts, but it will take a lot of time."

Hanna sipped her coffee, thinking about the duplicity of her so-called friend. Then, she whispered, "That sonofabitch." She reached for her cell phone on the counter and started a phone call.

"Who are you calling?" Frank asked.

"Maybe he'll pick up the phone for me," she said.

"Dillon?"

"Yes," Hanna replied, and held the phone to her ear. After two rings there was silence. "Thomas, are you there?" she asked. "Thomas, it's Hanna."

Then she heard his voice like he was standing in the next room. "Hanna, good morning," Thomas Dillon said.

Alex realized she had gotten through to the man and came around the counter to stand close so he could hear the phone conversation.

Hanna was trying to control her emotions and anger, but lashed out, "Thomas, what in hell have you done?"

She heard him say, "Hanna, please..."

"I don't want to hear any damn excuses!" she yelled. "Why didn't you tell me you were working with Ben on this project?" She waited for him to reply, but there was just silence on the other end of the line. "Thomas, answer me!"

"Hanna, you need to understand..." she heard him start.

"I don't understand any of this," she interrupted. "You need to help me with this, now!"

Dillon said, "Ben asked me to stay a silent partner in all the dealings related to Osprey Dunes. He needed my help understanding the housing development and real estate aspects of the project."

"Why have you run away?" she said, gripping the coffee cup in her hand so tight, her knuckles were white.

"Hanna, I'm sorry, but I can't talk about this on the phone with you," he said.

"Why the hell not!"

"I should be back soon, and we can talk," he said.

"You need to come back now and you need to bring this money that's missing." She waited for him to respond but didn't hear an answer. "Thomas, they have my son, Jonathan!

They're holding him until I get whatever money is missing back to them."

Again, there was no answer.

Then, quietly he said, "Hanna, I'm sorry about all of this." And then she heard the call click off.

Hanna looked at the phone in her hand for a moment and then slammed it down on the counter. She turned toward Alex who had been standing near, listening to the call. She felt her knees trembling and she stumbled. Frank reached out for her and pulled her close to him, holding her as she tried to fight back tears. She put her arms around him and held him tightly. She could feel his breath on her ear and then one of his hands gently rubbing her back.

"Hanna, you need to sit down." He led her over to the dining table and she sat in one of the old oak chairs, her face in her hands as she leaned on the table.

"I heard all of it, Hanna."

She looked up at him, wiping tears from her eyes and rubbing at her nose. "My God!" she said. "Who in hell can I trust?"

"We have the authorities in St. Croix looking for him, Hanna, but it's not going to do us much good today."

Hanna heard a phone ring and watched as Alex reached for his cell on the counter and took the call. He spoke quietly for just a minute and put the phone down. "That was Will Foster from the FBI," he said. "They're on their way." He looked at his watch. "Should be here around nine."

Hanna nodded, her tears coming under control.

"They're bringing a team with them to help. They'll explain when they get here."

Alex convinced Hanna to get out of the house for some fresh air before the FBI team arrived from Charleston. They took their phones and coffee cups and walked down to the beach and then north along the shoreline, both barefoot and letting the waves wash up over their feet. A few fishermen were set up on the shore several hundred yards up ahead. Otherwise, the beach was still quiet at this early hour.

They had walked in silence for a while and then Hanna said, "Alex, thank you again for being here with me." She looked over at him and he nodded back. "I can't begin to tell you how scared I am," she said.

Alex took her arm in his and said, "I know how hard this must be. We'll get your son back."

Hanna looked at him and his face was set and determined. "We better get back to the house," he said.

Special Agents Foster and Fairfield were waiting on the front deck of the beach house when Hanna and Alex walked up through the dunes from the beach. Alex still had Hanna's arm in his and he let her go ahead as they reached the stairs up to the deck.

Agent Fairfield greeted them first and then said, "We have a lot of work to do."

Chapter Forty-two

Amanda

Tanglewood Plantation, South Carolina 1866

Amanda rode with Tulia in the family carriage behind the single horse on the rough road leading back to *Tanglewood*. The morning was fresh and cool, a heavy mist still lying across the low stretches of pasture and farmland and through the heavy woods between. She handed the leather reins to Tulia and pulled a wool shawl tighter around her.

Tulia broke the cadence and soft sound of the horse's hooves in the loose dirt, saying, "Miss Amanda, me and Atticus, we spoke after the service yesterday."

Amanda turned to her family's long-time servant and her closest friend and confidant.

Tulia said, "We'll be stayin' on with you at *Tanglewood*, if you'll have us.

"Of course, dear," Amanda said quickly. "Of course, I'll have you stay. I need you to stay!" She reached her arm over and pulled the old woman closer. "You're all I have now."

Tulia smiled back and then looked on down the long road ahead as the horse pulled on.

Amanda found herself dozing, even on the rough road as the horse and carriage turned onto the lane up to the plantation house. She had slept little the night before, re-reading the lost letter from her husband's satchel again and again, trying to sort out how she would deal with all it revealed.

As they made their way up the winding drive to the house, she could hear muffled sounds of men talking. The house came into view and as Tulia pulled the carriage to a stop in front of the long porch, Amanda looked down to her left. Atticus was there talking to a man with shirt sleeves rolled up and an old hat pulled low over his eyes. A tall pile of lumber lay beside the burned remains of their old barn. She realized it was Robert Morgan standing there with Atticus. Both men turned when they heard the horse pull up.

Amanda got down slowly from the carriage and began walking toward the two men. She watched as Morgan came up the hill toward her, leaving Atticus behind.

When they stood just feet apart, Morgan said, "I hoped to be gone before you returned from town. I'll be on my way now."

Amanda said, "What is this?" looking down toward Atticus, the new pile of lumber and their pillaged barn.

Morgan said, "I had some money saved. I wanted to help with putting this place back together. It's not much, but you can get started on your barn. I wish I could do more."

Amanda couldn't find the words to respond.

He walked back down the hill. She saw his horse tied to a tree by the side of the old barn ruins. He said a few words to Atticus she couldn't hear. The old man nodded and shook Morgan's hand. Morgan mounted his horse and turned to look up the hill to Amanda, then pushed his horse forward toward the long road away from the plantation house. And then he was gone.

Amanda had been talking with Atticus down by the new pile of lumber. He was going to go to a couple of the nearby share farms where some of her father's former servants had started working small plats of land after the war to enlist their help on the new construction of the barn.

"Do you think they'll come?" Amanda asked.

"No doubt, ma'am," the old man said. "Your father was good to them. He treated them as best he could. They'll want to help."

She turned when she heard a horse and buggy coming up the lane toward the house. Her anger flared when she saw Orlando Atwell driving the buggy. She stormed up the hill toward the house, her emotions raging as she tried to collect her thoughts before her encounter with the man. She knew she mustn't let on yet what she knew about his treachery. She wasn't sure who she could turn to, but she needed to better understand what this man had done to compromise their holdings of her family's farm.

"Amanda!" Atwell called out, his face with a wide smile, his hand raised in greeting as he pulled the buggy to a stop in front of the house. "I didn't have a chance to speak with you privately after the service with so many around," he said, climbing down. "I wanted to personally give my respects and condolences. Your father was a fine man. The whole town will miss him. While I..."

Amanda interrupted, again, trying to remain calm. "You've done enough," she said. "Trust me in saying, you've done enough."

He looked at her with a quizzical expression. Finally, he said, "Of course dear." He looked down at Atticus and the new lumber beside the barn. Before he could ask about the new building material that clearly she was unable to pay for, she said, "It's a gift from friends."

"So, you'll want to start rebuilding?" he asked.

She nodded.

Atwell continued, "As I've said, I can help with selling off some of the outer parcels of your land."

Amanda's anger swelled again, and she almost lashed out. She breathed deep to calm herself and said, "We need to let the dirt on my father's grave settle before we talk of selling off his land."

"Of course, dear," Atwell said. "Whenever you're ready to discuss this." He looked back to her, waiting for some response. When he received none, he said, "Well, I'll be off then." He bowed slightly, "My deepest sympathies, Amanda. You know where to find me. Let me know if there is anything I can do."

She wanted to scream out at him for his deceit but held herself back and said nothing as he climbed back into the buggy and drove away.

The next morning Amanda stood with Atticus, Tulia and three other black men and two smaller boys who used to live and work here for her father, as they continued to clear the burned lumber and debris from the old barn site. The men had come back with Atticus the previous night and they'd all been working for several hours since dawn. She and Tulia had just brought what little food they could gather up and some water for the men and boys. They were all taking a break now.

As the sun rose that morning, Amanda came down the hill to find the men already working. She had thanked them for leaving their families and their own land to help with this project. She worked alongside them through the morning, the building site slowly revealing itself beneath the long-abandoned pile of burned lumber.

As the workers sat to rest and eat in the shade of a tall oak, Amanda walked out to the first levy beyond the old barn. The low field that once held the watery crop of rice plants waving in the wind now sat abandoned, more swamp-like and wild after years of neglect. As she stood there overlooking the massive amount of work needed to bring this farm back to some sense of abundance and harvest, she thought again of Orlando Atwell's last letter to his son and her husband and the clear message that the Atwell's would take a controlling interest in the property.

It had been three days since Robert Morgan's departure from the plantation and Amanda had seen no sign of the man, still wary of his intentions. The work crew had finished with clearing the build-site for the new barn the previous day and left to go back to their own farms with promises to return the following week to begin the new structure. Amanda had hugged and thanked each of the men and their sons before they left. She sat now on the porch of the house, looking down the hill, past the area where the new barn would slowly rise in the coming weeks.

Her old diary sat in her lap, a quill and ink bottle on the low table beside her porch chair. She had been writing down her thoughts of her father's passing, the work that lay ahead on the plantation... and then of Orlando Atwell's last letter to his son and the uncertainty now in the future of her control of the family's land. She thought now of how many others may have fallen victim to the greed and deception of Orlando Atwell. There was little trust left in her heart.

She planned to leave the next morning for the island with Tulia. She knew her father kept some of his papers there during the war where they were less likely to fall into the hands of the Yankees. She needed to sort through what he had left in his office there, having found nothing here at *Tanglewood* to help clarify his dealings with Jeremy's father.

Their journey had been long, but uneventful with no sign of Robert Morgan or anyone else out on this lonely road back to Pawleys Island. Amanda felt raindrops on her face. They were coming off the last bridge over the channel and out to the island. The wind had continued to build through the morning and now pushed the rain into their face as they made their final way down the beach road to the house. Dark purple and gray clouds rushed overhead. The smell of dank swamp and muck was strong. The horse plodded through the puddles in the road, it's coat dripping and wet with steam coming off.

They had the horse put up in the stable and Tulia had left to take their bags up to the house. Amanda walked out into the rain which was falling more lightly now. She thought of her recent time here with the man she now knew to be Lt. Colonel Robert Morgan, their ride on the beach and her growing feelings for him. She quickly chastised herself for such foolish thoughts and then followed Tulia up to the house.

She walked around to the front on the beach side and climbed the stairs up onto the long porch looking out over the ocean. She stood at the rail and looked over the dunes to the swirling dark blue waves of the Atlantic washing up onto the shore in loud rumbles. There was no one in sight in either direction down the beach. A heavy steamer was making its way north, far out on the horizon, a black smoke trail lingering behind against the dark sky.

She sat on one of the chairs up against the house and pulled *Jeremy's* last letter from her purse.

Dear Amanda...

It was past midnight and Amanda walked through the kitchen in her nightclothes to blow out the last candles before going up to bed. She'd fallen asleep earlier on a couch in the parlor, her late husband's letter beside her. She held the candle to blow it out when she heard someone coming up the steps to the veranda along the front of the house. She put the candle down and walked back through the house, in dark shadows now.

In the dim light outside she saw the figure of a man come up on the veranda. She felt chills of fear race through her body and thought immediately of her bag and the gun she kept. She knew it was in the kitchen and began backing in that direction, keeping the man on the deck in sight as he walked along the row of windows.

She jumped when she heard the man yell out as he stopped at the back door, "Amanda! You home?"

She recognized the voice of Jackson Atwell. As usual, his speech was slurred from drink. She stood motionless, watching as he tried the knob on the door. She had locked it earlier.

"Amanda, wake up! I need to see you," he yelled out.

Her anger got the best of her and she walked purposely to the door, Jackson Atwell watching her come up through the glass. "Jackson, I don't know what you want, but get off this property now!"

"Amanda, just let me in, " he said. "I need to talk with you."

"We have nothing to talk about. I want you to leave, now!"

Atwell tried the door again and Amanda thought of the gun back in the kitchen. He rattled the door now more forcefully, "Let me in, goddammit!"

Amanda started moving toward the kitchen and screamed when the door crashed open, the windowpane shattering and Jackson falling into the room on top of the broken glass. She turned and ran now toward the kitchen, the one small candle lighting up the room. She could hear him trying to get up behind her, cursing loudly. She thought of

Tulia, but she was out at the servant's cabin. As she came into the kitchen, she looked desperately around the room for her bag. Behind her, she heard, "Amanda, wait..."

Then, she saw the bag next to the sink and ran in that direction. She reached for it and then felt the man's arms around her waist, pulling her back. She screamed out, "Jackson, let go of me!"

He put his mouth behind her ear and whispered, "Amanda, settle down," the smell of whiskey overpowering on his breath.

She struggled to pull away, but he tightened his grip and pulled her toward the large counter in the middle of the kitchen.

"Jackson, I swear I'll..."

He turned her around and forced her up against the counter. Amanda tried to free her hands to hit him, but he held her fast.

She looked into his eyes in the dim candlelight. They were glassy and distant. He leaned in and tried to kiss her neck.

"Jackson!" she yelled out again. She struggled and tried to knee him, but his legs were pressed too tightly against her. Then, she felt the stinging pain of his slap across the side of her face. It stunned her, and she went slack in his grasp.

"You've needed this for a long time, woman," Atwell said, lifting her up on the counter. She struggled again and this time he hit her on the side of her face with his closed fist. She fell back onto the counter, dazed from the blow. She could feel him pulling at her robe and nightclothes and the sound of his belt unbuckling, but she was too stunned to move.

"Jackson, please..." she managed to whisper, then felt his hands pulling at her clothes. When she tried to pull away again, another blow hit her on the other side of her face and she felt herself starting to lose consciousness.

A loud explosion of sound caused her to flinch.

Atwell's grip on her loosened and then he stood back. Amanda managed to look up and saw Jackson Atwell stagger backward a couple of steps, a look of surprise on his face. A round splotch of blood widened on the white shirt above his chest. Amanda looked down and saw many drops of blood across her white robe. His legs grew wobbly and then he fell to his knees. Amanda could now see Tulia standing behind him, the pistol held out in front of her with a trace of smoke leaking out of the barrel.

She sat up and met the gaze of Atwell, seeing only a blank stare now before he fell over on his side on the wood planked floor of the kitchen.

Tulia was crying as Amanda struggled to get down from the counter. The old woman came into her arms. Amanda looked down and saw the blood leaking out from the wound in the middle of Jackson Atwell's back. She gathered herself enough to kneel beside him. His breathing was labored and blood now dripped from the corner of his mouth.

Then, he seemed to regain some sense of consciousness and he looked up at her and smiled, his teeth covered in blood. He tried to speak and then coughed on the blood gathering in his mouth.

She heard Tulia behind her say, "Leave him be, ma'am. He don't deserve tendin' to."

Slowly, his hand moved up and pointed to his coat that he'd thrown on the floor beside them. She thought he might be reaching for a gun and she held his arm. He mumbled something unintelligible and then pulled some papers from the pocket in the coat.

Amanda watched as his hand fell back to his side, the papers falling on the floor beside him. A low moan escaped from his mouth. His eyes grew distant again before he took one last gasping breath and then was still.

Chapter Forty-three

Hanna

Pawleys Island, South Carolina *Present Day*

It was four in the afternoon and Hanna had been with Alex Frank and six agents of the FBI for most of the day. Her fear and panic at the abduction of her son had been growing throughout the day and nothing the law enforcement officials were telling her provided any sense of relief in the situation she faced. In four hours, a deadline would pass where some group of dangerous people wanted money she had no idea of its whereabouts, or her son would face some unspeakable fate.

Hanna had spent two hours searching through her husband's office again, hoping to find some clue or insight into the missing money. She knew it was a long shot. Every drawer and file had been searched on numerous occasions, but she had to try. Her efforts also included another session in the attic, going through old boxes and furniture. Nothing.

Two minutes ago, she had pulled Special Agent Sharon Fairfield aside in her kitchen and asked, "Please tell me you have a plan."

Fairfield looked at her for a moment and then held up a hand when her cell phone began to ring. The woman walked away into the dining room to take the call. Alex Frank had been standing nearby and heard the exchange between the two women. He walked over to Hanna and said, "You need to give them time to pull this all together."

"We are running out of time, Alex!" Hanna pleaded.

"I just spoke with Foster," he said. "They expect you'll be receiving a call at any time. They have some sort of technology to tie into your cell signal to try to trace these guys."

Hanna looked down at her phone and then back at Alex, shaking her head. "I don't want to do anything else to put Jonathan in more danger."

Alex said, "I'm afraid we're past that now. We need to find out what they want and where they want it. Foster is right. They'll call soon."

Agent Fairfield came back into the kitchen, ending the call she had been on. "Hanna, we need to talk," she said. "Let's sit down." She walked over to the dining table and pulled out a chair for Hanna to join her. Alex and Hanna were sitting down when Will Foster also came in to join them.

Alex said, "I've told Hanna about the call trace."

"Right," said Fairfield. "We should hear from these guys at any time. Hanna, we need you to keep them on the line as long as possible. Ask a lot of questions. Ask to speak to your son. Ask for specifics on the money. How much? Where?"

"They'll know what I'm doing," Hanna protested.

Foster said, "You need to keep them on the line as long as possible. We should be able to get a call link traced quickly. If we can get any connection to where these guys are, we have teams here, in Charleston and up in Chapel Hill to respond."

Hanna looked across the table at Alex. He nodded back at her.

Fairfield said, "We also need to be realistic about this. They may well be using some throw-away phone, but again, we might be able to get a GPS link on it. Regardless, we need to find out specifically what they want and where. We suspect they won't be looking for some big cash delivery, rather, they'll want you to electronically transfer whatever money they're expecting to another account. That's what we need to know."

"Why do they think I have this money?" Hanna said in desperation.

Foster said, "We don't know. They obviously have some reason to believe you and your husband put it away somewhere."

"I'd give them whatever they want," Hanna said. "If I had anything to give!"

Alex said, "They obviously believe you do, and we have to keep them thinking that until we can get your son back."

"How much signal do you have left on your cell?" Will Foster asked.

Hanna looked down at her phone. It was at 80 percent. "It's fine," she said. "I had it on the charger earlier this afternoon. "Why haven't we heard anything from them?"

Agent Fairfield said, "It won't be long."

Hanna stood at the rail of the deck along the front of the beach house, looking out over the dunes to the ocean. She couldn't help thinking about earlier times here, happier times with her husband and son; friends and family who shared this place with them. She also thought about her family from the early days, many decades ago when the Paltierres and Atwells lived here and stood on this very spot. She looked out to a place on the beach where she and Ben and their son, Jonathan, would always set up their chairs and umbrella to spend the day enjoying the sun and the sand and the water... a picnic lunch, cold drinks in a cooler, music playing.

There were a few other clusters of beachgoers out there today, young children running into the water; adults watching or napping; all oblivious to the situation she was enduring at the moment. She thought of her son and took a deep breath trying to keep her panic in check. *Where were they keeping him? When would she see him again? They surely won't hurt him? Oh God!*

And then her phone rang.

She looked down and saw the screen light up as the phone buzzed and vibrated on the deck rail. *Unknown Caller.* Hanna was aware of Alex and Sharron Fairchild coming up beside her as she reached for the phone. She looked over at Alex who gave her a reassuring nod. It had buzzed five or six times before she pushed the button to accept the call.

With all her will to keep calm, she said, "This is Hanna Walsh."

There was silence on the other end of the line for several moments.

Hanna said again, "Hello, this is Hanna."

"Mom?"

"Jonathan!" she said, almost dropping the phone. "Jonathan, is that you?"

Then she heard another voice, the voice of the man she had met here at the beach late one night at the fire pit down below this deck and in Charleston.

"Hanna," the man said. "We're very disappointed."

"Let me speak with my son!" she screamed.

"Listen to me carefully," the man said. Agent Fairfield had moved in close to listen to the call. "You haven't followed instructions very well, Hanna. We told you not to bring in law enforcement and yet you're there on the island with an army of Feds and cops."

Hanna blurted out, "What did you expect me to do? You have my son!"

"If you want to see your son again, you need to listen very carefully," the man said, his voice maddeningly calm and quiet. "We want you back in Charleston tonight, alone. You don't want us to see anyone following you and or waiting for you there. Am I clear about this?"

Hanna looked desperately at Alex and the FBI agents. They nodded back at her and Fairfield twirled her finger, reminding Hanna to keep the man talking.

"Where do you want me to go in Charleston?" Hanna asked.

The voice on the phone said, "Just get in your car and start driving back. We'll tell you where to go."

Hanna was trying to keep her fear and agitation in check. She said, "I don't know what you want from me. There is no money. How many times do I have to tell you that?"

The man said, "Come now, Hanna. Let's stop playing games. You and Ben took almost $3 million from the escrow accounts and development funds and we want it back, today!"

"$3 million!" Hanna said, incredulously.

"Please don't act so surprised, Hanna," the man said. "Let me be very clear. You will not see your son again unless you follow our directions precisely and we have that money by the end of the day."

"There is no money!" she screamed.

Very calmly, the man said, "Get in your car now. Alone. No one is to follow you. We will know." The line clicked off.

Hanna looked at the silent phone in her hand and then up at the men and women standing around her. She shook her head, bewildered, afraid, at a loss for what to say or do.

Agent Foster turned when another man from the FBI came out on the porch and spoke with him briefly. Foster listened and then turned and said, "We have a GPS location on the caller. He was standing on the Battery in Charleston in the park. We're sending a team down there now, but it's unlikely they'll find this guy. The phone was a generic prepaid minutes model. We won't be able to trace an owner."

Hanna looked around at the beach and at the neighboring houses. "Where are these people? Who's watching me?"

Foster said, "Hanna, we need to get you on the road to Charleston. We will let you go on ahead without any of us following. We'll make arrangements to have someone reconnect as you get closer to town. They won't know you're being followed again."

"They sure as hell know now!" Hanna protested.

"They will call you on the way with further instructions," Foster said. "You need to keep us informed. Keep your phone on speaker so they can't see you making a call after you talk with them, if they're following closely. You have my cell number on the card I gave you. We'll put it in your speed dial, so you can reach us as easily as possible."

Hanna looked over at Alex. He said, "Hanna, they're right. Do exactly what they ask and keep us informed as best you can. We'll wait a reasonable time until you're on the road back."

Foster said, "We have a chopper at the Georgetown airport. We'll be back in Charleston long before you get there, but we'll keep our distance, as will the police and FBI teams we have on standby in Charleston."

Fairfield said, "We have a tracker in your car already, so we'll know where you are." She turned to the side and spoke quietly with Agent Foster for a moment, then said, "Do you have a laptop with you?"

"Yes, I have it my bag," Hanna said.

Fairchild continued, "They will likely want you to transfer some money electronically."

"And how can I possibly do that?" Hanna asked, the exasperation in her voice clear to all.

Agent Foster said, "We may want you to make that transfer. We are setting up a dummy account for you to access."

"You're going to give them the money?" Hanna asked.

"Maybe," Foster said. "If we think we can trace it to the receiving bank, account number, owner..."

"Three million dollars!" Hanna said.

Ten minutes later, Hanna was at the front door of the beach house, ready to leave. Alex stood with her and handed her the bag that held the laptop. He said, "We'll be with you all the way."

"Why am I not feeling so confident about that?" she asked.

"They have the tracker in the car and our teams are on stand-by in Charleston," he said.

She looked at him for a moment, then said, "Thank you."

"We're doing all we can."

"No, thank you for being here with me through all this," she said. "I'm not sure how I would have kept my sanity." She leaned in and put her arms around him. He returned the embrace.

He said softly into her ear, "Just do what these guys tell you and we'll get through this. Understand?"

She nodded and then turned to leave. She took one more look at Alex before she went out the door and closed it behind her.

Chapter Forty-four

Amanda

Tanglewood Plantation, South Carolina ...*one year later.*

Amanda stood in the door of the new barn that had been completed in early spring. The smell of cut lumber and horses mixed with a fresh breeze blowing up across the fields from the west. She watched as ten men worked across the land, dry now that the levees had been breached and the water drained. The men were clearing the land and cultivating a new crop for *Tanglewood.* Tobacco would be their future now and markets were strong for the first crop they would bring in next year. Other fields had been drained and planted with vegetables for food and hay for the horses.

Atticus came up beside her from inside the barn. "A good day's work out there, ma'am," he said.

"They're doing a fine job, Atticus," Amanda said. "I wasn't sure I'd ever see this place back on its feet."

"You been workin' hard, ma'am."

"We all have been."

They heard the loud clang of a dinner bell and looked up to see Tulia on the porch of the house with the big triangle chime, banging away. She yelled, "You all get up here for dinner now! Bring them men with you!"

After dinner, when the men had gone home to their own farms and to the cabins down by the field for those who were staying on for the planting season, Amanda sat out on the front veranda of the big plantation house alone. She sipped from a glass of water as she made new entries in her old diary. These past months she had recorded the stories of the recovery of *Tanglewood*, as well as the fate of her father-in-law, Orlando Atwell.

His son, Jackson, had died from his gunshot wound the night of his attack at the Pawleys Island house. The papers he had brought with him proved to shed light on all of Orlando Atwell's treacherous deeds, not only with the Paltierre family and their holdings at *Tanglewood*, but also several other families and their property in the area. The records showed the illegal skimming and other transactions her father-in-law had used to steal from the Palteirres and their neighbors without their knowing. Atwell seemed to have a hand in every pot and was a silent partner in more deals than Amanda could believe.

She remained in the dark on why Jackson Atwell had brought this evidence with him that night. His final act of revealing them to her seemed clear in his intent to reveal his own father's criminal ways, perhaps in hopes of gaining her favor and furthering his "romantic" interests. She shuddered when she thought again of his drunken assault that night. Thank God, Tulia had heard the man come on the property that night and dealt with him accordingly with a bullet from Amanda's gun.

She had gone to the sheriff and then the County Attorney's office. Charges were quickly filed, an arrest made and trial prosecuted. Orlando Atwell was just days from being transferred to the state prison in Columbia, South Carolina when he was found dead in his cell in Georgetown from an apparent heart attack. *More likely, a deadly dose of regret,* Amanda had written in her diary on news of the man's death.

The incriminating records revealed by Jackson Atwell were detailed enough that the authorities were able to return considerable funds from Atwell's accounts to families who were victimized by the old attorney. For those no longer in the area, or unable to be tracked down, the County used the money to help with the new hospital being built in Georgetown. They didn't name the building in honor of the disgraced Orlando Atwell for obvious reasons.

Amanda had been stunned at the amounts stolen or skimmed from the profits of her father out at Tanglewood. There had been more than enough to repay debts, finish the barn and begin the process of investing in men and materials to put the plantation back on its feet. The old weathered family house out on Pawleys Island also got a new roof and fresh coat of paint and stood now as a shiny beacon up in the dunes from the blue Atlantic.

Amanda continued to wonder at her husband's delay in revealing the treachery referenced in the letter from his father found in the old leather satchel he carried. She reasoned he had received the letter just a short time before he was to have returned home following the cessation of fighting in Texas and the end of the war. He likely wanted to deal with his father personally upon his return.

There were also pages in Amanda's diary chronicling the death of Jackson Atwell during his assault that night on Pawleys Island. Amanda and Tulia had loaded the man's body in the wagon the next morning and taken it into Georgetown to the sheriff's office. Knowing it would be difficult to defend a black woman shooting and killing a white man in South Carolina, Amanda had convinced Tulia she would take the blame for shooting Jeremy's brother during her struggles with his attempted rape. The bruises and cuts to her face were clear evidence of the man's attack and no charges were filed against her, though there were lingering questions regarding the man being shot in the back.

She had also written in her diary of the arrest and conviction of the two Northerners who eventually came around to confessing to the accidental death in self-defense of her father. Amanda wrote in the journal that it was most likely the old Georgetown sheriff who threatened to hang the two Yankees if they didn't confess to their true crime. They, too, were sent off to serve long sentences in the state's faraway prison.

A more recent entry that she was now reading back through was of an envelope received this past winter, postmarked from Philadelphia, Pennsylvania, but with no return address. Inside, Amanda had found no letter or message of any kind, other than a newspaper article clipped from the *Philadelphia Inquirer*. It was dated, Monday, January 17, 1867. The news story told of the discovery of a prominent local businessman's body in the cold and muddy waters of the Schuylkill River. The article wrote that authorities deemed the death accidental as the former U. S. Army Colonel, Terrance Barnett, had a significant head wound, likely incurred from a fall from a bridge or high bank.

Amanda was, at first, surprised at the news of the man's violent death. She thought of Robert Morgan and his promise to deal with the man's past ignorance and transgressions. She had never believed he would carry out his threat, but indeed, someone or something had done Colonel Barnett in.

She continued writing in her journal of the day's work and the progress they were making with the new plantings. When it became too dark to continue, she closed the diary and placed it by her side on the table. She pulled a shawl more closely around her shoulders as a chill breath of wind blew up onto the porch.

Chapter Forty-five

Hanna

Charleston, South Carolina *Present Day*

Hanna had been driving over an hour on her trip back to Charleston for some, yet to be determined, encounter with the people who were holding her son hostage for money her dead husband had apparently hidden away. Since leaving Pawleys Island, she had continued to check her mirrors to see if anyone was following her but hadn't seen anything that seemed to be a trailing vehicle. Her sense of dread and panic was rising by the minute and she tried to block out any thoughts of possible harm that might come to Jonathan. *When will this nightmare end?*

She had set her cell phone on the passenger seat where she could get to it quickly, expecting to hear either from the FBI or the kidnappers at any moment. Next to her on the seat was her laptop with a window loaded to an online bank website and a dummy account the FBI had set up for her to transfer money when the kidnappers provided the instructions. They had assured her the money would be sent but quickly recovered when her son was safe.

She had her cruise control set at the speed limit. The last thing she needed was to get pulled over and delayed by local law enforcement. The phone suddenly buzzed, and the screen lit up, catching her by surprise. Hanna looked down and saw a familiar name. She reached for the phone and pressed the green button to accept the call, putting it on speaker as the FBI had instructed.

"Grace? Is that you?" Hanna said.

"Honey, where the hell are you?" her friend asked, her voice agitated and concerned.

"On my way back to Charleston from the island."

"I've been worried sick about you since you left in such a hurry," Grace said. "Are you okay?"

Hanna was looking down the road and letting the question sink in. *No, she was not okay!*

"Hanna!" Grace called out. "Are you there?"

"Yes... yes, I'm here."

"Hanna, I really need to speak with you."

"Go ahead."

"No, I need to see you," Grace insisted.

"This is not a good time," Hanna said, trying to keep her voice calm. "I'm right in the middle of something."

"Hanna, this is important. I need to see you tonight."

Hanna hesitated, then said, "I don't think so... maybe later."

A car was coming up quickly from behind. It was just starting to get dark and the headlights on the car were bright. Hanna couldn't see who or how many people were in the car. She held her breath as it came alongside to pass and then sped on by without slowing. She exhaled and then heard her friend on the phone again.

"Hanna, what's going on?"

"I can't talk about it now," Hanna said. "I really need to hang up. I'm expecting a call."

"Are you coming back to our house tonight?" Grace asked.

"Hopefully, later," Hanna said. "We can talk then." She hung up the phone before her friend could respond.

Hanna began seeing familiar road signs as she approached the city. She still hadn't received any word from Jonathan's captors and her desperation was becoming unbearable. She thought for a moment about a call to either Alex or the FBI but forced herself to continue to wait.

She turned at the road that would take her downtown and near the neighborhood of their old house on the Battery. As she pulled up and slowed for a red light, her phone buzzed. *Caller Unknown.* Hanna took a deep breath and touched the call button and then placed it on speaker.

"Hello?" she said, tentatively, trying to breathe.

The stranger's voice said, "Hanna, we need you to pull into the parking lot at the Walmart up ahead on your right."

Hanna was stunned they knew exactly where she was. She looked around in panic, trying to see who was watching her. She was in heavy traffic now and realized they could be in any of these cars.

"What do you want me to do?" she asked, looking up ahead for the Walmart sign.

"Just pull into the lot and find a place to park, away from other cars," the man said.

Three blocks further down the road, Hanna pulled into the parking area and found a space away from the store with few cars around. She stopped the car and put the shift in Park, taking a deep breath to try to calm herself.

She heard the voice on the phone say, "Hanna?"

"Yes," Hanna said. "I want to know that my son is okay!"

"If you do as we ask, you'll be with him soon," the man said. "And you have the money ready to transfer?"

"Yes!" she said, "But, I want to speak with my son."

The man said, "He's on his way to you now, but you must do exactly as we say."

Suddenly, there was a knock on the window of her passenger-side door. Hanna jumped in surprise and then saw the shape of a large man standing next to her car with a cell phone to his ear. The man leaned down, and she saw the face of the stranger, his familiar ball cap and sunglasses. He motioned to the lock and she reluctantly hit the button. The man opened the door and got in, picking up the laptop resting on the seat.

"Hello, Hanna," he said.

She didn't respond, holding on to the steering wheel with both hands to control her shaking.

The man said, "You're going to come with me. Turn your car off. Remain calm. Do not do anything stupid."

"Where is Jonathan!" she demanded.

"I've told you, he is on his way," he said. "Now, let's go.

She opened the door, reaching for her purse on the floor. She saw the man walking away across the parking lot with her laptop and she followed. He climbed into a black SUV and motioned for her to get in on the other side. As soon as she closed her door, the man handed her the laptop and sped quickly away and back out onto the street. She looked behind her and no one else was in the car. She looked over at the man who was intent on driving. Hanna looked around, knowing the beacon the FBI had been tracing was behind her in the car she had just abandoned. She had no idea if anyone had been close enough to see her get into this vehicle.

After several minutes, the man turned down a dark street and then in behind an old commercial garage that looked abandoned. He parked behind the building and reached for the laptop Hanna was holding. He quickly began booting up her computer and pressing keys quickly. She realized he was trying to connect with some local wifi signal, probably from the nearby building. Finally, he said, "And you have your bank access online?"

She pointed to the link at the top of the browser menu and he clicked on it, bringing up the screen to the account the FBI had set up. He handed her the laptop and asked her to log-in to the bank site. She typed in the numbers she had memorized from the FBI and then looked over at the man.

He said, "Set up a transfer for $3 million even, a nice round number to include interest on the money your husband stole from us."

Hanna didn't respond and continued to set up the transaction. When she finished, the man took the computer back and continued to type in information to complete the transfer. In less than a minute, he hit one final button, looked down at the screen for a few more moments and then turned to Hanna.

"See, that wasn't so hard," he said.

Hanna didn't respond. The man closed the laptop and handed it back to her. He said, "You are three blocks to your old house on the South Battery. Start walking."

"Where is Jonathan?" she pleaded.

"If you've done as we asked and there are no surprises from your cop friends in the next hour, your son will join you," he said calmly.

"I want to see him now!" she demanded.

"Get out, Hanna."

"I want to see my son!"

"Go to your old house. Don't call anyone. Don't stop along the way. Do exactly as we've asked."

Hanna looked at the dark hidden face staring back at her. Finally, she said, "I need to know who killed my husband."

The man just looked back for a moment, then said, "I've told you, why would we kill someone who owed us so much money? We don't kill people like that, Hanna. It's bad for business. Now go!"

She reached for the door handle and slowly got out of the truck. She turned back to the man and said, "I swear to God, if anything has happened to my son..."

"Hanna, go now! You'll see him soon."

She slammed the door and backed away as he quickly pulled out and was gone around the building. She stood there, breathing deeply, feeling a cold chill rush through her body. She started walking.

Ten minutes later Hanna was standing on the sidewalk in the park across the street from her old house on the Battery along the riverfront in Charleston. The lights were out. The new owners hadn't moved in yet. The sounds of crickets and tree frogs broke the stillness of the night. She had resisted the temptation to call Alex or the FBI agents. Occasionally a car would drive by and she looked on, hoping one would stop and her son would get out. She looked down at her watch and saw there was still nearly forty-five minutes to the one-hour deadline the man had set for her to continue to cooperate.

And then a car she recognized did pull up and park directly across from her in front of her house. She watched in complete surprise as Grace Holloway got out of her long Mercedes sedan and started looking around as she closed the door to her car. Hanna resisted the urge to call out and slipped quietly into a darker shadowed area behind a large live oak tree. She watched her friend walk up onto the sidewalk in front of the house, a streetlight illuminating her as she turned and looked both ways down the sidewalk.

How in hell does she know I'm here? Hanna thought, her mind racing to understand what she was seeing.

Then, she jumped at the sound of her cell phone buzzing in her purse. She reached for it quickly and saw it was Alex trying to reach her. She wanted to answer but thought of the stranger's warning to not contact anyone for at least an hour. She sent the call to voicemail and put her phone back in her purse. She looked across the street. Grace had apparently not heard the phone. She had gone through the front gate of the house and was sitting on the porch steps, looking up and down the street.

Another car drove by but didn't stop. Hanna watched her friend for another minute and then started walking across the street. As she got to the far sidewalk, she came under the streetlight and watched as Grace noticed her approach.

Grace stood quickly on the porch steps and yelled out, "Hanna, oh thank God!"

Hanna walked through the gate and up the walk and met her friend halfway. The woman was holding out her arms and Hanna reluctantly hugged her and then stepped back. "Grace, what are you doing here?"

The woman hesitated, then said, "Is Jonathan okay?"

"What do you know about that?" Hanna demanded.

"Oh, god, Hanna," she said. "I've been so worried."

"What do you know about Jonathan?"

Grace just looked back at her for a moment and then shook her head, obviously trying to hold back tears. Finally, she said, "Hanna, I'm so sorry!"

Hanna watched as the woman wiped at the teardrops starting to streak down her face. She turned when she heard another car pulling up to the curb. She watched as Alex Frank ended a phone call and then got out of his car and quickly came through the front gate of the house. "I thought you might be here."

Hanna panicked as she thought about the stranger's warning about the police. "Alex, you can't be here!" she said. "They'll hurt Jonathan!"

Grace walked around them and was trying to leave when Alex grabbed her arm. "You need to go sit down over there," he said to her. "You're not going anywhere."

"Alex?" Hanna started to say, her confusion growing.

Alex said, "I just got off the phone with Ms. Holloway's husband, Phillip."

Hanna looked back at her friend who was sitting down on the front steps of the house again. "What is going on?"

Alex reached out and took her arms, looking past her at Grace. "Hanna, your friend has a long story to tell you, but let me give you the highlights."

Hanna nodded back and reluctantly said, "Okay."

"Your *friend* will have a lot of explaining to do. The Feds will be here shortly. Her husband called me a short while ago and told me a very interesting story. Apparently, Grace finally let on to him what's really been going on. When Grace found out that these men had kidnapped your son, she panicked and went to her husband for help." He looked back at Hanna and she could see his eyes reflecting in the glare of the streetlight. "I'm sorry, Hanna," he said. "It seems Grace and your husband were more than just friends. They'd been having an affair for quite some time before his murder."

Hanna was stunned. She just started shaking her head and she turned to look at Grace who had her head down in her hands, still crying.

Alex said, "She was also quite close to your other *friend*, Thomas Dillon."

"Thomas?" Hanna said, still stunned in total confusion.

"Dillon was apparently working with your husband on this land deal and Grace was behind the scenes... forgive me, but screwing both of them."

Hanna heard Grace yell out from behind, "Hanna, honey, I'm so sorry, but..."

Hanna turned and said, "You were with Ben?" She watched as Grace nodded and then started shaking her head from side to side. "Honey, I'm so sorry..."

Hanna interrupted, "Stop!"

Hanna heard Alex say, "She and Dillon were working together to steal the money in the land deal. I think we'll find these two so-called friends of yours were probably responsible for your husband's death."

Grace yelled out, "Hanna, no! I didn't know what Thomas was planning. I swear to you!"

Hanna felt her knees wobble and she sat down on the sidewalk in total bewilderment.

Alex knelt down beside her as a Charleston police cruiser pulled up down from her house with their flashers on. Two officers got out and walked down the sidewalk toward them. Alex motioned the two cops over to Grace Holloway and they went to her on the porch, had her stand and led her over to Hanna and Alex, who said, "Read the woman her rights and take her down to the station. I'll be down soon."

The two policemen led Grace Holloway away. She turned as she passed Hanna and said, "Honey, I really didn't know what Thomas would do. You have to believe me."

Hanna shook her head in disgust and looked away, "Just get out of here!" When the woman was gone, Hanna turned back to Alex and said, "This can't be happening."

"I'm sorry."

Hanna's phone buzzed in her purse. She pulled it out and felt her spirits lift as she saw the name of her son on the screen. "Jonathan!" she screamed into the phone.

She heard her son say, "Mom, it's me. I'm okay."

Hanna started crying and struggled to answer, "Where are you, baby?"

"I'm coming down our street. They just dropped me off around the block."

She stood and looked down the street in both directions, running to the front gate. Then she saw him down the block, coming into the light of a streetlamp. She ran through the gate and down the sidewalk and then rushed into her son's arms, holding him tight and letting the tears come freely. She sensed Alex Frank coming up behind them and felt his hand on her shoulder.

Chapter Forty-six

Amanda

Tanglewood Plantation, South Carolina 1867

Amanda had been dozing on the long porch at Tanglewood. She heard the horse approaching before she could see it. Only the shadowy outlines of the tall live oak trees lining the lane up to the house could be seen in the darkness against the fading light in the sky. Then, she saw the form of a man walking, leading his horse up toward the house. As always, she had her bag at her side with her pistol and she reached for it now as the man continued to approach. She pulled the gun out and held it in her lap beneath her shawl. Her eyes strained through the fading light to see who was coming.

She stood and walked down the steps, the pistol still in her hand at her side now. The man stopped ten paces out from the porch and his horse bent down to nibble at some grass. He just stood there and waited as Amanda closed the distance between them.

In the stillness of the night, she said, "I told you once I should shoot you."

The man looked down and saw the gun in her hand. Amanda heard him say, softly, "You'd have every right."

She took two more steps and now was directly in front of him. They both stood staring at each. She could hear him take a deep breath in the darkness, but he stood silent. She dropped the gun in the dirt and then moved into him as he tentatively took her in his arms and then held her close. She laid her head on his chest and said, "Welcome back, Colonel Morgan."

Chapter Forty-seven

Hanna

Pawleys Island, South Carolina ... *one year later.*

Hanna Walsh felt a cool rush of breeze off the beach, a welcome relief from a hot day, now fading past dusk. The family next door had set chairs around a beach fire and the black smoke drifted up into the wind, torches lit and flickering in a circle around the gathering in the sand. She could hear the laughter of the adults and children moving around the fire.

Her own son, Jonathan, had left earlier in the day, on his way back to school in Chapel Hill. He had a beard now and she couldn't believe how much he'd grown and matured in his first year away at college. He had come with his new girlfriend, Elizabeth, to spend a long weekend at the beach. Amanda thought she was a delightful girl and was happy for her son, but she missed him already and was plotting in her mind for the schedule of his next trip home to the island.

She had been sitting on the long veranda on the front of the beach house since they'd left, a glass of red wine now half empty at her side. She had tried to start again on a new book she had been reading, but then put it aside and went in to bring out another book, her distant great-grandmother's old worn journal. She had read it through several times in the past year and always found comfort in the stories of her family from the past.

Hanna found particular joy in learning of the renaissance of the old plantation after the war. She remained fascinated with the story of Amanda Paltierre Atwell and all that she endured. The return of Lt. Colonel Robert Morgan had proved a true blessing. The two had wed some months after his return from Pennsylvania and the surprising death of his former commander. No further news had been written in the journal of that affair. They had welcomed three children in the early years of their marriage. The last, a young son lived only a few days before succumbing to an illness not disclosed in the journal. Hanna found herself in tears every time she read that passage from Amanda. She could feel her real pain and grief but could not begin to imagine the actual loss of a child as she herself had come so close the previous year.

Apparently, *Tanglewood* prospered through the years of management by Amanda and Robert Morgan. Their son, Charles, took on the role of overseeing the land in the later years of their lives. Amanda wrote of her pride in her son's steady hand with the land her own father and loved so dearly. She also wrote of the joy of grandchildren on the old plantation and then the grief at losing her husband, Robert, in 1886, to a bout of fever that swept through the region.

Hanna had learned through her own ancestral research that Amanda Paltierre Atwell Morgan lived into her seventies and stayed on at the plantation and during summers out here at the Pawleys Island house until her passing. She was buried with her husband, Robert, and mother and father in the family plot in the Georgetown cemetery. It was unclear if Captain Jeremy Atwell's remains had ever been returned to South Carolina.

Hanna had also learned in her research from old records in the Georgetown courthouse that another generation of Morgans would run *Tanglewood* plantation until there were too many siblings and grand siblings disagreeing on the fate of the old farm. It was sold out of the family in 1906 and gone forever. Fortunately, one branch of the family had insisted on retaining ownership of the Pawleys Island house over the years and Hanna sat now on the very porch so many generations of her ancestors had enjoyed over the past decades.

It was growing too dark to read, even with the porch light overhead and Hanna placed the old journal on the couch beside her. She thought again of Jonathan and his recent visit and too soon departure. She knew he had his own life to live, but it was so hard to see her only child leave after every infrequent visit. She thought of the year that had passed since the troubles they had all faced. Her deceased husband, Ben, had left them with a terrible mess. His deception and infidelity still left her furious every time she thought of it. She shuddered again when she thought how close they had come to an awful and even fatal end.

Hanna touched the old journal again and remembered the pages that described the revelations of the second letter her great-grandmother had received from a man she knew then as Heyward; the woman's father-in-law describing his treacherous financial dealings to his son. That letter and documents reluctantly shared by her dying brother-in-law after his brutal attempt to rape her had revealed the many illegal acts of Orlando Atwell that eventually led to financial relief for Amanda and apparently many others in the area.

She took another sip from her wine, looking out across the dark beach and thinking again about the revelations in her own situation that came to light that night after her son,

Jonathan, had been safely returned and her *friend*, Grace Holloway, had been led away by the police.

Grace had proven to be a very cooperative prisoner, frightened nearly to the point of hysteria at her role in the whole situation and the legal impact she faced. In great detail in her interrogation with the police and FBI, Grace shared her romantic relationship with Ben Walsh and later with the realtor, Thomas Dillon, when Ben brought him in to the Osprey Dunes land deal. Over time, Grace found some attraction for Dillon as well and ultimately, the two plotted to steal money from the project when all signs pointed to failure and dissolution of the deal. Hanna had been surprised at the greed of her former friend when she had so much in her life with her husband, Phillip. *Apparently, there is never enough for some people.*

During that session with the authorities, Grace confessed to her knowledge of details behind the death of Ben Walsh. In a tearful account, Grace had shared a conversation with Thomas Dillon where the man admitted that Ben Walsh needed to be silenced. Ben had apparently threatened to go to the authorities with his knowledge of the corruption and illegal dealings of the mob in Miami. Thomas Dillon was convinced that would end his chance to make away with funds held in various escrow and development accounts. He had confronted Ben Walsh about it one evening in an alley in downtown Charleston. He had successfully made the crime scene look like a failed robbery attempt. When Dillon eventually shared this news with Grace when she continued to press him, he had also threatened her with a similar end if she ever divulged any of their plot.

Hanna had no idea how long her *so-called* friend had been sleeping with her husband. They never spoke after her arrest and Hanna did not attend the trial that sent Grace Holloway to prison.

Grace's husband, Phillip, had shown up at her door a few days after Grace's trial. Hanna had reluctantly let him in and watched incredulously as Phillip actually cried out his grief at the loss of his wife to infidelity and now, years behind bars in prison. Then, not unexpectedly, he had shown his true colors by coming on to Hanna again, asking her to join him that evening for dinner and... *whatever*. Hanna had chased him from the house, wishing she had a broom in her hand to swat him as he went out the door.

Thomas Dillon was another matter. The FBI had filed extradition papers for his return from the island of St. Croix. Before that order could be executed by local authorities, Thomas was found dead on a popular beach one morning as a couple walked their dog. The bullet hole in the back of his head could still not be attributed to any particular assailant to this date, though the authorities strongly suspected the organized crime element in Miami. Fortunately, information leading to the recovery of the stolen funds *was* found in a safe deposit box Dillon kept on Pawleys Island that the FBI was able to access.

There had been no information or indication of the identity of the stranger who had pressed Hanna for days on the missing money and then kidnapped her son in a final attempt to recover the funds. Two months after the arrest of Grace Holloway and the death of Thomas Dillon, Hanna had received a call from Special Agent Foster. A man they had been tracking as they traced the government's money used to wire to the specified account in Jonathan Walsh's kidnapping, had indeed, been located. He, too, was found dead, in this case in a hotel room in Miami, Florida. The Florida State ball cap was found on the bed beside him. Forensic accountants within the bureau had been able to recover the funds used in the ransom transaction within just a few days of Jonathan's return. They were, as yet, unable to identify anyone working with this man, or who may have killed him. There were strong indications of the involvement of organized crime already linked to the failed land deal, but the Federal authorities were still investigating or weren't revealing all they knew.

After several months of contentious litigation from lawyers representing multiple parties, it was determined that some share of the recovered money from Osprey Dune's hidden accounts should, indeed, be returned to the family of the deceased lawyer, Ben Walsh. Hanna had been stunned at the news when called by her new lawyer and contacts at the FBI. It was far from a windfall, apparently personal money Ben had put in escrow to buy three individual properties as rental investments at Osprey Dunes, but the money had been enough for her to keep her family's house on Pawleys Island.

Hanna had moved into the beach house full-time until she could decide on her future pursuits. A chance meeting one night during dinner at a local island restaurant led to her partnership in a small law firm that did business in Georgetown and out on Pawleys Island. Hanna also kept hours open each week to work with clients unable to pay and her new partners had agreed to the arrangement.

Hanna often thought back to the law practice of Orlando Atwell in Georgetown back in the 1800's. She had found where his law office had been located and the building was still there, restored and in operation as a restaurant and brewpub. She found some irony in its fate, thinking of the stories of the drunken son, Jackson, in the journal from her many-times great-grandmother, Amanda Palteirre Atwell Morgan.

Hanna woke with a start when she heard a noise behind her in the house. She glanced at her watch and realized she'd been sleeping for over an hour. She looked at the empty wine glass on the side table next to her and poured a splash more from the bottle before walking into the old beach house. She closed the door behind her and saw Charleston Police Detective, Alex Frank, coming into the kitchen. She came up to him and handed him the wine glass before she pulled him close and said, "Welcome home, Mr. Frank."

THE END

A Note From Michael Lindley

Thank you for reading **LIES WE NEVER SEE**! You got this far, so I'm guessing you enjoyed meeting Hanna Walsh and Alex Frank.

The story continues in the Amazon #1 Bestselling **"Hanna and Alex Low Country Mystery and Suspense"** Series. Hanna and Alex's often tenuous relationship faces many challenges as they take on the dark forces of crime and corruption in the Low Country of South Carolina.

All the books are available to purchase at the Amazon links that follow for both eBooks and paperbacks. They are also available as a free download for those of you Kindle Unlimited subscribers.

Next up is **A FOLLOWING SEA... (next page)**

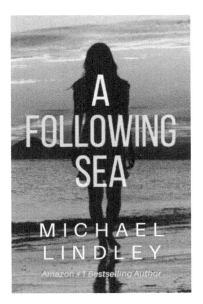

A FOLLOWING SEA Book #2 in the "Hanna and Alex" Series

A captivating and twisting tale of crime and suspense set in the Low Country of South Carolina and the continuing and often tenuous love affair of free legal clinic attorney Hanna Walsh and Charleston detective Alex Frank.

Amazon Five Star Reviews for *A FOLLOWING SEA*

"Once I started, I couldn't put it down."
"A very good mystery and thriller. A must read."
"I am a fan and will be eagerly anticipating the author's next book."
"I thoroughly enjoyed Michael Lindley's latest novel and highly recommend it."
"I have read all his books and loved them all!"

Free legal clinic attorney Hanna Walsh was starting to believe she might have a future with Charleston Police Detective Alex Frank until his ex-wife returns intent on making up for past sins.

GET YOUR COPY ON AMAZON AT THIS LINK:
https://www.amazon.com/dp/179160837X

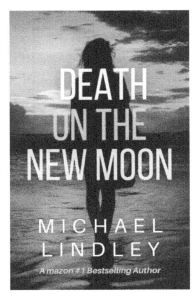

DEATH ON THE NEW MOON Book #3 in "Hanna and Alex" Series.

#1 for Crime and Psychological Thrillers; an engaging and surprising tale of love, betrayal and murder in the Low Country of South Carolina and the always precarious love affair of Hanna Walsh and Alex Frank.

Amazon Five Star Reviews for Death On The New Moon

"... a page-turning thriller."
"I love this author and everything I've read."
"This is a sit at the edge of your seat thriller."
"... a 10 Star thriller."

In **Death On The New Moon**, Hanna and Alex seem to have found a promising new start for their lives together when Alex encounters a tragic loss and near-deadly run-in with a dangerous crime syndicate. As Hanna tries to help him through his recovery and search for a dangerous killer, the surprise return of a lover from her past sends all hope of her future with Alex into a tailspin.

GET YOUR COPY ON AMAZON AT THIS LINK:
https://www.amazon.com/dp/B07SC3P9LP

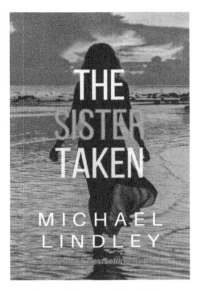

THE SISTER TAKEN Book #4 in the "Hanna and Alex" Series.

AN AMAZON CHARTS BESTSELLER.

A missing twin. A wayward sister. A "jaw-dropping" twist.

Michael Lindley's latest dark and twisting tale of corruption, betrayal and murder set in the Low Country of South Carolina and the precarious relationship of attorney, Hanna Walsh, and now former Charleston Police Detective, Alex Frank.

Amazon Five Star reviews for *THE SISTER TAKEN*

"... engrossing, thrilling, mind-blowing!"
"... a real page-turner with many twists and turns."
"... you can't wait to get to the end, but then wish it hadn't ended."
"... I STILL cannot believe how it all unfolded!"
"Totally loved this book!"

In **THE SISTER TAKEN,** Hanna and Alex again find themselves in the *troubled waters* of love and commitment. Alex returns to South Carolina with the promise of a new start but with strings attached that Hanna may never be able to live with.

GET YOUR COPY ON AMAZON AT THIS LINK:
https://www.amazon.com/dp/B083XTGVR2

Coming Soon!

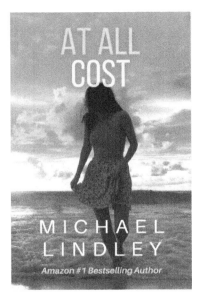

***AT ALL COST* Book #5 in the "*Hanna and Alex*" Series**

Follow Michael Lindley on Facebook at Michael Lindley Novels. If you would like to join his mailing list to receive his "Behind the Stories" updates and news of new releases and special offers, send a note to
mailto:michael@michaellindleynovels.com

Other Novels by Amazon #1 Bestselling Author Michael Lindley

"The Charlevoix Summer Series" Book #1

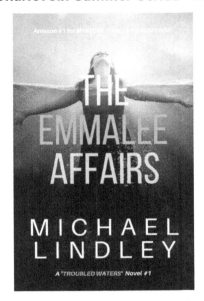

THE EMMALEE AFFAIRS

Amazon #1 for Historical Mystery Thriller & Suspense

One grand ship. Two love affairs decades apart. A quiet summer resort town torn apart by tragic loss, betrayal and murder in this *Amazon #1* romantic suspense tale.

Amazon Five Star reviews for *The EmmaLee Affairs*

"Engaging, captivating, beautiful writing."
"Wonderful! Loved every minute of every page!"
"A sweet reminder of loves lost and new beginnings."
"I wish I could give this book ten stars!"

GET YOUR COPY ON AMAZON AT THIS LINK:

https://www.amazon.com/EmmaLee-Affairs-Troubled-Suspense-Thriller-ebook/dp/B07QZ6W57G/

"The Charlevoix Summer Series" Book #2

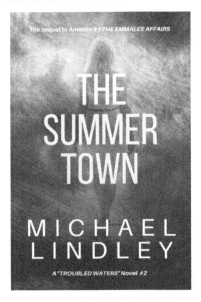

THE SUMMER TOWN

The sequel to Amazon #1 *THE EMMALEE AFFAIRS*

A captivating story of a shocking crime, bitter betrayal and enduring love, bridging time and a vast cultural divide..

Amazon Five Star reviews for *The Summer Town*

"… another stellar novel."
"… even more compelling than EMMALEE."
"… a great success."
"… a delightful read."
"… after falling in love with THE EMMALEE AFFAIRS, this was a must read!"

GET YOUR COPY ON AMAZON AT THIS LINK:
https://www.amazon.com/gp/product/B07646944J/

The "Coulter Family Saga" Series Book #1

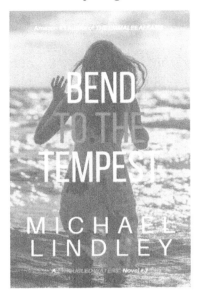

BEND TO THE TEMPEST

From Amazon #1 bestselling author Michael Lindley; an emotional story of love, betrayal and bitter compromise set in 1920's Atlanta and a remote village on the northern Gulf Coast of Florida.

Amazon Five Star reviews for BEND TO THE TEMPEST

"… wonderful character development"
"… one of my favorite authors"
"… hated to reach THE END"
"… WOW - totally impressed."
"… great characters and I love the author's style."

GET YOUR COPY ON AMAZON AT THIS LINK:

https://www.amazon.com/gp/product/B07QXG2SC1/

269

About the Author

Michael Lindley is an *Amazon* #1 author for *Historical Fiction/Mystery Thriller & Suspense* with his debut novel **THE EMMALEE AFFAIRS** as well as #1 for Historical and *Psychological Thrillers* for **LIES WE NEVER SEE** and **DEATH ON THE NEW MOON** with the more recent "Low Country" mystery and suspense series focused on the present-day story line of Hanna Walsh and Alex Frank in Charleston and Pawleys Island, South Carolina.

The settings for his novels include a remote resort town in Northern Michigan in the 1940's and 50's, Atlanta and Grayton Beach, Florida in the turbulent 1920's, and most recently, 1860's and present-day Charleston and Pawleys Island, South Carolina.

Michael writes full-time now following a career in Marketing and Advertising and divides his time between Northern Michigan and Florida. He and his wife, Karen, are also on an annual quest to visit the country's spectacular national parks.

"You will often find that writers are compelled to write what they love to read.

I've always been drawn to stories that are built around an idyllic time and place as much as the characters who grace these locations. As the heroes and villains come to life in my favorite stories, facing life's challenges of love and betrayal and great danger, I also enjoy coming to deeply understand the setting for the story and how it shapes the characters and the conflicts they face.

I've also been drawn to books built around a mix of past and present, allowing me to know a place and the people who live there in both a compelling historical context, as well as in present-day.

Acknowledgements

LIES WE NEVER SEE grew from the spark of an idea several years ago while looking through a collection of family Civil War records and memorabilia. My deepest appreciation to my deceased grandfather, Dr. Ross Matteson, for his tireless work during his life in documenting the history of our family.

While our family's past has no known connections to the Civil War narrative portrayed in this book, my grandfather's collection and recorded history certainly influenced my initial direction for this new novel. I would also like to acknowledge my mother, the late Janet Matteson Lindley, not only for her continued work on recording and preserving the family's ancestry, but also for her relentless support and encouragement for my writing. And to my father who taught me how to hit a curveball.

This novel is truly a work of fiction, though parts of the story are based loosely on the real events of the battle between Confederate and Union forces near an abandoned ranch on the Rio Grande River in Southeast Texas on May 12-13, 1865. With apologies to true historians who have documented this battle in considerable detail, I have taken some liberties with the events and outcomes of those two days of fighting to fit the narrative of the story.

Several real characters are depicted including Colonel Rip Ford, the commander who led the Confederate attacks at Palmetto Ranch. Other characters are based on real men who fought on those two days in May, although I have changed their names as their roles and actions were changed somewhat, again to fit the fictional narrative of the story.

It is certainly accurate to say the Battle of Palmetto Ranch was the senseless folly of a misdirected Union commander who fabricated a reason to attack Confederate forces weeks after the war had officially concluded. His actions led to unnecessary loss of life and many casualties.

Michael Lindley

Follow Michael Lindley on Facebook at Michael Lindley Novels. If you would like to join his mailing list to receive his "Behind the Stories" updates and news of new releases and special offers, send a note to
mailto:michael@michaellindleynovels.com

Your reviews on each book's Amazon page are always appreciated!
ML

Made in the USA
Coppell, TX
30 June 2021

58235358R00154